DATE			

FORGIVING

ALSO BY SHELLEY LIST

Nobody Makes Me Cry
Did You Love Daddy When I Was Born?

FORGIVING

Shelley List

E. P. DUTTON, INC. | NEW YORK

Grateful acknowledgment is made to Houghton Mifflin for permission to reprint from "Transformations," copyright 1971 by Anne Sexton.

Published in the United States by
E. P. Dutton, Inc.,
2 Park Avenue, New York, N.Y. 10016

Library of Congress Cataloging in Publication Data

List, Shelley Steinmann.
Forgiving.

I. Title.
PS3562.I782F6   1982   813'.54   82-2495
                                           AACR2

ISBN: 0-525-24132-9

Published simultaneously in Canada by
Clarke, Irwin & Company Limited, Toronto and Vancouver

Designed by Nicola Mazzella

10 9 8 7 6 5 4 3 2 1

First Edition

For Jonathan Estrin

throughout all eternity
I forgive you, you forgive me.

William Blake

I discovered that I had created my own pat-
tern, and I had to be responsible for it. I had
to forgive my parents for what they didn't
know and love them for what they did pass
down.

Cary Grant

FORGIVING

1

Mincemeat. They could make mincemeat out of her. Her. Naomi Lazurus Loeffler. Miss Accomplished. Like Oriana Fallaci who could intimidate anyone she happened to be interviewing, Naomi could make anyone choose his words very carefully—anyone other than her parents. Naomi was expert. In control: almost all of the time.

But old Sol. Sweet Esther. They could make Naomi's voice sound like a three-year-old's on the telephone. Those parents. The Lazuruses were a team dedicated to their pound of flesh. In the name of love. In the name of family.

Take Sol, who mustered up his intelligence only when famous people were around; Sol, who dropped names like Hansel dropped bread crumbs one by one on the forest floor; Sol, who used to be Naomi's "Daddy" and protected her when she was little, driving the car like a normal person as opposed to Esther who set her hair at red lights and read romantic novels at railroad crossings. Take Sol, who kept forgetting that Naomi was thirty-five years old and that the mayor of New York City utterly trusted her. That Gloria Steinem wrote her complimentary notes, admiring her intellectual courage.

Naomi Lazurus Loeffler had one foot in the fifties and the other in the year 2000. She was thirty-five years old and on winter days could be seen swinging along Fifth Avenue cushioned from the wind by her full-length fur-lined coat, protected by the cocoon of her own strength. Mistress of her own destiny. A queen. Her byline was her succor, her photo credit her quilt of satin. When she was working, some demon took over and all her fears evaporated. And she could never get enough praise. Approbation was food. Applause, sunshine.

Naomi, like a child of her time, ran. Tart, wry, she ran in and around her sadness, playing hide-and-seek with her pain. She went out every night, was indefatigable on assignment, interviewing people with a gusto and curiosity that exhausted and delighted her editors.

Success taunted her like a painted bird. Work was her reality, the rest of life to be dealt with after deadlines. She hid from contemplation, retreated from her dreams. The only place she felt safe was at her typewriter or behind her camera, her eye desperately trying to see it all.

That is not to say there were never men. There were. Always. But the thrust was to succeed, seek power. Love eluded her.

No one, especially Naomi, knew what made Naomi run. "Who is Naomi, what is she?" her husband had written on the last birthday card he had sent her before he went back to Wall Street and vests and bottom lines and brandy snifters and Fortune *magazine, the New York Athletic Club, and shiksas with turned-up noses.*

But Naomi ran. Her tall frame, rangy, could be seen racing the streets of Manhattan, cameras hanging from her neck; dark hair flying about her ears, brown eyes restless, darting. Naomi didn't know where she was going, but wherever it was she wanted to get there very fast.

Cannes, France

2

Naomi looked up at the fat man lying on top of her.

His weight was crushing her. It was as though the concentration of his belly flesh pressing into her was robbing her of breath, as though she would never be replenished.

He had just had an orgasm, and it had been a little-boy sound, a whine. Mommy, she thought, when will he say Mommy? Such a sound had come out of him, she thought, lying there, feeling his sweat on her chest, feeling his heaving and deep breathing into her shoulder. He was resting after that sound, as though the exertion of insertion and pumping, that loveless exercise in stamina had not been the point, that only the sound had been what it was about for him.

It was as though the girth and the beard, the flesh and the pinky ring, the telephone bark and the five-hundred-dollar suits were just air, empty pockets of air, compared to the little boy sound she had just heard.

"Was it good for you?" he said into her shoulder, the bristles of his gray beard cutting a harsh caress into the crevice of her throat. Why do they ask that, Naomi thought, why now, after that perfunctory journey over her body was done, why ask?

The words couldn't come. "You'll have to move," she whispered as she tried to wriggle out from under him.

"Oh, sorry." He rolled over onto his back, a giant sigh erupting from the mound of chest rising out of the sheet. He looks as though he is floating in water, Naomi thought. The whiteness stretching across his frame is filled with helium. Naomi squinted at it, watching the hugeness rise off the mattress as though it were a creature on a flying carpet, floating. She blinked her eyes and his image returned to the bed, his hands on his stomach, breathing up and down.

"Come here, kid." Stanley removed a hand from his swollen middle and put it around Naomi. The skin on the inside of his arm was white, whiter than the rest of him, white as the driven snow, she thought. Driven where, the snow, driven how, the snow, driven by a team of black horses. She couldn't stop her brain.

He pulled her face into his chest. He smelled of Canoe.

She winced, wrinkled up her nose.

"Too strong, cologne too strong for you, Naomi?" He seemed concerned.

"No. Just familiar." She felt small, minuscule in the bed next to the mountain of him. She pulled away, moving his arm from around her shoulders. She put her hand on her breast. He didn't notice.

"Been after you a long time, kid."

"I know."

Across from the bed, out the French doors, off the balcony, slept the Mediterranean. It was May in Cannes, and not yet warm enough to swim in the sea, but the swarm of visitors to the film festival didn't care. It didn't matter. The festival was always held this time of year. Always in May with only a hint of spring in the air. So far, for the two days Naomi had been there, the weather had been gray and forbidding, the Côte D'Azur not so azure as a misty torpor enveloped the terrain. The curve of the coast had been hidden for days by the heavy grayness, but this afternoon it had lifted; and in one hour it was suddenly summer and the beach was peppered with bikinis pasted on the taut bodies of young French girls with bracelets of gold around their waists. Awnings were unrolled and flapped in the new breeze, and the water had indeed become azure again.

In the morning it had rained, and by dusk there had been a brilliant sunset, as though the skies had finished their teasing. After all, this was the Cannes Film Festival, where years ago a buxom starlet had torn off her top to titillate a taciturn Robert Mitchum, where premieres had been studded with stars nodding graciously to their fans lining the streets. The flashbulbs had popped at evening screenings, and sequins and rhinestones had sparkled on dazzling velvet cleavages; years ago there had been some glamour, a flaunting of satin and silk, a blatant excessive love affair with the power of beauty. Today it was tacky, a Shriners' convention.

It was Naomi's third festival. Twice she had covered the madness for a newspaper she was working for, and this trip *Woman Today* magazine had asked her to write a story and take the pictures. There were precious press passes to the films and interviews in French and Jeanne Moreau for cocktails and the sudden surprise of Ingrid Bergman and her still compelling cheekbones. Naomi could have photographed her for days, the mysterious eyes peering out from under a gently aging face; the dark hair casually pulled back, the rubber band stretching it into a tight ponytail, a homey touch in the Carleton bar.

"Yes, a long time I've been after you. I'm a patient man," Stan said, lying back on the two pillows plumped high on the bed overlooking the French doors. His eyes were closed. "I remember you when you were sixteen, you know that? Skinny, you were very skinny then. You've filled out, Naomi."

This is not a romantic place to be, Naomi thought. Here in this bed, that is. I am definitely not in a romantic place. So what else is new. This gets the prize, though. Pin a blue ribbon on my chest for best in show. This man went to school with Sol. This man has lent Sol money, lied for Sol, played poker with Sol, cheated on his wife with Sol.

Out the window, across the Croisette and into the sea is a coast of azure, and here I lie hoisted on my own slothful petard.

Petard. What on earth is a petard. Whatever it is I lie in it, wallow in it. Love like sand like salt sifts through the checkerboard sieve of me. I will not think about love because it does not exist. Not for me.

"What did you think of me when I was sixteen?" she asked, pulling the sheet up to her chin.

"Skinny, I told you. Too skinny for my taste, that's for sure. Not enough tit."

You asked for that, too, she thought, interviewing herself for the Sunday society pages.

"But you had something, kid. Always had. Something in

the way you walked, a look in your eye. I knew I'd just have to wait around and the opportunity would present itself. And it did. It sure did, kid."

Stan had not moved. He lay, smoking, flat on his back with his eyes closed.

"Where'd you learn to kiss like that?" He interrupted himself. "Not from your ex-husband, that's for sure."

"How can you tell? You ever kiss Hank?" Naomi asked.

"You sure are a card." Stan opened his eyes. He looked uncomfortable. "Are you sorry?" he asked, the bluster fading for the moment.

"I don't know yet," Naomi replied. It was true. She did not know why she was in Stan's bed in the first place. In the second place, there were a lot of things she did that she didn't know the reason for.

Naomi had bumped into Stan that morning. She was wearing her expensively casual it-doesn't-really-matter-what-I'm-wearing-because-I'm-working look, baggy khaki pants and tweed jacket with suede elbows; she was tall enough but neither disarming nor casual enough to carry it off. Her cameras were around her shoulder, her hair was in her eyes, and suddenly in front of her, waiting on line to get the press package for the new Fellini movie, was Stanley Abel, movie mogul. Or movie something. She wasn't quite sure what he did for a living. He was one of those peripheral people in the film industry who talked animatedly about "percentages and distribution deals," knew a star or two, but—as far as Naomi knew—didn't have a real job.

The room was yellow, and through the cracks in the slats in the French windows, a slanting light played ticktacktoe on the floor. Naomi wanted to play hopscotch in the reflection of the slats. She wanted to dance on the ceiling; Naomi wanted to be anywhere other than where she was.

The sex had been executed with the dispatch of Stan booking a film into the Rialto Theatre in Corvallis, Oregon. He had frightened her with all that weight, his belly crushing her, depriving her of her own life force.

Earlier that morning, after Stan recognized her, his bear hug pressing her into his girth, she had felt, for a moment, warmed. He had then taken her for a sumptuous breakfast, for old-times' sake, he said, and she had missed an interview with

Jacqueline Bisset, but he had bought her champagne and steak and eggs at 8:00 A.M., and she had been enchanted by the one crisp carnation on the table. The exquisite crystal goblet in which her orange juice swam and Stan's continual touch on her arm to emphasize a point had held the promise of momentary comfort, despite the fact that she thought his hand seemed more porcine than human.

Stanley Abel, proud and able, get your elbows off the table. Stan the man Stan, lying there, catching his breath. Compelled, she had been compelled to follow him to his room.

The star sapphire on his pinky had been a beacon, a beacon to his paunch, to his yellow room, to his shrunken penis; a beacon to some secret unknown place inside herself.

Stan smelled the same as Sol. A Daddy Sol smell. A Canoe, an Aramis smell.

3

Bosoms.

Naomi was surrounded by bosoms. In the elevator going downstairs from Stan's room and in the Carleton lobby, breasts insinuated themselves at her, bouncing, boasting. Whether attached to the bodies of starlets (how obsolete the term now seemed, Naomi thought), or svelte and well-preserved producers' wives, portions, rounded hints of smooth or mottled flesh flashed and flaunted past her.

A muted hum hovered over the lobby, as seas of men dressed in linen jackets and paisley ascots, and women with tight, white gabardine pants and striped Saint-Tropez sweaters, entered and made their way to the reception desk. They gazed hungrily into their boxes for messages, keys, little white and pink bits of paper indicating an invitation for drinks, the promise of a deal, the hope of foreign distribution rights, some indication somewhere that somebody up there liked them. The cacophony was like American Airlines at Kennedy, or the buzz and vibrato of La Bourse, all resounding a J. Arthur Rank gong of delicious dreams—dreams of a killing, dreams of a hit, dreams, such dreams of millions.

"Naomi Lazurus!"

Dizzy from the activity, Naomi wheeled around as a heavy hand pressed her shoulder.

"Daniel, oh God I'm so glad to see you." Naomi looked into the thin face of Daniel Felske. "I didn't know you were here."

"Every year." Daniel took her elbow and led her through the lobby into a wide corridor where distributors had set up booths touting their films. Japanese posters picturing fierce-looking men brandishing samurai swords sat next to belly-to-belly photos of German pornos. Representatives of the distributors stood smiling behind tables covered with flyers and pamphlets advertising their wares. It was Orchard Street upgraded; the stakes were higher and the hawking more subtle, but the sounds and smells were the same.

Daniel led Naomi out onto the Carleton terrace. The weather had become almost balmy and, grateful for the softness in the air, people had removed their jackets and were sitting around small round tables, waving to each other, huddled in talk. A young couple, mirror images of one another in their leonine splendor, unwound themselves from their chairs and, each holding an elegant weimaraner on a leash, strode off the terrace onto the Croisette. Daniel pushed Naomi toward the table, almost knocking down a moon-faced Italian who had in tow a platinum blonde with two-inch-long eyelashes.

"What are you drinking?" Daniel Felske was a middle-aged journalist who had been writing film criticism for *Variety* for twenty years from Rome, where he lived alone. He had mastered the art of pithy language required for the paper and, sadly, not much else.

Naomi had met him ten years earlier, when she was a struggling reporter. After the obligatory pass had been intercepted with grace, they had become friends. Whenever they got together, they talked about books and about the novel for which Daniel had been keeping notes for the past ten years, which they both knew he would never write.

Naomi's legs were still shaking. She could feel her thighs quivering from her time with Stan.

"I cannot believe what I am seeing," Naomi said, watching Daniel's eyes move in the direction of a six-foot-tall blonde.

"She comes every year," he said, leaning over so he wouldn't have to talk loud. "She's got grandchildren."

Naomi watched the woman move in and around the tables. She was wearing a low-cut, red, skin-tight dress whose thin spaghetti straps were holding up the largest breasts Naomi had ever seen; whether or not stuffed with silicone, or sponge, or fat tissue, the effect was grotesque. The woman's hair was long and very blond, and in the late afternoon sun, there was something monumentally fading about her.

"You know, she's been in a few Fellini films," Daniel was saying, unable to take his eyes off her. "She's his type. I know she's got to be over fifty. She's always around here; been supporting herself for years as an extra. That's all, as an extra. Put two kids through college that way. A grotesque voluptuary."

Naomi suddenly felt tired. It was going to be a long week. She was getting jaded. It didn't seem like fun anymore. Tonight she would dress up in a long black gown and put flowers in her hair and carry her cameras and notebook in the Vuitton carrying case her father had given her before she left, and she would do her job. She was a good reporter and had mastered the art of making instant contact. Direct gaze, thorough research, succinct notes, and an excellent memory were the tools she had perfected. She felt complete when she was interviewing; it was a lifetime of a relationship encapsulated into an hour; an intimacy assumed. Most times. Other times, when it did not work, when there was no communication and she couldn't break through, the story turned out shallow, something was wrong.

Daniel had lost interest in Naomi. She watched his eyes move from the woman's breasts to a breathtaking young girl who had come tentatively onto the terrace. How could one live one's life without any pores? There was a simultaneous innocence and arrogance about the girl that was striking.

"They make me feel young," he was saying, anticipating her next remark. "Young girls might be less sophisticated in bed, but they are beautiful. And that's what I want. Ever since you turned me down, Naomi," he said lamely, trying to reinstate himself, "I've just been making up for it with young girls. What it is," he said, staring at the girl, cupping his chin in his hand, "is esthetically pleasing. A young body, a young face close up has a symmetry and perfection. What the hell, it's just nice to look at—to feel. It's good to feel something."

"Right. Hey Dan, what film are you going to tonight?" Naomi did not like the drift of the conversation. It had moved far, far away from her.

Daniel caught the sharpness of her tone and put his hand on her arm.

"I don't know, some American film about disenchantment with violence. Listen, so what else is new?" His gaze drifted away again.

Naomi stood up. "Daniel, I don't think I'll have a drink. Anyway, I've got to get dressed and get my head together." Naomi abhorred popular phrases like "get my head together" but found herself repeating them again and again.

"Oh, Naomi, don't go, come on, I really want to chat." He looked concerned, Naomi thought, but the hell with him.

He pulled her down into her chair.

"Come on, kid, you haven't given me any news. Nothing about anybody in New York and what's happening. Fiona Grant got Bureau Chief in Paris, you know. First woman ever."

"Yes."

"Who do you think will win the prize this year, do you know, could you care less? Oh my God, there's Gina Lollobrigida; that broad hasn't aged at all. It always surprised me how small she is; she photographs big, not just the tits, but big all over. Did you ever see the photographs we published? A slew of them in a book which wasn't half bad. The broad's got brains to want to get out of the tits-and-ass racket. Past thirty-five, maybe forty, forget it. You sure as hell had better have something else going for you."

"Dan," Naomi said, standing up once again. "I've got to go, hon. I'll see you later, maybe after the film here, or inside at the bar. There's lots more time. Maybe we'll have dinner some night." Something was wrong. She was probably getting too old for him, he didn't even want to flirt with her anymore. But so what, she said to herself, after Dan gave her a damp kiss on the cheek and swirled around in his chair, the better to see them with my dear, all those nubile morsels out there who Naomi was convinced had nothing to do with her, with whom she could certainly never compete, now or then or ever. And so what. Get back to work, my dear, she thought, where you feel safe.

Naomi took notes until 3:00 A.M. The transistor radio cooed to her. It kept the loneliness at bay.

She couldn't sleep, but lay with her head against the pillows. Suddenly she leaned over and dialed the long-distance operator.

Her niece's voice made her feel connected to something.

"Aunt Naomi, we went to a parade yesterday."

"What's it doing outside?" Naomi said, pulling the covers up to her chin.

"It's raining for a change. Miss Frankfurt said I was the best speller in the class."

"Wonderful, Janie. What time is it and where's Mommy? I want to speak to her."

"Mommy's asleep and it's nine o'clock."

"Why is she asleep? Who's with you?"

"Mommy. Daddy called and is going to take me away with him to Disneyland. What happens if you put a tushy thermometer in your mouth?"

"Why?"

"Loretta took my temperature and I wouldn't let her put it in my tushy, so I told her to put it in my mouth, and she said it wouldn't do any good, and she got mad at me. What's the difference? Naomi, I don't like things going in my tushy."

"Janie, what's the matter with you that you needed your temperature taken?"

"Cold. Just a cold. When are you coming home? Did you see Matt Dillon?"

"Who?"

"Naomi, he's the biggest thing. He's gorgeous."

"Where's Loretta?"

"Sick, everybody's got viruses."

"I'll call tomorrow. Is Mommy all right?"

"She had a fight with Daddy and ate seventeen Milky Ways. I counted the wrappers."

"Janie?"

"Yes, Naomi. Don't forget to get a good autograph for me. Bring me a surprise person. A mystery guest."

"Okay—Janie?"

"Yes, Naomi."

"I love you a lot."

"Me too. Mom's so sad. I jump around and tell jokes but she doesn't laugh."

"I know, Janie. We have to help her."

Naomi looked at her notebook. She had three interviews tomorrow. She took three sips of Scotch from a silver flask on the night table, and set the alarm. It would take her a long time to fall asleep.

14

New York

4

Philip Roth was walking toward her. It was Madison Avenue and Eighty-first Street and he was holding a long English-style umbrella, and a briefcase. His eyes glanced briefly at her. Naomi, enamored of her own chutzpah, was tempted but she didn't go up to him. Luckily she didn't say, "I write too." But she did look him squarely in the eye, and for the moment, in her imagination, Roth stopped; smitten. He could tell she had just returned from Cannes, he could tell she had just published the world's most definitive interview with Louis Malle. In her head he asked her for a glass of wine at the American Stanhope Hotel on the corner of Fifth and Eighty-first Street. She wondered if he knew that one glass of wine there cost a fortune. But before she knew it the moment had passed. He walked on by. Naomi turned to view his departing figure. She saw a small balding spot. Philip Roth was losing his hair.

"Philip Roth is losing his hair."

"I am not interested in Philip Roth's hair. I am interested in this magazine and your humble part in it. Sit down."

Taller than Naomi, intimidatingly chic, Helene Stanley had a loud voice, and a slight lisp that she always denied having. She had been Naomi's editor for four years. They had fought, disagreed, and were not exactly friends. The sisterhood thing had made it a bit confusing, since Helene was Naomi's boss and both women found power equally enticing. But they shared a mutual respect, a guarded intimacy. And it was only when, like Charlie MacArthur's trench-coated, battered-hat brigade in "Front Page", the two women went to the bar next door to the office after a long day and had their drinks, that they touched, momentarily.

"On the couch. I want to spread out on the coffee table."

Helene pointed to the extravagantly puffed couch in the corner of her mammoth office. Plants and trees and antique furniture and a view of the East River of heroic proportions bombarded the room. It was not a homey office. It was flamboyant, authoritative, like its occupant, with little evidence of humor.

But Naomi liked Helene. She was smart. Naomi knew where she stood with her. Always. And, strangely, if Naomi were ever in trouble she knew she could depend on her. But only up to a point. Only, mind you, if it had nothing to do with Helene's job security and that place in the sun she had fought so hard to attain. Sisterhood was fine, as long as you didn't tread on Helene Stanley's corporate toes.

Naomi collapsed into the couch.

"Soft."

"Just had it restuffed. The Louis Malle piece was really good."

Naomi looked sharply at Helene. The editor rarely gave compliments. Helene expected Naomi to perform beautifully. It was only when she didn't that Naomi would hear about it.

"Well thanks."

"Well, you're welcome. But forget about that. I want to go into a whole new area for us. I've been thinking about it for a long time. You want some coffee?"

"I'm trying to stop. I overdosed on the strong French stuff while I was there. My heart kept beating so fast all the time I thought it was MacNamara's Band inside my gut."

"Child molestation. Incest."

Naomi was used to her abruptness.

"What about it?"

Helene leaned forward, her green eyes shining. She pulled files of newspaper and magazine articles out of her briefcase which was sitting on the glass top of the table.

"In L.A., the County Grand Jury has just indicted nine men suspected of being involved in an international child prostitution and pornography ring." She slapped the paper down with an angry crack.

"Listen to this: 'Seven girls and one boy from the Los Angeles and San Diego areas ranging in age from six to twelve were the alleged victims of child molestation over a three-year period. One was believed to have been used for sexual purposes from the time she was four, the district attorney said. In some cases children actually were sold to adult men for prices ranging up to $1,000. One man is accused of selling his eight-year-old daughter for immoral purposes.' "

"I haven't read anything about that."

"It broke while you were away. You know what—I've had it. We've printed stories on this stuff before, but this time I want to go all out. I want to do a whole issue on child pornography, on pedophilia and molestation and incest. I've commissioned a few other articles and book reviews on the subject, but I have some specific things I want you to concentrate on."

"Four years old? Did you say four years old?"

"Wait till you see some of this material. You won't believe it. And you know who buys this stuff? You know who contributes to the fortunes of these creeps who make their living this way? Listen to this. 'For girl-child porn the average customer is white male, middle class, usually married.' So it's not just your run-of-the-mill raincoat Ralph sneaking into Forty-second Street porno house for a moment's relief from the day's occupation. These are the guys on the commuter trains and in the supermarkets who can't get it off with their wives and have to superimpose their fantasy onto a child. A child. It makes me nauseous."

As always, Helene's intensity and excitement were contagious. Naomi was listening very carefully.

Her ears were buzzing. A four-year-old. Having sex. Opening her mouth to an erect adult penis. Suffocating. Humiliating. An obscene use, an obscene abuse of power. Go away. Take it away, I cannot breathe.

"Here's another one. *New York Times* a few weeks ago. Incest is finally coming out of the closet. My dear, ninety—yes ninety—percent of all sexual abuse in this country takes place in the home. Home, as in there is no place like it.

"This piece says that it's finally coming out how widespread it is, fathers fucking their daughters, literally spoiling their chances for future normal relations. The figures quoted here about the percentage of prostitutes who have been sexually victimized by their daddies are staggering.

"Naomi, I want you to talk to girls who have been abused,

talk to psychiatrists, the authorities. I want to do a whole number on this."

Naomi took a deep breath. Slowly. She had to go slowly around Helene, the woman was too tightly coiled, charged. Naomi pulled a package of cigarettes out of her pocket, and slowly, deliberately took one out and began to light it.

"So?" Helene was swinging her foot, the long thinness of it eased easily into an Italian pump.

"I'm thinking. Now, in the first place I've got a vacation coming."

"You went to Cannes."

"Don't fool around with me, Helene. That was no vacation. Just because there's a beach there and a few palm trees. It wasn't fun and I'm not going to do that again, ever. It's no fun anymore. Stars don't interest me, and there weren't any anyway. I don't want to do assignments like that anymore." She felt tears beginning to come into her eyes. She had no idea she felt so strongly about it.

"All right, all right. That's just my point. You've got that Pulitzer Prize–winner Matthew What's-his-name coming to town. That's soon, isn't it?"

"I have to look at my appointment book."

"I think you should have a cup of coffee."

"I'm just tired and irritable." Naomi jabbed her cigarette out in the ashtray.

"Whose eyes you putting out? I'll put some milk and sugar in it. I think you need some dextrose. You never eat."

Naomi grinned. "We're trying the beneficent mother tactics now."

"It usually works."

Naomi was thinking.

"And you know what else? In the incest cases it's almost impossible to convict these bastards, no less get them treatment. If the kid finally does blow the whistle, the pressure from the mother, accusing the daughter of breaking up the family, causing the loss of financial support, is excruciating. Jesus, those poor girls. What a fucking lonely place. . . . Naomi?"

"I'm listening."

"You interested?"

"I'm interested."

5

"Come over and say goodbye. I want to talk to you about the will," Esther said evenly into the phone.

Every time her parents were going away it was the same. A promised trip for Becky and Naomi to the vault. Mysterious jewels glowing in the dark bowels of the bank; baubles, beads. But somehow the underground expedition never materialized. It would be like tempting that old Grim Reaper. So they never actually made the expedition.

Naomi threw on a raincoat, wound her cameras around her neck, and hailed a cab. She had an interview with an author in two hours, and was girding herself for the last minutes of her parents' pre-catching-the-plane freneticism.

The Park Avenue apartment, a duplex, where Sol and Esther lived, was the same one in which Naomi had grown up. The doormen were the same she had known when she was a child waiting under the canopy for the school bus to pick her up. The bedrooms were on the first floor and upstairs was an enormous living room where a fire was always blazing, except in the summer, and a high-ceilinged dining room which included a marble-faced fireplace. The place was stuffed. To Sol, acquisitions were affirmation of his existence, photos confirmation of his immortality.

Sol Lazurus had begun working his way off the streets as a pushcart peddler, collecting rags, and because he was a fast talker and very handsome, he had pushed his way into the garment center. He made a fortune early. He made his fortune so early that he had been able to go into semiretirement years ago.

Naomi walked into her parents' bedroom. The walls were weighted with hundreds of photographs. Contrary to the Indians' belief that a photograph would take away the soul, Sol somehow felt that if his image were there, hanging on the wall, if there he was, all great smiles, perhaps then he would never die. So there they were; Sol with Lyndon Johnson, Sol with Moshe Dayan, Sol and Esther with Mayor Teddy Kolleck in Jerusalem. Esther, always lovely, always hanging in chronological order, never appearing to age. The exquisite skin is intact, the perfectly coiffured hair is always regal in its white castle.

The room was dimly lit, so Naomi switched on the lamp next to the canopy bed. The thick canopy matched the wallpaper and the upholstered couch in front of the fireplace. She squinted at all the Naomis on the wall. Naomi at ten on a pony in the park; scraggly braids and a nubby knit sweater and the smile very shy. Two teeth are missing. It is her favorite photograph of herself. Naomi at eleven at sleep-away camp, the CB for Camp Bernice emblazoned on her green sweater. She is holding one hand behind her back and the look is a retiring one, even frightened perhaps. Sol likes that picture. He was proud of her then. "You were captain of the blue team and a fabulous volleyball player. I used to come up to camp and watch you hog the ball. What a hogger you were."

"Skinny, you're too skinny," he used to say, but he would be looking at her chest. After all, she was only eleven, but three girls in her bunk had already had their periods and their breasts were pushing out the CB emblem on the blue sweater. "Put some weight on, Naomi," he would say. When he said "weight," Sol meant breasts, Naomi was convinced of that, as though she could indeed grow breasts overnight. The little wads of Kleenex stuffed in the roomy bra did little good; she looked lumpy, lopsided, and they tickled. Oh, to have breasts, she had thought. Oh, to be beautiful and full and heavy, to feel the heaviness would be bliss, the ultimate in fulfillment and sensuality and acceptance.

But she was a long drink of water. A string bean when a voluptuous green pepper was the preferred dish.

"That Renee is quite well-developed," Sol would say at

Camp Bernice on the August visiting day. That was the word, "well-developed." Naomi was undeveloped; underdeveloped, she thought, as in country, as in Africa or South America, for example. "Am I pretty?" she had written home that summer. Such doubts. No matter. She would think herself pretty. She would conjure mountains of fantasy flesh onto her chest and buttocks. Some day Sol would look at her with the same covetousness that he reserved for the statuesque.

Naomi picked up her high school graduation picture. (Such a hot night; she was perspiring under her arms and couldn't stop crying as "Pomp and Circumstance" nudged her down the aisle. Ethel White had been pregnant that night and later had had twins and everyone had used their programs for fans.) I am so full-faced in this photo, she thought, the smile still tight, the knuckles white, fingers clutching the diploma. She moved on to Naomi and Hank Loeffler walking down yet another aisle, at the Pierre Hotel in some grand ballroom with yellow walls. Her smile is strained. He looks bewildered. He had loved her in his way. He thought she was funny and he liked her energy. But Hank was concerned with facts; Naomi with nuance. He wanted order; Naomi mobility. He was a good man. Earnest. But he lacked imagination. They had made each other up and when they discovered they each had married a stranger, they knew it was over.

Janie was pinned to the wall also. Janie as a baby, Janie graduating from kindergarten, Janie on her mother's lap, on her grandmother's lap. Esther looks especially careful with her grandchild on her lap. She is wearing silk and silk wrinkles easily. Her other daughter, Rebecca, sinks behind her own eyes. It is hard to see who she is.

Naomi moved on. There were pictures of Sol with bathing beauties, at Saint-Tropez, in Estoril, at Palm Beach. Sol is short and his stomach protrudes, even in the young pictures, but he has a full head of hair always. There is Sol with his arms around Sophia Loren, his hand around her waist. He is in profile and it is obvious that he is looking deep down into her dress.

There are pictures of Sol's parents, yellowing half-smiles, faded, loose-fitting clothes. Today Sol, in his sixties, talks about them as though they had only gone around the corner for a newspaper a few minutes ago and would be back soon.

Naomi sank down into the overstuffed couch in front of the fireplace. The room smelled of her parents. The expensive floral odor of her mother, the tart muskiness of her father. This was a room she had known all her life. Sunday morning the *New York Times* covered the king-size bed as Esther would hold court, zealously protecting the theater and book sections. Esther would drink cup after cup of black coffee dutifully poured by Sol into the Spode china pot, placed on a tray and brought to her bed with one rose presiding in a Steuben vase.

Naomi and Rebecca would crawl up on the satin quilt and read the funnies in the *Daily News*. Sol, in his pajamas, would look over the proceedings. Esther's face was smoothed with cold cream, Sunday being the day of rest for her face too. She would put her face up to be kissed.

But Sundays were good in that room. All of them sprawled on the oversize bed; Sol disappearing into some cavern somewhere returning with baby Tootsie Rolls or miniature Three Musketeers. Esther sitting up, straight through it all. Regal. In charge.

Her parents careened into the room, breaking Naomi's reverie.

"You're not, you're certainly not going to bring all those bags." Sol stood staring at the three enormous suitcases, jewelry cases, book bag that Esther had piled up at the door.

"Esther, you do this every damn time and every damn time I tell you, 'Esther, don't take so goddamn much.' Leave some stuff home, for God's sake. You need one bag. Who takes three? Nobody takes three for ten days. Nobody. Nobody but Esther Leah Lazurus. Besides which I am not carrying that jewelry bag all the hell over the place. Last time I almost put my back out."

"I'll carry it." Esther was hardly paying attention to her husband's tirade. She was used to it. She had heard the same words, seen the same fury, the same veins pop out of the same head for almost forty years. Forty years next June as a matter of fact.

"Sol. Don't get me nervous. Just don't get me nervous." Esther was shaking her finger at Sol. "I'm calm now. I was fine this morning. I did my meditation and my exercises. I have calmed myself. Naomi, when did you come? I didn't hear you.

Just don't make me nervous, tell Joseph to go outside in twenty-five minutes and get us a cab. In twenty-five minutes, if you leave me alone and stop ranting, I will be totally ready." Esther was trying desperately to be in control. It was a losing battle. Sol's short fuse made it almost impossible.

"Esther, I'm telling you right now, if you don't unpack one of those bags and take just two, we are not going. We are just goddamn not going. How dare you, how dare you. I'm the one who has to pay the overweight. I'm the one who has to schlep the bags if we can't get a porter and those porters charge an arm and a leg. So what the hell are you giving me!"

Sol's face had gotten very red and his hands were shaking. He turned to his daughter.

"Naomi be sure and keep in touch with Rebecca while we're away. I'm worried about her."

Esther looked him straight in the eye. "Sol Lazurus, I'm going to divorce you. I don't care about forty years or whatever. I've had it. I don't know how I've stood it this long. I'm going to call the lawyer.

"Oh, Mommy," Sol said suddenly, realizing he had gone too far, "stop it. Who would bring your breakfast in bed Sunday mornings? Who would warm your feet at night? Come on, baby." The tone had changed. The anger abated. It was a ritual, a mating dance. Naomi had heard it a thousand times.

"I am not fooling," Esther said, reciting her lines in this passion play. "I've had it. You yell and you scream. For what? For what, Sol Lazurus? Just to get me upset." Esther had begun to speak very softly.

"What's with the sotto voce? All of a sudden, you're speaking so elegantly. Come on, baby girl. Let's be all right. Let's get organized or we're going to miss the plane. Who's my sweet, sweet girly-girl?"

"Sol, stop already with that sweet, sweet stuff. We're too old and too grown-up for that." Triumphant, Esther put the jewelry bag on her little shoulder, folded her mink coat carefully so that the satin lining embossed with a rococo *L* was face up, patted her hair with a confident motion as she passed the bedroom mirror; and, not looking at Sol, put her face up to be kissed by her eldest daughter.

"Hold the fort, Naomi," Sol said, pulling Naomi up by her elbows out of the couch. He hugged her hard. Naomi felt herself stiffen as her breasts pressed against him. She contracted her stomach à la Martha Graham as he hugged her. He didn't say anything. Just picked up his wife's bags as she walked chattering out the door.

Suddenly, the house was quiet. The whirling dervishes had whisked out the door in a flurry of invective and shouts. So much whirling, so much dervishing, Naomi thought. Were they Turks the dervishes, and why on earth did they whirl? No matter. The house was quiet; her parents had gone.

Naomi's interview with Matthew Johnson, author, explorer extraordinaire was not scheduled for an hour. She walked into her mother's bathroom. She felt like a giant there. She was so tall and her mother was so small, this diminutive white-haired person whose essence was floral and organza, petals and veils. She faced herself in her mother's mirror. Big, she always felt so big next to her, a towering awkward bean of a girl. Creams and combs, pins and pencils lined the marble counter top. There were gold faucets and an elaborate frame surrounding the mirror.

As a little girl Naomi used to look in that same glass, adjusting the mirrored closet doors in back of her so that if she stood in such a way she would be able to see the back of her whole self. She used to wobble in heels high as the sky in there, with her mommy's dress of decolletage dreams hanging limp over her thin bosom. Naomi would stand, smiling, the silhouette's leg bent, curved seductively.

And she would become Esther then. And Naomi, drowning in her mommy's dress, tottering on her pointed stilts, dreamed of her mommy somehow disappearing, just vanishing like the wicked witch of the west, up and out into a poof of smoke, leaving only an empty dress and her shining, shimmering, pointed red shoes.

Leaving Naomi and her magic shoes alone with Sol in the castle in the mirror with Sol singing Rapunzel, Rapunzel, Naomi, Naomi let down your long hair, and he would climb up and they would shut the castle window and they would live happily ever after. In the castle. In the mirror. In Naomi's mother's bathroom.

6

The Palm Court of the Plaza was an odd place to interview a man associated with climbing mountains and writing books about the Depression and the South. But this was where Matthew wanted to meet. Or where his agent and/or publicity director wanted to make the appointment. He was only in New York for a few days publicizing his new book before he returned to Los Angeles where he lived high in the hills.

Naomi was not looking forward to the interview. Johnson had a reputation of being a womanizer, a macho Hemingway character of epic proportions. But she had been impressed by his last book, *Trager*. It was a lyrical evocation of the man's voraciousness for the outdoors and learning. No one intimidated Naomi as long as she had a notebook in her hand, a camera around her neck. But, riding over in a cab to the Plaza, she had pangs. Perhaps the afternoon might present something of a challenge.

She was right. Punctual, Matthew Johnson was waiting for her in the lobby as she raced in, ten minutes late. His beard was red, his hair dark brown and long, the residue, she would learn later, of a tow-headed boy, whose Danish heritage also gave him the palest of blue eyes and the broadest of chests. A Viking, she thought, as she walked over to shake his hand.

"Johnson, Matthew. You must be Lazurus." The hands stayed in the pockets.

"Lazurus, Naomi," she said grinning. She liked his face.

"Yes, Lazurus you have risen. It's about time. I'm dying for a drink. Let's weave in and around the tea-toting ladies, the petits fours and the petits sandwiches and get us a real drink, girl. They didn't tell me you were going to be pretty."

"Thanks." She couldn't think of a brilliant amusing cogent retort.

"You go everywhere with those cameras pulling your shoulders down?"

The maitre d' was leading them toward a table in the back. Matthew took Naomi's elbow and firmly guided her in back of a man who was wearing a tuxedo in broad daylight.

After three boilermakers, Matthew made it very clear he wanted her. After four, he got up from the table and walked to the men's room where, he told her later, he had taken a pee and called his agent and canceled his next three appointments. After five, he was talking about the importance of the soul in sex.

"Even at the soul's weakest," he said, leaning forward, not touching her, still not touching her, "the spirit's feeblest, befogged by booze, pain, starvation, whatever, in many there is still that soul's glimmer, a final soft word of love, a final goddamn. That is what we must save at all costs. Without it there is nothing but the machine. Without good soul, sex must become akin to torture, a gleeful debasement of others along with all value, a smearing with shit of everything reachable, a saving of shit as if it were gold, an obsessive involvement with shit in general. Naomi," he did not stop for a breath, "go see the toilets in Germany with the little trays where they can examine their feces before flushing. Perhaps the last sign that France yet has a sense of the soul is that you must often squat over a hole in the floor."

Naomi's eyes were wide. In all this time, she had not yet begun the interview. She had listened.

"So, Mr. Johnson." She mustered up her Barbara Walters voice. "You were born in the South, and . . ."

He moved on.

"I am involved in another thought. You see, I am not opposed to modern plumbing in the least. But its importance as cultural standard of excellence is highly overrated."

"Mr. Johnson . . ."

"Matthew, as in the Bible. Call me Matthew. Not Matt, as in door, it does not suit me."

She laughed, but she realized she was not the one in control.

"Your mouth is open, Miss Lazurus. I assume it is Miss since there is no ring on your finger, no bells on your toes, and since ladies of your persuasion rarely have the persuasion of wedding. Bedding yes, wedding no. Relationships perhaps, but no," he took a long look, "no, I don't think so. Your work is your everything, I would say. Your refrigerator is empty, perhaps except for a bottle of champagne and one avocado, in season, of course; you go out for dinner every night, you've got a lot of chrome around in your apartment, it's roomy and your office is perhaps the warmest spot in the place. An armchair perhaps, bulletin board over the desk filled with memorabilia . . . I think . . . "

"I think that's all rather presumptuous. I think we really should begin the interview," she said, reaching for archness. "I don't know how we got this far afield." Naomi unscrewed her ball-point pen. Set up her little tape recorder. She tried to stare him down.

"What is it about you that moves me so," he said quietly.

Naomi thought she was going to cry.

7

I will drown in his words, Naomi thought as Johnson helped her into a taxi. The liquor had barely affected him. If anything it made him more cogent, more mellifluous.

He put his arm around her shoulders as Naomi gave the cab driver the address of her apartment.

He took a long look at her.

She thought he was going to kiss her. She thought he was going to tell her he had fallen in love with her.

"Are you aware," he said, "are you aware that the Dani tribe, all five thousand members of them, who exist in the Grand Valley of West Irian, which used to be called West New Guinea by the way, do not make love during the first two years of marriage and abstain completely for four to six years after the birth of a child?" Spoken in all seriousness, a concerned paternalistic expression on his face.

"No, as a matter of fact I was not aware of that fact," Naomi said straightfaced.

"Treat this fact, if you will, with some respect," Johnson said, still not cracking a smile. "And indeed be more than grateful that I am not a member of this illustrious tribe. They do not have much drive, sexual or otherwise, and instead of expressing anger they usually move away from a threatening situation."

"Fascinating. But I hate to say it, I didn't get enough material for my story." And with chagrin, "I didn't get any pictures either. The cameras stayed around my neck. We have been talking for hours and I haven't been doing my job."

A strong turn flung her against him. He smelled of strong tobacco. In a passing street light she saw a large *G* for Givenchy embroidered on his shirt collar.

How come such an outdoorsman likes name brands? she thought. She stayed close to him, not moving back to her place. The man had the oddest effect on her. She listened; interrupted perhaps, changed the subject, perhaps, but was for her, quiet. Very.

"Actually, it certainly does give you second thoughts about Freud, doesn't it?"

The driver was approaching Central Park West where Naomi lived.

"I mean after all, if this low energy system is, as anthropologists seem to think, less genetic or biological and more cultural, well, then, shit, what do you do with the whole Freudian thing about the innate power of the sexual drive? What do you think Miss Lazurus who has risen, Miss Lazurus who shall rise again? I would like to hear your opinion on this."

"Some other time. Here's my house, my doorman, my bed and board." She was getting as silly as he was. "I know you're in town for only a short while but I've got to get the story on you with more information than about what you feel the Sexless Indians of wherever are about."

"Redundant. You used the word 'about' twice in one phrase, redundant you are, with unfortunately, disastrous syntax. I'll come up. You can take a picture of me raiding your refrigerator, pouring beer into your goldfish bowl, climbing a ladder to your bookshelves to find a copy of Karl Marx, standing in front of a print of my favorite artist Edvard Munch. 'The Scream' perhaps . . . or . . . "

He took a fistful of bills and change out of his pocket and let the driver pick out what he wanted. He started rubbing the back of Naomi's neck.

Naomi had heard it all. She had heard all their stories, from all those men out there. Since she was fifteen, as a matter of fact. For twenty years now she had listened to their tales of woe and wonder, of women and war. This was the first time she had heard something new in a long time. She was tired of their tales, those men out there, tired of their stories about other lovers, about those who could only have orgasms if *he* poured hot wax on *her* face and let it harden; or *he,* after spending a weekend in a country inn, discovered that *she* had one leg more than a foot shorter than the other. Men loved to talk about other conquests, other "cuntries," she thought. She was drunk and punning in her head and acting as ridiculous as Matthew. Matthew Johnson.

"No. No coming up. Not tonight."

They were standing on the street in front of the mammoth glass doors of her apartment house. The doorman, a bit disheveled, a bit weary from his brandy nipping in the basement, was peeking out, wondering about the Viking and the bean of a girl giggling out there as cabs whizzed by and stars fell, if not on Alabama at least on the Central Park Zoo.

"What do you mean not coming up."

"That's what I said."

"Bullshit."

"Mr. Johnson, I'm supposed to get this story to an editor in a week. At this point I don't know a thing about you except that you are charming and, like everybody else, just like everybody else wanting to end the evening in a predictable way. Well, I'm not feeling predictable for once and . . ." Again she was close to tears.

"What are you feeling? Lazurus."

"I don't know what I'm feeling but I want to go upstairs and find out." The tears finally oozed out of her eyes.

He took his cue from her.

"I've got two TV shows in the morning. Then I've got to go home to Los Angeles Sunday. Some people want to talk to me about making a movie out of my last book. There's not much chance to get acquainted is there? You got something against going all the way on the first date?"

Naomi, who at this point was at a loss to explain her actions as well as her feelings, was fighting for her composure.

"Your mascara's running."

"Lunch tomorrow," was all she could muster.

"I can't." He looked crestfallen.

"I still have to get my interview with you, in broad daylight with no alcoholic beverages."

"Don't be so flippant."

32

"I have to get a story. My editor wants a story on you for some reason."

"Come to L.A. then. We'll pick up where we left off."

At that point she turned and walked into the lobby, leaving Matthew Johnson on the sidewalk. She took refuge in Nick the doorman's bloodshot eyes, his blue frayed uniform badly in need of pressing.

The phone nestled in the crook of Naomi's neck. "So I'll kill two birds with one stone. I'll interview Johnson in L.A. The city has a special police unit on the sexually exploited child, and I could interview incest authorities out there." Naomi used her cajoling voice on Helene.

"I cannot imagine how you could spend a whole evening with the man and not get the glimmer of an interview." Helene was incredulous.

"A glimmer, that's just about all I got."

"Okay. So go. Call me when you get there. I've got three other calls. Gotta go. Bon voyage."

8

Naomi stared out of the airplane window. Her legs ached as she twisted them under the seat. Helene's secretary had specifically requested an aisle seat, the haven for the tall, but naturally the airlines didn't comply, and here she was pasted up against the window. A barrel of a man sat down beside her and proceeded to eye her long legs, which were trying to find a home. He took a large round cigar from his breast pocket, crinkled the paper off, and stuffed the cigar into his mouth. Naomi was trying to stop smoking this week. The third time this month. The idiot secretary had not succeeded in getting her into a nonsmoking section either. She tried to scrunch down into her seat. Putting the pillow against her cheek, she turned her face to the window.

Naomi shut her eyes. Several years ago, she had come upon meditation. Taking the meditation course had been a fad. She always went under the guise of reportage, research covering a multitude of indulgences. But, all right, so she would admit it; she was a faddist.

But when the Maharishi decided to levitate and proposed that people of her height do so also, that was the last straw. She turned in her TM card. But now and then, like now, meditation helped. She would will the man next to her away, whisk him off into Maharishi land. She drowned in her mantra. Over and over the word *Ala* lulled her as she felt the plane finally levitate into the clouds.

"Mind if I smoke?"

Here she was with her back to him and her eyes shut and does she mind if he smokes.

She did not move, nor acknowledge that he was a living breathing thing.

"I know a cigar can really affect some women, so if you're violently against it I won't light up."

Silence.

When she heard the match go, she couldn't help herself.

"As a matter of fact," she said, turning as sweetly as she could, "cigars do make me nauseous."

Crestfallen, he quickly made moves to douse the cigar, but not before taking one long, lingering puff. Naomi felt guilty for a single moment, but owed the debt to her sinuses.

"Thank you so much."

"Tannenbaum. Arthur Tannenbaum." He handed Naomi a card. She unwound her legs into some semblance of straightness. Vice President, the card said, of Burton, Barton, etc. He admitted to her in what proved later to be a characteristically honest yet irritating attitude that he was one of many vice presidents.

And Arthur Tannenbaum took over. Naomi was astounded by the avalanche of the words, not to be contained. She could not keep her eyes off his face. There seemed to be no upper lip, and under his grey eyes were deep circles. Smudges of coal.

He settled in. There was no escape. "I was born and raised in the Bronx. We were poor, and Jewish. Are you Jewish?" He did not wait for an answer. "After college I went to Washington to work for the government. At twenty-one I met my wife, got married, worked for the IRS, went to law school at night. God, did we struggle. I made thirteen thousand a year. Had two sons. Got an offer in '59 to come to New York, doubled, then tripled my salary. Listen, my whole life, I chased. You know? We had the house in Riverdale, the private schools, money. And I chased. Met a twenty-three-year-old in the office. I was forty-one. Fell in love or learned about sex, I'm not sure which. One or the other. I still can't tell. I was crazy. It lasted two years. My wife wouldn't divorce me. The girl wanted to get married, you know?"

He did not stop to take a breath. Naomi barely heard the words, they came so torrentially. She was repelled, fascinated.

35

"So I almost had a nervous breakdown. I went to stay with my brother in L.A. He fixed me up. I learned that I could have oral sex with anyone. You know what I mean?"

He looked quickly at her to judge her reaction. She would not bat an eyelash. Airplane survival tactics. She had long ago passed the commando course.

"So now, listen, I don't have the energy to fall in love. And you know what else?"

Naomi blinked her eyes in response.

"I can't bring myself to have oral sex with my wife. And don't tell me I should go see someone to figure it out. I'm not going to any shrink with that. Look, my relationship with my wife is okay. She doesn't think about it. Never says a word. And me, I lead an exciting life, I travel." He searched around for some wood to knock on. "Look, your work ever take you downtown? I could show you the sights of Wall Street. How about lunch some time?"

"I'm getting married in the morning." Naomi, in retreat, almost chanted the Lerner and Loewe to Mr. Tannenbaum who by this time looked quite exhausted, the coal under his eyes melting into a mausoleum pallor.

"I see. Well, look," he said, turning away from her, "I hope you don't mind but I'm going to catch forty so I'll be good and rested when we land. Okay, kid?"

Los Angeles

9

The police inspector handed Naomi a photograph. It was a picture of a nine-year-old girl lying on a bed. Her body took up most of the page. She was naked, with a flat, concave chest. She had one hand over her heart, as in the photographs Naomi's father used to take of her at birthday parties as she was blowing out the candles on her cake. Her hand had been over her heart then too.

The pubis of the girl in the photo swelled high. Without hair, it looked innocent, nonsexual in a way, oddly sweet. A man's finger was being inserted into the vagina. The girl's eyes looked straight into, almost through the camera.

Naomi did not blink. Inspector Porter did not look at her as he rifled through other pornographic photos. Other pamphlets.

It was late on Hill Street. Everyone else had gone home. Naomi was sitting opposite Chief Inspector Ira Porter of the Sexually Abused Child Unit of the Los Angeles Police Department. It was one of the few units of its kind in the country. His office was small and glass-enclosed, surrounded by a larger room that was dimly lit, echoing an emptiness, as ghosts of clicking typewriters and ringing phones hid in silent corners of the room.

Fiddling with her tape recorder, Naomi watched the little red dial flicker frantically; some indication that there was life in the machine, that for once it would work all the way through an interview without her sheepishly shutting it off, forcing her to rely on her notes, her memory.

Porter threw another photograph at her, then another. An eight-year-old wearing knee socks, lying on her back, legs straight in the air, was holding the backs of her knees as a finger was being inserted into her; a girl looking about ten with a flat boyish body stared at the camera, with a penis in her mouth; two nine-year-olds were playing with another's genitals.

"Sure, I'm obsessed by it," the short inspector was saying, fixing his eyes on Naomi. "You know when I first got into this, it was when I was on the vice squad, before we were able to get us this special unit, I saw a picture, just one picture started me. I have a copy of it here." Bending down to the bottom file standing next to his desk, the inspector found a folder filled with pornographic material. Naomi took notes about the Inspector's shirt sleeves, the tattoo on his arm, the careful, neat appearance. The enormous hands.

"Here it is, and I'm telling you someday I'm going to get him, that guy in the picture. Someday I'm going to get him."

He handed Naomi a color photograph. A boy looking about seven or eight had his mouth around the penis of a middle-aged man. The boy was looking covertly, fearfully at the photographer. He was afraid.

"That's it, that's what started me," the inspector said, his beefy hands folding and unfolding. He was impassioned, but Naomi heard words that sounded as though they had been repeated many, many, times. The inspector had been giving a lot of interviews recently, had testified before a congressional committee investigating child pornography, and was continually going to PTA groups.

It was eight in the evening and Naomi had been in his office for an hour. She was very hot. She yearned for a shower, fresh makeup, a magazine, a drink, but she sat straight. Efficient.

"Who do you think took the picture?" she asked.

"There's always somebody there," he said, "that's part of it. Listen, Naomi, Los Angeles is the child-porno center of the country."

Coolly, Naomi looked at copies of magazines the inspector had pulled from his files. It was odd. Here she was, sitting in this quiet empty building with this stranger, looking at photographs that were deviant, horrifying, blatantly sexual. She would not flinch, she would not blink, she would not in any way indicate a reaction to the material. She could not fathom why there was an automatic mysterious stirring. These were children, these pubescent little girls, each looking like Naomi's ten-year-old niece in the bath. Janie was buoyant and funny, rosy and lovely in the bath, talking grandly and eloquently to herself. Janie was a child, her sensuality primitive, appealing. Snuggling deep into her satin comforter at night, smellng of Johnson's Baby Powder, her cheeks dewy from the bath, Janie was loveliness, incredibly desirable. And Naomi, hugging her sister's child, sniffing the aroma of little girl, would delight in such natural pure sensuality.

But this was something else, this brazen puffy vagina, this erect penis being held by a small hand.

She pulled her camera out of its jacket and shot one round after another of the inspector as he was talking. She worked with quick precise movements. He was used to speaking about the inflammatory material, but Naomi detected the slightest intimation of his curiosity about how she was reacting. It could have been her imagination. All she knew was that this was her job, she was professional and it was important. She could not let her mind wander.

"Look," he continued. "These kids are what we call willing victims. They're seduced by attention and affection. It's the same way young men seduce women, with gifts and kindness." He settled back into his chair, smoothing the watchband on his arm. "Say you're a widow, or divorced, right, and you're the one who struggles to make the living for the family. Right? I'm the neighbor down the street, or something, and I try to be nice. So you think I'm after you. First off I bring a bag of groceries, try to get to know you. I take you and the kids out to dinner, come home, sit around and talk. Right? I don't make advances. I'm a gentleman. I'm a nice guy."

Naomi watched the tape go around and around. The little red light flickered. It was working, she thought, relieved. But she continued taking notes. She wished he wouldn't keep personalizing his story. She squirmed a bit, smoothed her stockings with her hand, and listened intently.

"So I'm going to take the kids to Disneyland tomorrow and, Jesus, you haven't been able to take the kids anywhere for a long time. And me, I'm just a good guy and I give attention and affection to your family. So the next day I take the kids to the beach. Now your oldest boy is twelve. So Monday I bring him a new bike. And you, you're beside yourself with this good guy who's come into your life. I take you all to dinner again, then just me and you. You trust me. You may make advances, or maybe I seduce you. At any rate then I move right in."

The inspector had a dramatic flair. He told his story well. Naomi's pen made scratching sounds across her pad. The inspector continued to build his case.

"And then what I do is I ask you if I can take Billy camping. Sure, you say, okay. So I pick him up Friday night. And then, the next day at about sundown I show him pornographic pictures. We take a bath together. I get the opportunity to touch him. I molest him. He won't refuse because I did all those lovely things for him, you see. And I say to him, if you tell anybody, I'll take the bike back. And we won't go fishing next week.

"And Billy doesn't tell, he's got no father you see. I'm the new father, you speak highly of me, and he's embarrassed. And you know what? I'm going to molest all of your boys. I might even marry you. Because pretty soon Bill will get to be too old for me and I will prefer the younger ones. And that, Naomi, is your ideal neighborhood molester. He can be anything from an unskilled worker to a corporate executive."

Inspector Porter took a sip of water from a thermos sitting on his desk. Naomi took the tape out and turned it over.

"A lot of these men are in protective marriages, some have incestuous relationships with their daughters. They are people who cannot receive fulfillment from sexual relationships with peers," he said.

"Look, let me show you something." The inspector delved once again into the recesses of the Pandora's box of a filing cabinet. Naomi did not stop writing.

He handed Naomi the declaration he had taken from a ten-year-old boy named Tom. She scanned it, divining the boy's explanation of what some forty-year-old man had cajoled him into doing. Words like "dildo" and "up the butt" and "big Bertha's butt banger" jumped off the page.

It was enough. Naomi's eyes burned. She put her notebooks away, shook the inspector's hand and thanked him. She walked outside and let the air calm her face.

Naomi had covered Vietnam and veterans' hospitals, she had seen the disfigurement and the excrement, the stumps and the scars, she had spent hours inside an eight-by-ten cell at the Tombs, she had interviewed a man who had confessed to committing five rapes. She was rarely afraid. She had won awards for her stories. She could take whatever the inspector had to tell her. In her professional life Naomi Lazurus Loeffler was one smart, sharp thirty-five-year-old lady.

Her personal life was something else.

10

Driving back to the Beverly Hills Hotel, Naomi began to let down. The material Inspector Porter had shown her was indeed the end of the world, she thought. She felt dirty, contaminated. She wondered how he could make this his profession; tracking down evil, day after day, dealing with men who preyed on children.

She went through a red light, but luckily there was not an officer in sight. She was not used to driving, being a New Yorker, and all she could see in her mind's eye was the last picture the inspector had shown her. He had told her that it was taken by the children.

It showed a stocky man, naked, smeared with blood, with torture machinery sticking out of different parts of his body. It was obvious that the children had had to operate these devices. He was tied up. Heavy apparatus was hanging from his testicles and blood was coming out of his anus. The inspector had quietly mused that this man was a masochist, but what would have happened had he been a sadist? He had explained passionlessly that bags containing the remnants of boys' bodies had been found throughout the city in the past year. Some fun. Some world.

The boy took her car in front of the hotel. She was tired, but exhilarated in some way. She knew she was tenacious, she knew she would write a good piece. Tomorrow she would contact the two judges and two psychiatrists who were consultants to the court on incest cases.

Naomi caught a glimpse of herself in the mirror next to the

phones on the way to the Polo Lounge. Gone was the smooth-
ness of six o'clock when she had first encountered Inspector
Porter and the Hill Street Station. Gone were the evenly placed
rouge and lash-lengthened eyes. There was a toughness, her
"coping look" as she called it. The big bang Bertha or whatever
the pleasure pain principle that poor sick man had titillated
himself with would not shock her; children in the most degrad-
ing and provocative poses would not give her tears. Being a
professional would protect her. When she had gone into the
veterans' hospital in the Bronx and had to hold a handkerchief
to her face to avoid the smell, the *Newsweek* reporter with her
had said, "Listen, you gotta get tough. We have to hide behind
our notebooks to stay sane." And so she did, stay sane and hide
behind her notebook and her cameras and her briskness and her
efficiency. Someday she would win a Pulitzer Prize, someday
she would write the story or the book that would move the
world. Naomi would make people cry. She liked to touch them
with her words and her photos. Her performance was exem-
plary on this field of battle. She was proud of her performance.
Cool. She had been cool.

But Naomi couldn't bear the thought of going up to her
room alone. She had called Matthew Johnson but he was out of
town. She told the female voice who answered that she would
like to see him. Her heart sped up when she heard the voice, but
she toyed with the idea that it was the maid. That was comforting for a while.

Here I am in my big pink house, she thought, this big
dream house of a hotel where Mary Pickford and Charlie Chap-
lin and this one and that one had their rendezvous in the bun-
galows out there by the tennis courts and here I am all expenses
paid in a big beautiful room in this big beautiful hotel, but I
don't want to go up to that room alone.

Walking into the Polo Lounge, she squinted into the darkness, trying to find the maitre d'. It was after nine, but the room
was very busy. A statuesque girl with long brown hair was
sitting at a table in the corner. She was very beautiful in a light
blue dress, low cut enough to reveal a tan freckled chest. An
elegant hooker. Hook and eye, hooked on love, hooking a rug.
Naomi's mind was racing. Words. Why hooker? Naomi smiled
at the maitre d'. He ignored her.

"I'd like a table for one, please," she said, shifting her camera more comfortably on her shoulder.

He continued to ignore her.

She began tapping her foot impatiently, as he kept looking around at three empty tables as though they were crammed with people.

"Naomi Loeffler, Room 802, *Women Today*, expense account. I'm sure there must be something," she said.

"Of course, Miss Loeffler," he said, "it's just that those tables are reserved. But wait. Of course I can place you. Please wait a moment."

A tall man wearing a sweater open at the neck came through the door and stood quiety behind Naomi. She glanced briefly at him.

"Having trouble getting a table?" he asked. The sweater was blue, the better to see you with, Naomi surmised, since it brought out the blue in his eyes. She knew it, and he definitely knew it. He was carrying a purse whose handle rested around his wrist.

"It would seem so," she said.

"Watch," he said.

"Felix. Two."

Felix raised one eyebrow, gave Mr. Blue Sweater, Mr. Blue Eyes, the once over and led them toward a table deep in the corner. He took Naomi's elbow and led her to it.

"All you need is to be a man." Naomi sighed. "Aren't you meeting someone?" she said, over her shoulder.

"You."

Predictable. Now, she could predict the next hour. He had to be the creative director of an advertising agency in New York, on the coast shooting commercials, or a writer whose agent had stood him up for a drink, or a married studio executive unwilling to go home.

Naomi began playing the game.

Yes, she was in town for a short time; no, she didn't like California; yes, this was her first trip; no, she didn't know her nose was shiny; yes, she would like another drink. He rolled up his sleeve and the hairs on his arm were curly and blond. Squinting at him she tried to remember his name and what he had said his youngest child had done in school that day. He asked if he could come up to her room and she hedged. She had to go over her notes and play her tape recorder, she had to wash her face and meditate, relax. She had to be one-directional.

Sharp words cut across the room.

"All I know is that it's either be a success and do what I want to do or not get fucked. It's become one or the other." An intense young woman was saying her piece. There had been a lull in the lounge hum and her words sang out. She was not embarrassed, she did not know that Naomi or What's-his-name had heard her. "I'm too strong for them. How is some studio ever going to come on to me when I'm more powerful than he is? When I can make things happen and he can't." She put her hand on her friend's arm.

"Women's lib is outsmarting itself. There are no men for us."

She had seen them before, Naomi had. These women. These hustlers and operators. They could get things done. They could manage millions and some day would run studios and couldn't find men to make love to them who would stay and care about them through sickness and health and all that. She would never admit an identification with them.

"Androgyny recapitulates ontogeny?" Naomi was feeling the drink.

"What do you mean, pretty lady?" Blue Eyes was moving in.

"Just eavesdropping." Blue Eyes was getting more attractive by the minute.

"Oh yeah. Those broads have more balls than anything. Not you. Not you, honey."

"Me. Me. I'm neither here nor there," Naomi heard somebody in her mouth saying. Somewhere some man was taking pictures of little girls with their little round bodies and some other man was buying these pictures for his own enjoyment. She took another sip of her Scotch. She liked to drink and could drink her liquor as well as any man.

Gin fizz. That's what Sol had told her to order when she went out on dates. "Gin fizz and don't let them lay a hand on you, kid. I know, I know men. Listen, I've been there myself. I know what they want. To get in. To get into your pants. Gin fizz forever, Naomi. That way you always know what's going on and nobody can take advantage. Keep your legs together. Someday he'll come along, that prince. And he'll be big and strong, the man you love." No, he didn't say that. That's a song by another name.

Naomi was unwinding. It was the way she unwound. Scotch. And . . .

Blue Eyes was tickling the inside of her hand. Her leg jerked forth. There was a direct line from her palm to her nipple to her crotch. The electric current was carried straight to the source. The last time she had taken a man up to her hotel room, in San Francisco when she was doing a story on Linus Pauling, he had given her some kind of disease. She had sworn to be more careful, she had decided that taking one's sex as a man does has drawbacks for a woman. "It's because you are the recipient," the resident psychiatrist at a magazine she once worked for said. That's why a woman can't be like a man. A man puts it in. A woman receives it. On top of which, the more partners, the more chance of cervical cancer. It doesn't matter, Naomi thought, responding to the tickling in her palm. Blue Eyes was pressing his suit. She would take him to the cleaners.

"What are you laughing about?" he said as she threw back her head and giggled. She delighted in the pun in her head but would not share it. She had to get up early in the morning. She wanted to take a swim before breakfast. Keep your legs together, Sol had said. Wait for Mr. Right. Good God. Mr. Right is the bluebird of happiness in your own backyard, Mr. Right is the center of the universe located right in the middle of your own stomach. And Matthew Johnson wasn't in town. Probably bedding down his thousandth lover. And Matthew Johnson wasn't in town.

"I have a masters degree in engineering," Blue Eyes was saying, the hand moving surreptitiously up the left arm. "But I don't use it. Boring. Commercials. That's my bag. But I'm working on a novel that would make a swell film. My agent has lots of interest."

"I have a masters too," Naomi said. She never admitted it much. In the circles in which she traveled, people really didn't care much about degrees. Journalists were more interested in how you covered the story and if you got the facts right and if you could spell.

"In what?" Blue Eyes said, stopping for a moment on his finger floating journey, forgetting for the moment his search for the erogenous zone in the crook of the arm, the back of the elbow.

"D. H. Lawrence. I read *Women In Love* four times before I was sixteen not understanding what it was about. It made me tingle." It was the longest sentence she had uttered all day.

"He was obsessed with sex," Flying Fingers said, discovering the infinite possibilities of the shoulder.

This was not going to be a fruitful conversation. Naomi shifted her attention to the two girls at the next table. "Celibacy or women is the only answer," she heard one of them say as she collected her coat from the back of her chair.

Naomi thought of lying next to Blue Eyes, his arm around her. She thought of dancing the swinging singles sexual liberation rag. He was nice looking and seemed all right. He was going back to Chicago tomorrow so she would not be distracted. So she could get some work done.

"Room 802," she said as they walked toward the elevator.

There was a small light on in her room. Someone had neatened up the chaos she had left. She put her camera and briefcase into a chair and looked at Blue Eyes. He was faceless except for the eyes, shaded by an extra layer of skin hooding them. It is November or December, she remembered as he began undressing her. It is near Christmastime, she thought as he unzippered her skirt. This morning I saw Santa Claus looking for chimneys, suspended as he was between two palm trees on either side of Wilshire Boulevard.

As Blue Eyes laid her down on the bed and began kissing her, his tongue intruding onto the textures of lips, she thought of that view of Santa and his reindeer flying across the sky with tinsel toys in his big bag glittering in the sun. The sky had been a sweet blue, she remembered, as Blue Eyes explored her body and murmured appropriate approval, and there was no snow, will never be any snow. It is early December or late November, she thought, putting her hands behind his head, touching the curling graying hairs. At least in New York they have the decency to wait until after Thanksgiving for the onslaught, but in

Beverly Hills it is November 10 or something and Santa is riding the Milky Way across Wilshire, the smile on his face garish in the white light.

Naomi grunted and made appropriate noises and touched Blue Eyes on his buttocks, soft, too full, like a girl's. She wondered what they do for Christmas here in this palm-tree place, this city of a pale dusk that slashes a six o'clock sky with pink. Do they have Salvation Army girls here with tambourines, and men with rimless glasses playing the tuba, oompa oompa? Blue Eyes, deciding she would not respond anymore than she already had, entered her.

Do they give Christmas turkeys here? she thought, as Blue Eyes danced the Peabody inside her. Do bearded men with watery eyes stand by store fronts waiting for cranberry sauce and mashed potatoes surrounding the bird? Maybe they don't even have them here, those bearded men with watery eyes and nervous tongues running over thirsty lips. Blue Eyes' lips were panting on her neck as he raced himself for peace.

Brass. There will be no sounds of brass in Beverly Hills, when Christmas comes, Naomi thought, just Santa Claus crossing the high wire on Wilshire Boulevard attached to two palm trees on both sides of the street.

Blue Eyes shuddered and Santa Claus came tumbling down breaking his crown with reindeer tumbling after.

He rested on top of her for a few minutes before she asked him to leave so she could play back her tapes.

11

John Kenneth Galbraith, like some long-out-of-place giant from Jack's beanstalk, looked down from on high in the hotel lobby. Naomi smiled at him and he smiled back as she heard her name being paged. It was eight o'clock the next morning and she had not slept well.

Naomi's back itched. It was so hard to find the spot. She twisted around, her fingers searching for relief. She needed Sol. Sol was the world's best back-scratcher. Sol liked to scratch Janie's back; usually after dinner, just like little Naomi, who, slim and pot-bellied like Janie, used to sit on the arm of the dining-room chair. Sol would pick up her sweater, creep under the undershirt, and to the tune of her "up a little, down a little, more to the right, Daddy, not so hard, you're scratching me . . ." Naomi would move in and out of ecstasy. It was a game they played, Sol and Naomi. How he had loved her. My doll. My doll baby, he used to call her and after dinner, when she would be finished with her bath and her homework and her phone calls, Naomi would lie in bed, in a majestic four-poster with an old-fashioned canopy acting as sky to her fervent dreams. There, with the hall lights on, shadowing the flowered wallpaper outside her room, she would conjure puppy dogs and rabbit heads out of the flowers, castles and rooftops, fingers and clouds. Ordinary petals and flowers clinging to the wallpaper, matching the drapes, caressing the window, became demons or friends of the night as the case might be. Waiting. Naomi was waiting not for the Robert E. Lee, but for Sol, Daddy. And he would bound up the stairs, still smelling of chicken from dinner, his fingers strong with paprika stains and string bean odor. Daddy would come into the room and sprawl himself across the bed. The quilt had been chintz, Naomi remembered, and Sol would press himself against his little girl. And he would tell stories, about Winken, Blinken, and Nod who went to sail in a wooden shoe on the open sea. And he would smell of chicken and paprika and string beans. Of Daddy. And then they would wrestle, and he would scratch her back again. Short fingers. Stubby. Good. Smooth on her back. Daddy.

The lobby was sparsely furnished with beige flowered couches and chairs looking as though they were growing out of the green-grass carpet. Naomi followed the bellman to the phone.

Matthew Johnson. Perhaps he was back in town. Her step quickened.

"Hello dear."

Her mother's voice was girlish. High and familiar. The voice triggered other Esther voices in her ear, other phone calls at college, and when Naomi got married, and when Naomi lived alone. Why didn't Naomi remember her birthday and why didn't she love her enough and why, when she was so good to her, did she not love in return and why was she so ungrateful; ungrateful, a popular Lazurus epithet hurled often, with abandon.

"How are the interviews going? Did you call the Feldmans? Be sure to call them. They're expecting your call."

"Fine, mother. I'm on my way now to do some research. How are you?"

"Don't ask. It's been raining since we got back, the whole block is flooded, your father's asthma is acting up and I'm thinking of firing Jasmine. I may have to get a cleaning service and I think we'll just do without anybody and I'll do the cooking for a while. Nobody else can make fish the way your father likes it. I'm not feeling so well myself but don't worry it's nothing to worry about. The last thing I want to do is worry you."

Mother, ask me how I am. Ask me if there are any Blue Eyes in my life. Or what my favorite color is. Or, here's a neat one, how about if I'm lonely.

"When are you coming back? Your father hasn't been feeling too well and I'm the one who gets the brunt of it. He doesn't mean to, but I'm the only one around. Your sister has her own problems and you're never here. By the way, I know it's a long way away but we're planning the fortieth anniversary party now. We're definitely having an orchestra."

Naomi didn't hear the rest. There was no point in saying anything. She was getting a headache.

"We're running a house tour for the hospital and I was able to get Stuart Mott's place. It is very gratifying the work I'm doing for the hospital. They love me there; the women say they've never had such an effective chairman. I'm very tired and it is a lot of work but it's what I have to do. They need me. Oh yes, some insistent person named Matthew Jones or something called. He said your machine wasn't answering. He called you too 'bicoastal' for him, who's he?"

"Johnson. How'd he get your numb . . . "

"He didn't say. How's the weather out there?"

"What time did he call?"

"I don't know, maybe dinner time."

"Mother think, how did he sound? Did you chit-chat with him? Did you give him my number?"

"Naomi, we exchanged three words. When are you coming home?"

Mother, Mother, Mother. When did we get to be strangers? Naomi sighed when she hung up the phone.

12

"My brother molested me when I was nine. After that I became invisible."

Naomi adjusted herself in a chair located in the middle of a circle. She was in a large loft building downtown. The room was white-washed, with about ten pillows scattered in the middle of the floor. There were six television screens around the room. A different face filled up each screen. One of the screens was talking.

"I didn't tell anyone till I was sixteen. No one believed me, and it's taken all these years to gain back my self-esteem. I don't know if I'll ever get rid of the insomnia."

Naomi looked around the room. About forty people were intently watching an experimental project about incest. She began to take notes. Six women were sharing the results of a ten-week consciousness-raising group. All had been sexually abused by a member of their family and all, in this case, were lesbians.

"My stepfather would always watch me pee. He would make me wash his penis when he was taking a bath. And he would come in and watch me when I was taking a bath."

"I would wake up some nights finding my brother fondling my breast. I felt paralyzed. I didn't move. I figured if I didn't pay attention to it it would go away. He was eleven and I was ten and he had total control over my body."

Naomi looked around the room, observing the reactions of the women seated around her.

Another voice: "I was Daddy's special little girl, he loved me the most. And he molested me in strange ways. Like in a public situation he would force me to sit on his lap and then he would get a hard on. And when he would beat me it would be in a ritualistic way, he would remove my underwear and get off on it somehow. I knew it; I sensed it. I could never figure out whether he really loved me or he was abusing me. At fourteen, when my mother died, I ran away."

"This hurts me more than it does you, Naomi," Sol would say when he put Naomi across his knee. She couldn't remember, the photograph in her mind was dim, blurred. But she was wearing white tights and Mary Janes. There was a pulling down, a feeling ashamed. Naomi cleared her throat to banish the images fluttering in her head. Hoping the intrusive sound would frighten them away.

". . . And I would sit on the priest's lap and he would get a hard on."

This face was a serene, Oriental one.

"I couldn't tell anyone."

"I just felt like such a bad girl; sometimes I would eat all night long, until I couldn't eat anymore. I figured if I got fat he would stay away from me. I turned into a watchful, suspicious person."

"It was the trust. I couldn't trust anyone. My mother too. She wouldn't protect me from him. I can't trust either of them. Ever."

Soon the short film was over. Many women in the audience had glazed eyes. Their own memories, their own inner photographs had snapped inside their heads. Naomi had filled almost half a stenopad.

One of the young women who had participated in the film stood up to lead the discussion, asking for reactions. They came in a rush. At Naomi's left, two women were holding hands. One began to speak. All eyes turned to her.

"My father came into my bed and began to fondle me. I was about ten. And then he spoke the words I will never forget. 'Be a good girl. Open your legs.' . . . I was my daddy's girl. He loved me. He wouldn't do such a thing to me; and it has taken me twenty years to put it away. Three marriages, lots of self-destruction. Six years ago, finally, blessedly, I went into therapy at Christopher Street in Minneapolis. And now I work as a mental health counselor and lead groups of women who have been abused."

The leader passed around a roll of toilet paper to accommodate the tears in the room. Naomi thought she wanted to say something, tell them how she felt. She could not. She didn't know how she felt.

"I always go with married men who I can't have, or have a relationship that is only sexual. It's an endless cycle. I don't know how to separate sexuality and love. When my father became sexual with me in my teens I was afraid I'd lose his love if I told. And I loved my daddy." The woman was weeping openly. "My father was loving, gentle, kind, viewed by the world as a terrific husband, but he was always right, never wrong. He told me he loved me so much. But he never checked out what he was doing to me. He betrayed me at such a deep level. I can never trust anyone now who really loves me. I can't."

Naomi took off her glasses and put her hands over her eyes. She had to stop the pictures snapping in her head. She got up abruptly, making quite a clatter as she gathered her cameras and paraphernalia. She was the first to leave the room.

13

Matthew Johnson came back to town. He had been in six cities, pushing his book. Naomi couldn't believe how happy she was to see him.

They saw each other Wednesday, Thursday, then Friday.

"I've slept with a thousand women," he told her. She believed him.

"Big deal. I don't want to hear about your other women after we've made love. Your timing stinks."

She would never be the same, she thought. The man had played ticktacktoe with his tongue over every inch of her body. The man had moved in on her bones and flesh. A celebration.

Henry Loeffler, Hank for short, that faraway husband who had said she preferred her father to him, Hank the vest-wearer with the vested interests had said she was frigid. But now she knew. Finally. Hank's touch had been too tentative, always hoping to get on to the next, on to his turn. He had said she couldn't love, ever, so wrapped up she was in dear old Dad, in portly powerful Sol. She had scoffed and laughed and gotten furious at him when he said that. So she had not been able to respond. So she had gotten bored with his diddling and fiddling with her electric circus of a body. At times she could have slept through it all. Tepid he was. Lovemaking without love. Sex without sex.

But now she was determined not to tip her hand. Ever. She would not tell Matthew. She would not share this miracle.

"I love you," he said.

"Impossible." Naomi looked at the freckles on his hairless chest, the well-shaped but scarred legs. Skin grafts, he explained, borrowed flesh from accommodating borrowed thighs. In the Navy at fifteen he had lied about his age. Burns. A boiler room had blown up all over his legs. There were initials, designs blued into his arms, tattooed sixteen-year-old dreams.

Matthew had appeared at her door that second day at noon, carrying a copy of *The Red and the Black*. "Stendhal's cleansing," he explained. There was a Blass label sticking out of the pocket over the right breast of his belted khaki director's jacket. A little studied, she thought. As were the cowboy boots. But his beard had glistened in the sunlight and there were great puffs under his eyes.

"Not impossible. I love you."

"How can you love me? You don't even know me." Naomi was irate.

"Sorry. I know my own mind. Today I love you. You are long in the tooth and long in body and I love your limbs, long like Modigliani. You are not the tough broad you pretend to be, but I like them both, the tough broad and the baby girl underneath."

Baby girl, that's what Daddy Sol used to call her. Still does.

Daddy loved me. Matthew says he loves me. Daddy, Daddy, as in he who Mary Martin's heart belonged to.

Matthew moved his hand over her body.

"I love touching your sex. I do so with reverence, everlasting wonder, sheer loving curiosity and delight."

Words. He made love to her with his words.

Matthew smoothed her hair away from her brow. They had never gotten out to lunch, but he had brought purple grapes and champagne and had put them on the night table. He leaned over and took a sip, fed her a grape.

"Lazurus. I want a lot more than a lovely fuck. I don't know if this is it. But I am telling you I do not care all that much about the mechanics of the fucking. I want to give myself to you, Naomi, and find myself pleasing to you. I want to come in you knowing that there is a home on this planet I can share with a woman."

She did not know what to make of his intensity, his strangeness. She just knew that she had discovered a man who all but swallowed her alive, who all but sucked the sweet out of her like the pits from his purple grapes, who all but burst her with his tenderness, smoothing her lips with his fingers, moving on to a place he discovered he liked, on the neck under the ear before the shoulder started.

Like warm milk baths her grandmother used to take, his tongue slid over her; a cat lapping his meal, a small snake gliding, and she sank, disappeared under it. She felt as though she were swimming, the sheets her pool, the pillow her moon. The light shining in from the window made loving shadows on his face.

It was a joyful secret. For the first time her body felt beautiful, it was as though she were eating herself, her tongue becoming his. She felt inside her own body. She put her head into his mouth like a lion in the circus and dreamed swirling dreams; she was a belly dancer swaying and dipping, her breasts halvah to all the men in her head, she felt sweetened, sauteed, basted, tenderized by tongues. She laughed, she cried. She screamed. She became silent. She rested. She slept a sleep of deep completion. It was joy to the world, Naomi had come.

14

She clicked around. The car radio beamed its Southern California cacophony.

God. Masturbation. Orgasm. On the radio.

Whatever happened to Brahms? Whatever happened to Barry Gray? Long John Nebel? Southern California radio was a receptacle for anything and everybody. You could find God at 6:00 A.M. while riding some highway watching the ball of a sun sitting there, hanging between a thin layer of mist and the emptiness of the desert. God was there. The man on the radio said so. You could be saved. If you just opened up your heart and let Him come in. Jesus was there, coming over the air waves into your car on a Southern California highway. Naomi was mesmerized by the sounds. The minister's voice lulled her with its promise, cooing his seductive view of a world inundated with goodness once sin was cast out.

Click.

Enough God for the moment.

"Get rid of those zits in a flash. . . . Try . . ." Click.

"And why are you so rude when I come to your restaurant, just because I'm not Robert Redford or a big celebrity."

Naomi turned it up a bit louder. She was almost at the end of Venice Boulevard. Suddenly it was the sixties: someone crossed in front of her who resembled the Moondog of old who used to hold court on Forty-seventh Street and Fifth Avenue, resplendent in his flowing robes and heavy beard, his rod and his staff in his hand. Oblivious. He was communing with the sun or the heavens or perhaps the sea. He was leftover mellow. Obsolete.

"Yes I certainly wouldn't go to your restaurant again."

"Well, Monsieur Alain, you've heard what one dissatisfied customer of your eating establishment thinks of the so-called snobbery you seem to engender, what do you think about that?" Michael Jackson's mellifluous British tones moved into the car. Naomi leaned forward. She wanted to know what the owner of one of L.A.'s poshest places was going to say to this dissatisfied customer who was really giving it to him.

"I utterly deny it. It is true that many film people eat at our restaurant, and we must cater to them, however, the rest of le public is always welcome."

"So how come your restaurant has an unlisted number? Whoever heard of a restaurant having an unlisted number?"

The caller was getting belligerent. Naomi almost went through a red light. In California one is so easily distracted, what with orgasms and maitre d's and masturbation inundating you over the air waves, bombarding you between Hollywood and Vine, Venice and Pacific.

Click. Naomi moved on. Enough of that. She had been to that restaurant and agreed with the caller. The owner-maitre d' had indeed such hauteur, such elitist eyes. Naomi was glad he was getting it, right there inside her car on the radio at ten in the morning.

". . . and so it seems to me that most people have some kind of experience as a child with incest, don't you think, doctor?"

She almost went through a stop sign.

She wanted to hear what Miss Southern California Radio Shrink had to say about this.

". . . and," the caller continued, "I do think there is pleasure in it for the child, since as we all know, children can feel sexual pleasure at an early age."

Dr. Somebody was furious. Naomi pulled over to the side of the road. She had come to her destination. She was on a side street adjacent to the beach. She had to hear this. She sat in the car listening.

"I am going to say something to you and I want you to listen. I get a very odd feeling from your call. There is something not quite right. One can never excuse incest. Never. What it is, is a betrayal of innocence. Your father is there to protect you and to nurture you. There should be no sexual innuendo in the relationship whatsoever. If there is you have been betrayed. Over and over we find that the child lives with the guilt and the pain of this forever. Of course a father dotes on and admires his pretty little girl. But that should be it."

"But children know about sex. They can tell pleasure. Fathers always touch . . ."

"Excuse me, I would like to finish. From one to five, children are very sexual. Yes. And they can feel pleasure. From six to about eleven they are in a period called latency and they become social. There is a whole world of peers and life to explore out there. It is at this time that if a father betrays this, he does undeniable damage to a little girl . . . and—"

Abruptly, Naomi turned off the radio. She had heard enough.

15

"You're a grown woman."

"I know. But I always spend Christmas with them if I'm in the country."

"Whose law? Sol's? The Jewish equivalent of Murphy's?"

Naomi and Matthew were eating dinner in a restaurant called The Original Pantry Café. It was downtown and very inexpensive and had more food than anyone could ever manage at one sitting. Matthew had introduced her to it during these whirlwind weeks in his effort to expand her education about the town he loved.

"No one loves Los Angeles," she had admonished, her prejudices shining virtuously through Big Apple eyes.

"You got to move around, kid. You sit up there in the hills, in your fancy hotel, you never see or feel anything. Too bad you didn't know me when I lived on the houseboat. Could have really shown you the sights then. Have a steak. You won't believe the steak here."

Naomi looked up over Matthew's head at the menu chalked on a large blackboard. The waiters were all ex-convicts, she had been notified, and there was a line around the block to get in. Huge baskets filled to the brim with thick carrots and cucumbers, onions and radishes, embellished each table. Their waiter had just dropped off a basket filled with obscenely thick slabs of bread. Naomi loved the place.

She looked across the table at Matthew. He was very ruddy, his eyes bloodshot.

"I've got to go back. I've got to see Helene. I haven't even handed in the story on you yet."

"Two steaks . . . baked potato and beans."

Before she could protest the waiter had scurried off.

"I can't possibly eat all that."

"You're too skinny. Shapely. A good shape for a thin girl, but you could use some meat on those . . ."

Two round red spots appeared on Naomi's cheeks. She was in flames. "I am not too thin. I like being thin. This is my body and if you don't like it go sleep with Sophia Loren."

He clasped her hand with both of his. "From your mouth to God's ears." He crossed himself and looked up to the heavens to see if anyone was listening.

In spite of herself Naomi laughed.

He tried another tack.

"So I figure we should spend Christmas together. We seem to hit it off."

"Hit what off. First of all, if we get along so well together, how come you just took off on a fishing trip in the middle of this passionate affair. Coitus interruptus so to speak."

"That's different. My buddies needed me."

"Bullshit."

"Naomi. We get along. Right?"

"Fair. Listen, Matthew, you've got your cast of thousands waiting in the wings. Lonely you're not going to be. I've been working hard on this child molestation material and I'm just beginning to get somewhere with it. The whole thing is beginning to obsess me a little."

"No kidding. But what's that got to do with going home for Christmas?"

Naomi absentmindedly buttered a piece of bread. She never ate bread.

"Look. As a matter of fact I don't even want to go home for Christmas. But it's not worth the hassle and the carrying on they're going to give me if I don't go home. I've been here a month already."

"Guilt. They make you feel guilty?"

"Let me tell you something; I have nothing to feel guilty about. My conscience is clear with them."

The waiter dropped two enormous steaks in front of them. Four truck drivers would have difficulty finishing them. Side dishes of cole slaw took up the remaining space on the table.

"So in other words, they don't make you feel guilty."

"Listen Johnson, don't patronize me."

"My love. This is not patronizing. I realize I don't know you very well but I don't believe I have ever known a grown-up person who could zing around the world with cameras wafting in the wind and talk herself into a free ride from Saigon to Da Nang, who could survive the stench in Vietnamese hospitals where babies were dying like flies all around, who is so unbelievably connected to Daddy and Mommy and what they think and what they say."

Warming to his subject, Matthew flourished his fork like Zubin Mehta at an open-air concert.

"You seem to forget that you have jumped out of an airplane, covered wars and assassinations, and are a rather accomplished person. Or so you tell me. So your résumé says. They're people, your parents. Just people. You know? You're a thirty-five-year-old person. Look, when you go to bed with me, it's of your own free will, as a mature adult. Right?"

This man made her feel very nervous.

"I don't think this is any of your business. How I conduct my affairs with my mother and father." She sounded terribly formal to herself, as though she were responding to an invitation from Prince Charles for tea. "Some of us didn't have the luxury of exorcising our parents in our work."

"Big deal. The point is that I came to terms with them. The good and the bad."

Matthew took a cigarette out of his breast pocket and began playing with it. He kept staring at it and not at Naomi.

"And it wasn't easy. It might be hard for you to believe, but I was, am, a gentle soul in an ungentle world. Sure I've written about them a lot. It's what I know. My father was not a very nice man. A con man, a drunk. He'd beat up on me a lot when he was drunk. He threw me through a window once. Until I got bigger than he was. Until my size and self-respect got to be too much for him. That old sucker loved to make me feel puny and worthless, it made him ten feet tall. Poor bastard, he didn't know any better."

He was still looking at the cigarette, twirling it between his first and third fingers.

"And my mother. She knew from nothing; scared shitless of him, she died before she made thirty. Her folks raised me. The old man was hootin' and hollerin', but my grandparents would have none of him."

"Did you see him much after that, your father?"

Matthew looked straight into her eyes. His eyes were watering.

"Old and sick and filled to the brim with cirrhosis. That's when I saw him. Hard to believe he was the man I'd hated so. The man I was so pissed at I thought I would die. He was lying there in that hospital bed all wrinkled and puny like some old prune. Who needs to hold on to all that shit. He didn't ask for it, but I forgave him, right then and there. I forgave him everything. Poor bastard. But I felt better."

"Well, we all can't be as terrific and well-adjusted as you." Naomi wiped her nose with the back of her hand. It was not very ladylike, but tears kept dripping out of her eyes, and her nose was running. "Besides, what makes you think I'm angry at them in the first place?"

"It's written all over you. You've got to get good and mad first, honey, and then you can forgive them."

Matthew gently gave her his napkin. She threw it back at him.

"It's got cole slaw on it."

Out of his back pocket came a handkerchief.

"They're just parents, they drive me crazy but everyone's do. They're getting old. They don't mean it when they hurt me," she said.

"Will you cry when they die?"

Naomi looked at Matthew quickly.

"What kind of question is that? Now what kind of question is that?"

Matthew was silent. He was pouting. He wasn't changing her overnight. He wanted to make her over into his own image of her. He would have to go slow. He ate his food.

"Okay, there are all kinds of stuff between me and my parents," she admitted. "Underneath. But I can't deal with those things now. Our relationship is all on the surface now and that's all right. I'll be the daughter they want if it doesn't cost too much to my soul. I hate them and I love them. They've hurt me and I've transcended it."

"But you hold grudges."

"That's what I am, Miss Grudge. But let me tell you something. There was a time," Naomi said, not looking at him, "there was a time when I thought they would kill me. When their screaming would get out of hand, when I would cry and choke and bellow in frustration, because I couldn't reach them."

Matthew sat back far into his chair. He put his fork down. "Do you still feel that way?"

Naomi was very uncomfortable. She was not used to this kind of interrogation.

"I don't know. They can still make me very angry. It's complicated."

"Everything is."

Naomi looked down at her hands, the fists were clenched so tight the nails were almost drawing blood in her palms.

Matthew moved over into the booth and sat next to Naomi. He kissed her nose. Her forehead.

"I blame them. I blame them for a lot of things." She closed her eyes.

"Blame is like Blake's 'Poison Tree.' The resentment poison sits there like yesterday's sauerkraut. Forget about blame." He paused. "If I can, you can."

There was a long silence. It was time to change the subject.

"Naomi. A dark, mysterious, Biblical sound. I am enamored of your darkness. Your dark eyes, the dark Russian soul lingering under all that drive. I am attracted most strongly to a certain darkness in a woman. Semitic, Indian, Oriental mysteries in which I can touch something that transcends the orderliness of the German-English view of reality. Why the hell do you think my Viking ancestors got into those long boats and went voyaging?"

The man loved to talk. He loved the sound of his voice and the way his words finally ended up together in a sentence. And so did she. "Why?"

"Oh sure, there were those interested in commerce, but they were not my ancestors. Mine were the romantics who swung their legs over the leeboards, dreaming no doubt of some tawny beauty with whom they could cuddle, stretched out to the full rather than cramped in a sit-up bed back at the farm."

Matthew took a long swallow of the dark beer the waiter had brought in a heavy glass pitcher.

"Naomi, I don't know what this is between us. But I do know there are so many things I would like to reexperience with you in this world, hear you talk about as we look at them, share your reactions. Friends I would like to share with you. I want to know you because I perceive you to be a person worth knowing, one who adds something good to my living. Spend Christmas with me. Last offer."

This man was moving in. He would probably get her over-come with feeling and then move on in and then out, on to the hordes waiting; the armies of bright incandescent career ladies, wealthy too-tan literati groupies, latching on to his every endless word, his every movement, as he went about the world giving credence to his reputation. She had better get out while the getting was good anyway. She had never been very good at this, this feeling business.

"First of all I'm not Christian." She ran her fingers through her hair. "It's not my holiday. And second of all, you went away. How do I know you've been fishing this last week. Just because your eyebrows are bleached means nothing."

He looked at her in all innocence, shocked that she would doubt him.

Who did he think he was kidding? Trusting Matthew Johnson was not what she was about to do.

Besides, if she didn't go home for Christmas, her parents would kill her.

New York

16

Naomi was back in New York.

It was Sunday morning. It was her first day at home. Janie was coming to breakfast, but there were no eggs. It was the first meal she would cook for her niece in a long while, so eggs were important.

She envied her sister her daughter. Especially since she had fears that she was getting too old to have a child. She loved Janie.

Outside, on the way to the market, the trees were bare along Central Park. Naomi found a grocery open on Amsterdam Avenue and Ninety-fourth Street. She saw several old people there stretching their dollars, counting their change carefully. The fruit was not as succulent as in Southern California. They did not take pride in the display here. And the eggs cost twenty cents more. She kept comparing. But coming back was like seeing the letters of her own name.

When she emerged fifteen minutes later, there were two police cars on the street. An ambulance. A crowd. New York, she thought. Always something.

Then she saw the body, covered by a sheet. And the blood where the head was. Legs in black stockings protruded out from the whiteness of the sheet.

"She jumped out of the seventh-floor window," the woman next to her said. "Right onto the sidewalk." She could have landed on me, Naomi thought. I walked past that spot moments before. She looked up. The window was still open.

During the time Naomi was in the grocery, the woman on the seventh floor had opened the window and stepped out. While she was choosing apples, while she was drumming her fingers on the counter as the checkout man changed a hundred-dollar bill for the man in front of her, the woman had decided she had had enough.

And when she left the market, out into the newness of Sunday, savoring her first sweet day back in the city, missing Mr. Platinum Eyebrows and his showering of verbosity, there was the woman, fallen on the sidewalk. They had covered her with a sheet in moments.

"She lived on my floor," the woman next to Naomi said, shaken.

"Was she depressed? Sick?" Naomi heard herself say. The woman had one shoulder much lower than the other.

"No," she said.

"Did she live alone?"

"Yes. Her children had all gone away."

Naomi felt a chill. But Sol and Esther always have each other. No, not always. Some day they would be gone. No more Daddy. No more Daddy long legs, Daddy dearest. No more Daddy Sol.

In Los Angeles people jump out of windows. But you don't see it. You're in your car. You don't stop with a bag full of groceries and the *New York Times* lying on top smudging your white blouse. You don't see it.

Naomi was back in New York.

17

"I want to take a bath."

"What do you mean you want to take a bath? You came here for breakfast."

Janie was adamant.

"Mom never lets me take a bubble bath much. Come on, Naomi. I'll be your best friend."

"Oh well, that's different."

Naomi got up, went into the bathroom and ran the water. She poured a generous serving of her expensive L'Air Du Temps bath oil into the tub. It was a kind of ritual. Sundays at Aunt Naomi's. This year, when she turned nine, Janie mastered the crosstown busses perfectly and always came for breakfast by herself when Naomi was in town. Her mother, Becky, always slept late on Sundays (and Tuesdays, Wednesdays and Thursdays) but it was their day together. Naomi wouldn't miss it for anything. Back in the bedroom Janie began to undress.

"Do you have that health food shampoo you had last time?"

"Yup, I went and got you some."

"I love that shampoo," Janie cooed. "It makes my hair very shiny, don't you think?"

"Indubitably." Naomi tackled Janie on the thick white carpet and started kissing her madly on the back of her neck. Her niece was getting so old so fast she wouldn't be able to do shenanigans with her pretty soon. Right now Janie screamed with delight.

Exhausted, Naomi lay on her back, looking up at the ceiling. "Okay, kiddo, you go into the tub and I'll go start beating up the eggs."

"Remember to beat the whites separately from the yellows. It makes them fluffier." Janie started to throw her clothes all over the room.

"My, you sure are well-versed in things. Pick up your clothes and put them on the chair."

A cloud of petulance settled over Janie's expression.

"Momma says . . ."

"You're in my house now. Different rules. Naomi's nest. The birds here do what Naomi says."

No problem. Janie picked up her clothes and took her roundness, her porcelain bottom and sloping back into the bathroom. Watching her from the rear, Naomi felt a visceral tug. Her niece's back was probably one of the most beautiful things she had ever seen. The curves sweetly sensual, the fleshy hard thighs almost aching in their innocence. Naomi marveled at Janie's unself-consciousness, the utter confidence in her own flesh.

"Hey, kid. I don't want the water to overflow."

"Oh, all right." Janie said.

"Got to get a hug. Can't live another minute without a Janie special."

"You're such a smoocher, Naomi."

"Ears. I'm mad about your ears. Especially this inner part right here where it curves like a sea shell."

Janie was convulsed in giggles as Naomi trapped her one more time into the disgusting lick-the-ear game which Janie went to great pains to explain was gross and revolting.

"Come on, you're going to have a floooood."

She toddled off into the bathroom. Naomi got up and went into the kitchen to beat the whites and the yellows separately. The kitchen was fairly far away from her bedroom and bathroom but she still could hear the child splashing and carrying on, talking a blue streak to herself.

Naomi set the table. She smiled as she thought of Janie's body scooting through the room, the apple of a rump, such sweet roundness. The girls on the television screens in California in the whitewashed room with the pillows on the floor, talking about what their daddies had done to them, they had once been round and young too. Like Janie. And squealing and beautiful. And innocent. And me too. And me.

Abruptly Naomi cut her reverie and walked quickly into her bedroom. She went to her purse which was resting on her desk and took out a Bufferin. As she walked toward the bathroom for a glass of water, she stopped in her tracks. A voice, a terribly television voice was coming from the neighborhood of the bathtub. She peeked in, making sure she could not be seen, and saw Janie soaping her hair high up to the skies, making Cinderella castles out of her thick blond tresses. She swirled and she twirled, fashioning pompadours and page-boys, up-sweeps and down-sweeps. Chattering the whole time.

"You see you must always remember to get underneath each follicle. This is one of our main problems in this world and only a good shampoo like the one I have in my hand can help. In my personal opinion it is the very best in the world. So many people neglect their follicles, you know. Now if you're an older person like my age, thirty or above, then washing your hair a lot is necessary. I'm not saying to wash it every night. Now that's terrible. Let's say at least Sundays. But of course if you're invited to a ball on a Tuesday by all means wash it on a Tuesday . . . "

Naomi was fascinated by the monologue. She had stopped in her tracks, listening.

"Now what you must do is get down under the water so you can soap yourself, so you can free your hair from all the shampoo . . . " The voice disappeared and only a gurgling sound could be heard as Janie submerged herself into the water to get the soap out. In a moment she had resurfaced.

Naomi leaned on at the bathroom door. She looked at the rosy figure in the water. For a moment Janie turned into a little Naomi, her concave chest dotted with little nipples, the face shining, the arms round, beckoning.

Just one more time Daddy, ten more slipslops, ten more slides back and forth. I'm polishing the tub with my tushy, Daddy. Daddy, watch me, watch me, Daddy.

Abruptly, Naomi was back.

"I suggest you clean the tub with the sponge on the side after you get out," she offered.

"Sure. Can I have a towel?"

Naomi threw her one. As she walked away she heard the commercial begin to conclude.

" . . . As I was saying before she came in, you see I'm rinsing out now. As you can see I have not neglected one solitary follicle . . . "

There was a bouquet of flowers on the dining table.

"How come I haven't lost all my teeth?"

"Some people do things like that late."

"I've only lost ten teeth. I'm going to go to my sweet-sixteen party with not a tooth in my mouth."

Naomi looked at her. She was very serious.

"I decided that I want to be a writer when I grow up."

"Okay."

"Like you."

"Okay."

"I brought something for you to read."

"Okay. I'd be glad to. How are the eggs?"

"Scrumptious, and I love these brown muffins. You're against white bread? You eat funny since California."

"White flour kills, sugar kills, caffeine kills. Everybody knows that."

"Not around here. Can I read you my story?"

"Please do." Naomi lit a cigarette.

"It's called 'Saturday Night.' 'It was Saturday night. Fiona wished that someone would call her. Her mother was in a terrible mood, and sulking in her room. Mr. Graham was never really in any kind of mood and this particular Saturday was no different from any other night. Since she was an only child, to her, nothing terribly exciting was going on at the Graham house. Fiona wasn't really the reading type so she obviously wasn't about to pick up a book and start reading.

" 'Fiona felt like she didn't have anything and she was all alone. All of a sudden Fiona began to cry. She ran on the terrace and called for Sidney, her dog. He casually trotted over to see what his owner was troubled about. Fiona quickly put her arms out and hugged Sidney harder than she had ever hugged anyone before. Sidney licked her face. She pulled in her tears and got up, leaving Sidney looking up in a bewildered way.

" 'The phone rang. Fiona ran to answer it. It was Valerie Fitzhoff from across the hall. Valerie wanted to know if it was all right for her to come over and borrow a few eggs so that in the morning her dad could have some. Fiona asked her why her mother couldn't go to Wipples in the morning and Valerie gave the smart answer of 'the stores are all closed on Sunday, stupid.' So Fiona said, 'Yeah come and get the dumb eggs, but if you're not here within six and one half minutes you can't have 'em,' and hung up. Sure enough, Valerie had come and gone before even five minutes had passed. That, thought Fiona, was a perfect sample of Valerie Fitzhoff.' "

Naomi was spellbound.

"Now that's just a sample. I mean, more is going to happen."

"Let me see it."

Janie handed over the carefully typed manuscript.

"I love you, Janie. You will be a writer and I will help you and I hope we will be friends forever."

Janie's body felt tight and close. She smelled of French perfume and cheese omelet and little-girl freshness. Such freshness.

"Janie, I have a new friend." Naomi wanted to share Matthew with her niece.

"Boy or girl?"

"Boy. Man. He's a writer. He could really help you with your writing. He's written a bunch of books."

"Neat. Can I meet him?" Janie's eyes were bright.

"He lives in California. How'd you like to meet him on the phone?" It seemed the appropriate thing to do. She missed him. She missed Matthew Johnson.

"Sure." Janie jumped up. "Let me dial. I love dialing long distance."

They tried a few times, but there was no answer.

18

Christmas.

Even though it wasn't their holiday, it was family time. Family. Family. Naomi had to participate.

She used to berate Hank when he would go down to Wall Street on Yom Kippur. That was their holiday. Sol used to say that it was a shanda for the goyim but Hank didn't care. He was Jewish by definition, not by persuasion or proclivity, he used to say. He had liked to use words like that to cloud rather than clarify issues. To Henry Loeffler being Jewish had to do with just the circumstances of your birth and nothing else. Naomi would stay home on the High Holidays and listen to Jan Peerce records. Sol and Esther had belonged to a temple for years; it was a given that Naomi and Becky would go to Sunday and Hebrew School. Naomi had been confirmed and they had given her a white Bible with gold lettering on it. She had made a speech whose subject she could no longer remember. Being Jewish to her had meant fasting and sitting next to Sol in temple on Yom Kippur, atoning like crazy, then having to give up her seat to Esther who always came, glowing in her finery, for the last hour of the service. Sol never had a son, so Naomi was important to him sitting there. Becky was there too, but Sol made it clear that he wanted his oldest girl next to him for the whole time. He would daven and beat his breast and pretend to read the Hebrew which he couldn't. He was a fierce Jew, a proud one. He thought, as a matter of fact, that Jews were not only chosen but better. Not only better but best. He collected Hebraica; any painting with a rabbi wearing a talis and a spiritual look was bound to be bought. Being Jewish meant belonging. It was one great big club of which Sol was self-proclaimed president. Naomi had never quite figured out where God fit in.

The Tavern-on-the-Green sparkled with Christmas. A giant tree presided in the corner, embellished with green and red glass ornaments. It was huge and lorded over the room. There was snow outside that made a postcard backdrop to the scene. Inside was elegant and glittery and the waiters looked debonair in their tuxedos. Janie's blond hair was loose and fell almost to the small of her back. Without her braids and without her glasses there was the promise of beauty that would later be staggering. At the moment it was less Sleeping Beauty and more Raggedy Ann.

Janie was wiggly.

"Stop wiggling." Rebecca, puffy in green velvet, gave her daughter the elbow as they and Naomi waited for the maitre d' to lead them to the table where her parents sat.

"I am not wiggling; it's the way I move around. Standing still is boring."

"Oh my God."

"You told me not to say that. Which, by the way, is pretty stupid since you should hear what the kids in my class say. God is nothing."

The three of them followed the fashionable maitre d' across what seemed the enormity of that Christmas room. They were different, Naomi and Rebecca. Becky was small and fair-skinned and very round. Plump. "A plumpkin," Sol used to say when she was little. It was adorable then, this round curly headed plumpkin, but as she got older and made food her primary passion, it was no longer cute or adorable. She was just a fat person.

Becky ate. She couldn't stop. It was her raison d'être; as peanut butter bars and croissants became her bed companions, morning crumbs remorseful reminders of her indulgence. A binge eater, a fudge eater, a secret eater, a compulsive eater, nothing helped. Overeaters Anonymous, Weight Watchers, Atkins and Pritikin, Scarsdale and Stillman; bedfellows all, all followed religiously with varying degrees of longevity and rigidity.

They all failed. There was a great cavern inside Rebecca that had to be continually stuffed. A faraway husband had long ago ceased his efforts to help Becky feel full.

It was something she and Naomi shared. That cavern. For Naomi there would never be enough success, enough attention. For Rebecca there would never be enough bread, enough chocolate-covered marshamallow to satisfy. Ever. Satisfaction, satiety eluded them.

"Hello Mother." Naomi bent down to kiss Esther, as they arrived at the table. Esther was wearing a suede pantsuit. In her sixties she looked as svelte and trim as any thirty-year-old, with a silk scarf at the neck fastened at the knot with an enormous Scotch pin. She was wearing her good diamonds, the six carat engagement ring Sol had bought her for their tenth anniversary, and large diamond studs in her ears. She looked more beautiful than ever, the white hair recently trimmed and curled. She had the look of a woman who had been protected and buffered through the years; the way she sat back and waited for her cigarette to be lit, the way she expectantly looked at the waiter as he pulled out her chair, the way she put her left hand on her left shoulder, waiting for a fur to be placed there, anticipating a chivalrous gesture. It was expected. Sol had spoiled her. He excused her most inappropriate behavior, her most outrageous demands as being "adorable," or "cute." She held all the cards. Esther walked into a room and deference was paid— automatically. Attention was definitely paid.

"I do not know about this severe period, Naomi." Esther scrutinized her daughter's outfit. Naomi was wearing gray, a tweed suit cut close to the body. "I'm not so sure it suits you. You look so much better in softer things. Don't you think so Sol? Don't you think Naomi looks a little *Gentlemen's Quarterly*? Janie dear, tell me everything now. What did Santa bring you? Are you anxious to get back to school? How is Miss Frankfurt these days?"

"Well," Janie began, taking a sip of her water. "I got the Blondie album that I wanted and . . ."

"Sol, don't you think that look is too tailored for Naomi? Do you have to go back to Los Angeles?"

Naomi turned her head. Usually she could get into her

mother's non sequiturs, her staccato rhythm. But she was a little tired today.

"Pretty soon."

"I thought you were going to be here for your father's birthday."

Becky buttered some bread for herself and Janie. She kicked Naomi under the table.

You knew I wouldn't be here, I told you that on the telephone yesterday, Naomi said to herself in her head. She was determined not to have a scene. There was something about restaurants that brought out the scene syndrome in her family, something about waiters and plates, tablecloths and crystal, the dark intimacy of an adjoining bar, that collapsed inhibitions and control.

Sol took restaurants as license. A place to let go in. Once, he had slammed his napkin down into a plate full of fettuccine, staining the pristine whiteness of the cloth as he stormed away from the table, wheeling straight into the arms of Charles Bronson. The rage had immediately disappeared from Sol's brow, the flush instantaneously subsided. That time, not long ago, the family had watched him become deferential, jovial, hand on the shoulder—I'm a fan of yours Charlie Bronson boy. Mr. Bronson, at that moment, had been bemused and not at all put off by this rotund smiling man.

When Sol came back from the bar with a fresh Scotch, when he came back from the men's room all scrubbed and sweet-smelling, he had been truculent, unforgiving. Naomi could not even remember what that fight had been about, but she was struck by the abruptness of the change, back in the bosom of his family where he knew he could get away with whatever scene he wanted to play. When Naomi was nine, ten, eleven, Daddy would, in utter frustration, fling himself out of the dining room, his temper laced with illogic, unreason. The fear had made the little girl in her shake, and made her forget sometimes that he was, indeed, the daddy she loved. Becky remembered hiding in the closet when Sol was enraged. And she remembered reading Frank Harris when she was twelve, Sol finding out and slapping her.

Naomi looked at her father. He looked benign. It was

Christmas Day and he had, surrounding him, as he proudly put it looking around the table, the women for whom he would give up any throne.

"I really had planned a beautiful dinner party for your father. You know how he likes to have his family around on auspicious occasions." Esther spoke about him as though he were in the other room.

Esther was hurt. Sol rubbed her wrist.

"It's not that." Naomi began peeling the petals off a large radish to distract her parents from her irritation. "It's an assignment. I have to go."

She heard a ten-year-old voice come out of a thirty-five-year-old mouth. She heard an apologetic whine come out of a carefully made up, very attractive face. When do we ever grow up? she thought. Is there such a thing as a grown-up?

"You could get out of it. You've been gone for the last three years now."

"Well I've sort of been looking forward to the . . . "

"Is that the blouse I gave you last year, Janie? It looks so marvelous on you. It's much more in style this year."

Janie knew how to handle her grandmother. She buttered her third roll before her mother's firm grasp on her wrist stopped the breadmobile making its way into her mouth.

Putting the knife down, Janie put her hand inside her grandmother's white one with the blue veins puffing up, like worms under the skin.

"Grandma, you look neat-o today. That outfit's sexy. You sure don't look like a grandma. Edith's grandma is younger than you, she isn't even sixty-five yet, and she looks like your mother."

While Naomi was eyeing the waiter to order another Scotch, Janie zeroed in on the bread plate again.

"Stanley Abel . . . How the hell are you?" Sol boomed. He stood up and embraced a man who stopped by the table. The Stanley from France Stanley. The Stanley who used to come to the house on Sundays and ogle her friends when Naomi was a teenager. That Stanley; of the French windows and yellow room Stanley. There was an Anne Sexton poem about her father putting his tongue down her throat. Or was it her father's friend?

At any rate, every time Naomi read the poem it made her think of Stanley Abel, and his eyes ogling her and her friends. Naomi looked at his face but all she could see was his belly, white, whiter than the sheet it was breathing on, whiter than the towel hanging over the Louis XIV chair by the antique desk in front of the French doors looking out over the sea. Jonah had gone inside the whale, boat and all; well, Stan's belly could accommodate the French Navy, so gargantuan, yet so pristine, so untouched it was, since no sun, no wind had bruised its ivory countenance. He was all belly—this man standing before her— and she had caressed, smoothed his swollen self, she had made him groan with pleasure, she had cupped the penis living below . . .

Stan's eyes blinked their greeting. I remember you.

Sol proudly surveyed his kingdom.

"You remember the family. Esther, Becky, Naomi. This is the the sheine maedele. The prettiest grandchild in town."

"Grandpa."

"True is true."

"Becky. Esther. Naomi, you're looking well. Since when you started wearing glasses?" Stan peeked at Naomi.

The better to see you with, my dear. She let that one pass. How was he ever going to button that jacket?

"Stan was in Cannes too. Hey Naomi, Stan was tripping the light fantastic in Cannes with the French chippies. You happen to run into my girl, Stan?"

"Sol, you look swell. Never age at all. What's your secret? Let me in on it, you know what I mean? Gotta run, pal. Nice running into you. I'll call you for lunch. For sure. I'm only in town for the holidays." He embraced his old friend. He towered over Sol, and patted his back like a mother burping her baby. Stan waddled away, back to his table.

"God, he's gotten fat. He's the pits." Becky was observant.

"That should be a lesson to you," Sol said. "That's the way he is. That's the way he looks. Stan's all right, got out of the market while the going was good. Lives abroad. Got a great life."

"He left his wife for a twenty-two-year-old," Esther added. "She almost had a nervous breakdown, then she took up with a thirty-year-old herself. Francine's rich and had her face lifted. Her whole body lifted. I saw her in the gym once. She has no belly button."

Janie stared at her grandmother.

"No belly button?" Janie's hand moved involuntarily to her stomach.

"I'm starved, why don't we order?" Naomi had had enough.

"Right. Waiter," Sol bellowed.

Cannes seemed so far away now. It didn't matter. A red-bearded Viking had established residence in her brain. She would have to brush him away before he gave her the brush. Becky was quiet. Sullen, yet as plump people are inclined to be, very beautiful. At thirty, she had the sweet unblemished roundness of a young girl.

Naomi impulsively kissed her sister.

"You look so lovely in green. What happened with the job?"

"I didn't go. I had a stomachache. Naomi, don't look at me like I did a terrible thing. I postponed it till Monday."

"Top of the morning to you," Sol said as a handsome young man hurried over. "And what may you be serving this morning my good man?" Hank had been the same way. Joking with waiters, making immediate contact. When Naomi was young it had been an asset, as Sol's extroverted personality would open doors. Today it made her cringe, now that she could open her own doors, now that she saw in herself the potential to do whatever she wanted.

Janie spilled her water, but Esther showed great restraint as the spill left a round prominent circle in the middle of her thigh.

"Where did you get that scarf, Naomi?" Esther said, patting the spot with her napkin. "I'd love one just like it. Could you order it for me? I'm so busy these days I don't have a minute to shop. Where, where did you get it? I love it."

"I don't remember."

"Of course you remember. How can you not remember? It's new so you must have bought it recently. Think dear. It would go beautifully with my beige dress."

"Mother, it was Bonwits or Bloomingdales or something. I . . ." She was fighting for control.

"If you don't want me to get it, I won't. You always do that when I want what you have. Honestly Naomi, sometimes I just think you don't like me." Her eyes filled with tears. They weren't even up to dessert yet.

Esther had Charlemagne on her left to protect her. She plunged in.

"Naomi, did it ever occur to you that I want things you have because I want to be like you? That it's my way of being close to you?"

"No, can't say that it has." She couldn't let this go by. She would probably regret it but the Scotch had given her some kind of false courage. "You know what? This may come as a shock to you, but you know what I feel every time you do that? I feel robbed." She spoke so quietly Sol and his bad ear and Esther with her good ears had to bend forward to hear her.

"You never seem to understand. I've told you this a thousand times. To my way of thinking I've had to fight for every moment of myself. Even down to the last fucking silkness of a scarf. Leave me that. Would you, please?"

Janie's eyes watered, Becky held her own elbows, Sol drummed the table, his mouth set in a purposeful pout. This bean of a girl was ruining his perfect day.

And Esther, Esther blinked continually, as though a thousand bats had just descended onto the table, bent on quenching their thirst in the thin cracked crystal glasses with their long, graceful stems.

"Why do you do that to your mother?" Sol erupted. "She loves you so much. Your mother is your best friend. Do you know that? Both of you. Your mother is your dearest. Do you know that there is no mother better in this world than yours. And do you know what? Do you know that you don't appreciate her? Do you know that? Do you know that your mother would do anything for you?"

Naomi turned it off. She turned him off. She had to. She was shaking so hard she could barely hold her Scotch. She had to turn off that daddy she had loved so long ago. Or she would kill him. She had to turn him off because he never once stuck up for her or took her part over the Queen of the May sitting over there on her throne of feathers. You say you love me, that I'm the best. So stick up for me once, Sol. Just try it on for size. See how it feels.

She had to turn off the daddy she had loved. And the daddy who had made promises he couldn't ever, ever keep.

Los Angeles

19

Matthew forgave her.

Big deal, she told him. She hadn't done anything deserving forgiveness. She railed at his presumption.

She didn't ask him what he did on Christmas, and he didn't tell her. He perpetuated the mystery. However, in truth, he had begun a new book, and nothing could equal that joy, that sweetness of finally breaking through and letting the new tale come out. Which is not to say that Matthew toasted Yule celibate and alone. For Matthew, out of long experience, knew how to cover himself. There was always a chance Miss Naomi might never come back. So he did find some adequate female companionship. To share the festive time.

Because in his most honest moments, when he did not hide behind the verbiage, Matthew might admit that he was as vulnerable as the next man. That he, with all his success with women, was wary of rejection, prickly at the thought of not being accepted totally.

But this impossible woman was getting to him. So he decided to forgive her even though she preferred spending her holiday with a bunch of middle-class crazies back in New York. Matthew had no patience with the middle class. He had no patience with their angst, their petty concerns. Theirs seemed to him somehow not the most crucial problems on earth. He was more committed to the political theory which addresses its constituents with the "aw, suck it up and get on with it" theory. The credo that exhorts, "There are people all over getting sliced in two, so stop your bleating, for God's sake."

But because he liked her so much, he forgave her. And when she called on her return, her bravado such a thin layer of tissue, he laughed out loud, and invited her to his lair in the sky.

It surprised him how happy he was to see her.

How much he had missed her. He hadn't missed anyone in a long long time.

Matthew had not been married for thirteen years. But before that there had been two wives. A hopeless romantic, he had adored both, been obsessed by them, and cried when they left. His wooing was always attentive; giant strawberries and chilled champagne, flowers and books, and then he would be up and off for months at a time, exploring some obscure mountain range in Africa, some Alaskan streams, a small border town. He loved women, but he had become wary. Marriage had not lasted, love had not survived. His wives had found him charming but inaccessible, and he had never found a woman who traveled well.

In order to visit Matthew Johnson you had to take an outdoor elevator. His street was in Hollywood off Camrose which was off Highland near the Hollywood Bowl. There was no parking on the street, so you had to walk a long way up a hill to get to the elevator, the only way to get to a series of houses that nestled at the top of a cluster of hills. Except for the steps, over a hundred. Naomi did that once. Only once.

She still couldn't get used to it. Los Angeles was a thousand things; the Mediterranean and Queens, Levittown and Amalfi, Forest Hills and the Riviera. Full of surprises. To get to a person's house, you turned off a busy street and took an elevator that looked like the Leaning Tower of Pisa turning toward the sky. In the middle of everything. Raymond Chandler had written about this street and the district and the elevator, Matthew said, but he just lived there. No point in writing about it. At the moment people left him and his neighbors alone to enjoy the Tuscan view from the top. Up in those hills they could be anywhere and that's the way he liked it.

Outside the bedroom the hills were pinpointed with white lights. A giant cross, brazen in the corner of a hillside, electrified its message: *Jesus Saves.*

Inside, the room was lit only by a bar of light coming from the open door of the bathroom. It cast a whisper of a shine on Naomi's body. She felt the texture of her own flesh, stretched out on the sheet, lengthening itself in front of Matthew's eyes. She sucked in her stomach knowing that the waist would indent, the hips billow just a bit, just a rounder bit more. Matthew had told her that he had held many bodies, seen many hips billow, many waists indent, and that Naomi was no more beautiful nor more sensuous than any other, but it was an organic familiarity, a tautness surrounded by such roundness that drew him to her again and again, that connected his body to hers. It was chemical and he could not explain it. It was just that his mouth belonged in, on her.

Matthew parted her lips below, and, finding the protuberance, judging by its exquisite sensitivity, he moved in on her with his hands. The one on her breast teased the nipple; he touched her everywhere: behind the knee, inside the arm, back of her neck, her toes, between her thighs. Everywhere. Everywhere she shivered. Everywhere she was aroused.

His other hand moved deep inside her. And somehow the rhythm of his fingers, playing her, his mouth tasting her, was right, and, like Alma Mahler Gropius Werfel, as the rush began, Naomi eventually reached another place, almost expiring in her frenzy; screaming; and then, nearly dazzled by her own exhaustion, she came back to him again, hungry.

What was it Mahler or Werfel or Gropius had said about Alma, that woman who had married them all at one time or another . . . what was it they had said about her? As though she had died, that's what it was, as though she had lost consciousness, disappeared. At the moment of climax, Alma would go away, lose breath, visit another place. The orgasm, *le petit mort*, was like dying. I have the Alma Mahler Gropius Werfel passion, Naomi thought. I go somewhere else too. So far away.

This night she went too far away. She said, after it was over, that she felt she would never come back, that that place had been nothing and everything. This night she almost stayed away, she told him, and she was afraid her heart would stop, and when Matthew felt it, her heart, when she was finished, it sounded like John Philip Sousa, it sounded like the thump of a thousand boots in Trafalgar Square, it sounded like the ocean on some black Maine night. But she did come back. And as Matthew held her, feeling her subside, feeling the seas in her calm, there was, at that moment some peace, finally, for both of them.

Matthew had delayed his own release because her pleasure had been so full for him, almost equal to his own, and so he began once more. A hand kneaded, stroked. He entered her, delaying once more his climax, wishing only to feel her.

But still he did not come. He wanted to see her yet another way, and turned her over, putting her on her knees. Matthew entered her again, riding her waves, feeling her deeper than before. He steadied himself with his hands on her haunches, and he noticed how sweetly the waist curved. If only she could see herself from this place how delighted she would be. And then, only then, did he allow himself release. And he screamed. He had learned how to scream from Naomi. And, as with a good full sneeze, Matthew gave in to the sound of his own cry.

They rested. He lay on his back, his arm around her, her head on his chest. Matthew felt Naomi begin moving again, her stomach undulating. She was not yet finished. In some ways, she would never be finished, each encounter serving only as continuation of the last. It did not matter how many times or how intense her orgasms, her excursions into her other place, she always began again.

Matthew touched her softness once more, now more relaxed, more moist than before, and he played with her, tempted her, teased her textures, slithery, and at the same time put his mouth on her nipple in the way he knew, and Naomi came and went away, Naomi died and came to life, over and over again.

20

Somehow Naomi and Matthew managed to see each other almost every night. This was not easy since Matthew was researching and writing his new book, and very quickly Naomi again became totally immersed in her own work. She found the names of the authorities in the field of child abuse and incest. One contact led to another. There seemed to be more people associated with the courts and the psychiatric professions who were accessible to her in this city. Or so she told herself. She convinced Helene that she had to stay at least another month or two. It was a Pandora's box. She was able to switch apartments with an actress she knew who was trying out a play off Broadway.

The apartment was in Venice on a ticky-tacky street whose backyard was a working canal. The apartment came with a canoe for traveling up and down the waters on bright sunny days, moving in and around the ducks who settled in the area thanks to the kindness of the residents and tourists who overfed them nonnutritive white bread in their misplaced philanthropic zeal. It was a two-story house and the apartment Naomi had was upstairs. From her deck she could see the mountains when the smog did not hover. The soft charm of this unlikely oasis enchanted her. The apartment was quiet and calm, while outside on Washington Boulevard, the streets crackled with action.

Roller skaters with bikinis and high socks weaved in and out, up and beyond. Weightlifters whose muscles fairly burst from their skin swaggered by. Bicycles wheeled and rolled on the streets and sidewalks; flesh was the order of the day. Bare flesh. Mostly young, mostly nubile, mostly firm, mostly too too solid, tight, tan, mostly perfect flesh. Youth was on display, and they made the most of it. At thirty-five Naomi felt ancient, ready for the discard pile, but they didn't last long, those feelings, since she knew in this place a girl of twenty-two might feel the same way.

It was the world of the fifteen- to nineteen-year-olds out there enjoying this feast of the flesh festival. It was their time. They were entitled. Before they turned around it would be over.

Naomi had worked very hard on her piece on Matthew. The photograph Helene had chosen to use for the story was not her favorite, but it was the more glamorous of the shots. In it his eyes were opaque, one could almost see through the lightness of the blue, the puffs under them more subdued, but he bore them proudly. It was as though nights of heavy drinking and philosophizing, weeks of no sleep as he struggled over a book had entitled him to these swollen signs of decadence, or maturity. Because of the lighting his hair seemed blonder, whiter than it was and the lines etched by the sun deeply into the side of his face indeed made him seem the strong Viking, with a forty-five-year-old face that looked fifty. A face that liked itself. That Naomi liked.

The interview was very alive. He could talk about anything, Matthew could, and make it interesting, even compelling. Naomi had reread all seven of his books, spent three days in the library reading everything she could find that had been written about him. She was stunned by the ferocity of the man's words, his passion. She had forgotten. She had wanted the piece to be the best she had ever written. But the force of him stood over her chair as she typed into the night, and she did not like that. His specter haunted her. She was snared by and she retreated from the force of the man.

Things were all right. Her price had gone up with this last story. A publisher had contacted her about a book, a cable company had approached her about doing her own videotape interview show. She was moving. Exactly as she had planned. Exactly as she wanted.

But she wasn't quite sure what to do with this man in her

life. And it occurred to her that, like many of her friends, it was possible that a fascinating job and lots of money might have to suffice as her priorities until that time when the sonography and amniocentesis tests in the hospital would reveal that she was sadly too old to have a proper, undeformed baby because of her age, because inside her body her eggs were getting old.

Everything else was fine. She was working, tracking down a story that was important to her, traveling; her life was all right. What would she do with a man in it? And what would she do with a baby anyway? Oriana Fallaci had gotten pregnant and had written a whole book of letters to the child growing inside her, revealing how she had tried to stay in bed the whole time but just couldn't. How, restless, she had then lost that baby, that baby whose every breathing moment she had detailed as it expanded in her womb. The pictures over Fallaci's desk had explored what stage the fetus was in, each month, as it lay there in her belly waiting to be born. But Fallaci didn't let it come out because somewhere deep down, as much as she wanted a baby, as much as she wanted to be a mother and hold the infant and suckle him, she knew it would change her life and her sense of herself and her sense of freedom. She knew that. Deep down.

Me too, Naomi thought.

Maybe.

21

"Dr. Allen, I do thank you for seeing me, I know you're very busy." Naomi put out her hand.

Dr. Grant Allen shook it vigorously. "I'm sorry we'll have such a short time, since I'm due to testify in court fairly soon." Dr. Allen was shorter than Naomi. Bearded. He was the consultant to the court on incest cases. "I must admit there was something quite compelling about your note that convinced me to see you right away."

The psychiatrist's office was small. No plants, no photos offset the grayness of the room. Only books. Books and periodicals everywhere. There was one framed lithograph over his desk. It was a surrealistic picture of a family. The father was seated in his easy chair, his dog at his feet, one hand over the dog's eyes. His wife was standing behind him; her hands over both his eyes. The son had one hand over his mother's eyes, the other over his own. It was the same with the daughter.

"Secrets," the doctor said, noticing Naomi looking at the picture. "It has to do with family secrets, the things we know and don't know, the things we hide and don't hide. The things people just don't talk about until, sadly, sometimes it is too late."

Secrets.

The poet Muriel Ruykeyser had written about the secrets in her family. She never understood why her mother and her mother's sister never spoke, after a time. The woman was her beloved aunt. And when her mother died her father married the aunt. They had been lovers all along. And the child Muriel had sensed it, felt it, knew something. Something.

"Family secrets," Naomi said. "That's what incest's about, isn't it? According to the reading I've been doing, such secrets are usually about power and independence within the family unit, love and hate, about the wish to take care of and the wish to hurt, feelings inevitably bound up with sex. Do you think that what ultimately becomes the 'family secret' often is the result of someone's inability to work through incestuous yearnings?"

Dr. Allen thought about this for a moment. "Perhaps. But in my job I only encounter actual incest cases, not the Freudian temptation, the Oedipal unspeakable, but the actuality.

"I don't know if you know this, but Freud discounted incest, the reality may have seemed too threatening. He and his colleagues relegated most revelations of his patients to fantasy. The average adult cannot believe that a normal, truthful child would tolerate incest without immediately reporting it, or that an apparently normal father could be capable of repeated unchallenged sexual molestation of his own daughter. You see, the child of any age faces a disbelieving audience when she or he complains of ongoing incest."

Naomi looked directly into the doctor's eyes. He was an attractive man, whose direct intense gaze was disarming.

"I'd like to say something about incest before you begin to ask me any questions, something I feel very strongly about. It is very important to understand that the objective distinctions between loving support from a father and lustful intrusions are disquietingly subtle."

Loving support. Lustful intrusion.

"I feel that the parent bears the entire responsibility to define and maintain appropriate limits of intimacy with the child. When there is difficulty it is because of a lack of impulse control on the father's part, or a confusion of roles, where the child is regarded as something other than a child, a surrogate someone else.

"You see there is a vague borderline between loving sensuality and abusive sexuality. We have to understand that, as parents and professionals. I mean, some women get an erotic response to breast feeding. To one woman breast feeding is a bonus in her life. Another despises it and will never do it again. Some mother touches a baby's penis and when he gets an erection she doesn't know what to do with that. By the same token, some father might feel odd bathing his daughters. Sometimes the sexual tension may be diverted into games involving teasing or mock spanking or wrestling . . ."

Naomi's pen stopped, the doctor was looking out the window as he spoke, Naomi's thoughts galloped through her head.

The bathtub was wide and spacious, a veritable ice-skating rink, a regular roller derby of a tub. Only the organ music and the dragon's breath of a Saturday afternoon were missing . . . She and Becky would squeeze the giant sponges of soapy water over each other's heads and squeal, and in would come Daddy with the lights and the camera and the action. Becky, you've got some chest already there, or is it just plumperinos there, wave to the camera, look this way Naomi give us a smile honey, what a sourpuss and listen when the water goes all out, I'll come back in and watch you do your slipslops, see how many you can do tonight honey lamb. Mommy's going to love these pictures of her girls, you have got to be the cutest in town. Becky's getting boobs, I'm telling you, already. Four years younger than Naomi and she's getting something there, at almost seven. Is that possible? No word about Naomi's ten-year-old chest, just because she happens to be a bit concave. No matter. Daddy is staying so long in the room, it was their tub time, their fun time, he should go out, he should take pictures of the cat or somebody . . .

Twenty-five, I did twenty-five slipslops, Daddy, up and down the tub, I am the queen of the slipslops, I can slide back and forth better than anybody in Tubland. Becky can't do it she slips and falls all over the place the water goes gurgling down and then the tub is all pearly and empty and I slide uuuup and baack no hands, no hands Daddy, watch me do my slipslops. Oh I'm all clean we scrubbed and scrubbed. We washed each other Daddy . . . Daddy . . .

". . . With adolescent girls two kinds of behavior are usually reported," Naomi heard the doctor say. Father either withdraws when he is threatened by his potential attraction for his daughter. Or, he is overtly seductive. Again, it is very tender for an adolescent girl growing up, and she needs support to keep up emotionally with her sudden rush to womanhood. And at this period especially, her most trusted allies should be her mother and father.

"Girls flirt with their fathers. Fathers should be harmless to flirt with. He should be approving, admiring, responsive to her growing sexual attraction and he should provide a controlled self-limited prototype of the sensual experiences she will develop with other men as an adult. As a matter of fact both father and mother should have a shared sense of the appropriateness of this prototype romance, and both should be comfortable in recognizing and defining the appropriate limits . . ."

Naomi was sixteen and the boy was telling her her body was like a Stradivarius, that he'd never known anyone as responsive, the boy was kissing her on her earlobes, his lips barely brushing her eyebrows. In the Marquesan Islands they bite each other's eyebrows in the heat of passion, he was saying. He was an educated boy, as she remembered. The moon was shining onto their faces as they sat on the living room couch, and his hand lightly, so lightly, brushed across her breast barely moving under the sweater, soft, so soft. She thought the moment had no substance, no end and no beginning. She could not breathe for no one had ever touched her breast before and it felt as though the nipple would cut its own hole through the brassiere through the whiteness of the cashmere. It was so strange, so new, so new . . .

What the hell's going on in here! Sol had flipped on the light, having the audacity to not jiggle the key loudly in the lock, having the unadulterated gall to not bang the elevator door loudly shut. His face was all red and Esther obviously was letting him handle this scandalous affair alone since she stood quietly by, holding her little bag that matched the little pillbox comfortably settled in the middle of her newly feathered feather haircut. Well, Sol did everything he could to embarrass the boy, Naomi couldn't even remember his name anymore and except for the fact that he was the first to touch her small but welcoming, quivering, all too tender, yearning breast he had remained nameless through the years . . .

She had been frightened and she couldn't look at Sol for days afterward. She hadn't done anything, just feel good, why had he gotten so angry, as though he were jealous, as though it were his breast someone had brushed, for God's sake. She didn't understand and it became so difficult between them after that and at their big parties, when the women looked so perfect, especially Allison Snow the doctor's wife. Simon Snow had almost gone to jail for performing an abortion. He had a Southern accent and they had moved out of New York after that, back to his Southern town. Allison had red hair and shiny skin, a flawless full figure that Sol loved, and they would dance cheek to cheek at the Lazuruses' big parties. Sometimes they had an orchestra in the enormous Park Avenue living room, and Allison Snow would snuggle up to Sol, and he would hold her tight around the buttocks. Simon Snow didn't even look since he was always in the corner drinking Pimms Cup, sporting a worried look. Sol would always ask his Baby Doll, his Naomi, to dance after he had done his dapper doings with Mrs. Snow. He would always ask her to dance then. But after the night in the living room with his getting so red and making her feel as though she were Caryl Chessman or somebody, it was hard to go near him, hard to. . . . Dance with me, darling. Stop it Naomi you're so tall you always think you're supposed to lead, men lead, girls follow, that's the way the dance is done, and he would hold her close just the way he had held Allison Snow. But she couldn't do it. She kept tripping over her own feet, kept moving away so that those breasts, meager and forlorn as they were, those breasts whose size it just so happens she was considering augmenting by putting falsies into the cups of the bra which she couldn't possibly fill out no matter how thirty-two it was, no matter how the lady who sardined herself into the dressing room with her had said she would grow. Sol would hold her close and she would pull back. This isn't the waltz, Naomi, this is cheek-to-cheek time. But she couldn't do it. It didn't feel right. He would get angry at her because she danced so badly, because she kept tripping over his feet and then her own, because she kept looking down at her feet and kept counting the steps. She would never be as debonair as he, cheek-to-cheek and holding the arm way out that way and then folding it to his chest that way holding hers. She was glad her generation danced without holding each other, you just had to express your own rhythms and . . . she could not press herself into Sol after that time, even just to kiss him, not after his red face and sweating that time. There was something so odd about it, and she hadn't done anything wrong . . . but still she knew he loved her. . . . She knew she would always be the girl he loved . . . but he had been acting so odd with her lately . . .

"Now these are not essentially classified as sexual abuse, of course. Like when adolescents complain of parental voyeurism, fathers who compulsively station themselves near where their daughters are undressing. Usually they are sure their daughters are unaware of it, but on the contrary most girls are aware and are usually disturbed by it. As clinicians it is very important for us to listen carefully when a teenage girl says to us, 'Dad just isn't the same as he used to be.' "

Naomi tried to please the question carefully. "But when incest does indeed actually take place within a marriage situation, would you say it is planned?"

"Rarely. As I indicated at the beginning, it is a surprisingly subtle distortion of normal family relationships. No matter how collusive a mother may be, and often unconsciously she is, the responsibility of the father must be constantly emphasized. He is the key to the disturbed dynamics, and he is responsible for the choice to eroticize the relationship with the daughter. And when it happens it is a vicious cycle, he feels guilty and frightened, but still there is a compulsion for repetition. The child feels used and betrayed, and feels she has no worth except as a sex object, she feels alternately courted and demeaned. Then the girl seeks escape and often the mother will not believe her."

"Does incest necessarily mean intercourse?"

Dr. Allen leaned forward, his elbows on his knees. "To my mind incest is any sexual activity of intimate physical contact that is sexually arousing between nonmarried members of a family."

The buzzer on Dr. Allen's phone broke the intensity in the room. He picked up the phone, listened briefly and hung up.

"I've got to leave in five minutes. Naomi, I feel you have much more to ask, but I must get to court." He picked up a pencil and drummed it on his desk.

As though she had not been listening to this last, Naomi said, "So you are saying that even though there has not actually been intercourse, but a girl feels that something along the way, uh, untoward, happened, that is considered incest?"

Dr. Allen got up and studied her carefully.

"If a girl or a woman feels strongly that something was not quite right, that the trust and loving support we spoke of earlier was in some way crossed over, then yes, I would say, depending on the extent of her malaise, a lustful intrusion took place, due to the father's ignorance, inability to understand his sexual feelings for a beloved daughter, whatever. Yes, I feel strongly that this is a betrayal, a form of incest."

22

Naomi was exhausted. She felt drained as she drove down Ocean Park Boulevard. She had come out of her way on this route so she could be greeted with the miraculous surprise at the end. A miracle loomed in front of her after she passed Main Street, after Pacific, as the giant yawn of the ocean appeared suddenly, welcoming her at the end of the long wide street. It made her chest open up when she saw it. Like a proud robin she swelled with air when she saw the sun glistening on the caps of the waves, shining on the endlessness of it. How blessed, to be able to drive down a street that suddenly turns into an ocean.

As she drove down into her street, she barely missed hitting a mallard who was waddling off after a haughty white duck who had the telltale markings of a gang bang on her neck. The skin had been bruised raw by the mating game. Living on the canal, Naomi had been conducting an unofficial survey on the sex habits of the ducks. They didn't seem to fornicate in pairs, their operation usually involving two or three mallard brutes chasing after one female, pinning her down on the ground by the scruff of her neck and giving it to her, one after the other. It was painful to watch, but the lady duck didn't seem to mind; since after the acts were consummated she would pick herself up, shake herself off contentedly, and start all over again. But Naomi wanted to kill the mallards she saw drag one lady duck off the nest, away from her babies.

As she was struggling with her key she noticed the woman with the cape approaching her.

Accosted.

The woman pushed her face so close their noses almost touched.

"Hello."

Naomi knew something was wrong.

The woman's eyes were too bright, her tone too intense. She was holding a French newspaper.

"God is alive you know," she said, tipping her head so that her hair almost brushed Naomi's cheek. "Yes my dear, he was sighted in 1953 in the south of France and that is where he is living now. Do you read French?"

"No." She did, but she was damned if she would let on.

"Oh, what a shame, then you cannot read this newspaper which tells all about God and what he is doing. He has been sighted, you know, in the south of France."

"I'm Jewish," Naomi said, for some reason thinking this bit of information would be a deterrent to the onslaught.

"Oh, that's all right. You believe in God, don't you? It's all the same. Aren't you relieved to know he has been sighted? Living in the south of France?"

Let me pass or I will knock you down in the middle of this duck-inundated street.

The woman must have sensed the demon in Naomi's eyes. She moved on.

Matthew was sitting out on her deck, his yachting cap over his eyes, his feet up on the railing. Seeing him there made a round warm sun settle in the middle of her chest. Her next reaction was one of irritation, of intrusion. This was her space, to coin a revolting phrase she ordinarily refrained from using, how dare he come unannounced; and then she let it happen. The good feeling. Unfamiliar. How lovely to see him there, his bulk awkwardly arranged on her deck chair, on his lap an extravagantly wrapped present.

She threw off her shoes and tiptoed out to the deck. She bent down and gently lifted his cap and kissed him on both eyes. The sun spot was still there, spreading, warming the whole inside of her chest.

"Where you been?"

"Incest."

"You still involved with dirty old men?"

"What's in your lap?"

"That's a loaded question. Would you like me to unzip and . . . "

"On top of your lap, not inside your lap."

"Oh yes. A present."

She tore it open. It was a cookbook. Beautiful, with lots of illustrations in color.

She didn't know whether to be insulted or to thank him.

"I just got a little tired of doin' the cooking. And I thought maybe this would inspire you all."

"Me and who else."

"You all. Southern talk."

She decided to thank him instead of being angry, and crept into his lap. All five-feet-almost-ten of her wound herself around the squareness of him. She breathed into his neck. "I love getting presents."

"Don't I know it. Underneath all that capable shit and achievement business is one little old Jewish princess."

She didn't have the energy to fight him on that one. True, Daddy Sol had spoiled her and given her a lot of stuff when she was a little girl. But a Jewish princess? She couldn't even think about it now.

"Do I have to start using the present now? Why don't we just go to the corner and have sushi?"

He smoothed her hair, this big baby all wrapped around him, all legs and bones wrapped around him.

"When I was a kid in my little Texas town, you're the kind of middle-class lady we would have had a field day with. If you were stopped at a red light I would just open the back door of your car and walk right through. Or bang on it from the outside and scare the shit out of you."

Naomi lifted her head and looked into his eyes.

"That's disgusting."

"And I'm most certain that if I had been a kid on your block, I would have been in your pants. I mean if you were the Jewish princess on the block, the Miss Middle Class on the block, I would have come over to your house and would have done chores, come in for cookies, y'know, and then would have got to you. And then, my dear, right into your pants."

"You take such pride in your working class origins. You wear them like a medal of honor."

"I don't want to argue. I want to get into your pants; didn't you get the hint?"

"I got the hint." She unwound herself from him and walked into the living room dropping her clothes as she went. In seconds they were on her friend Maria's Japanese-style sleeping mattress lying on the floor, in each other's arms.

Into her hair. "I missed you today. There was no one to complain and carry on, no one for me to tease. No one to kiss." He nuzzled the back of her neck.

She settled into his arms. He smelled of the sea. Or was that fish smells from the canal?

She pulled back and looked him in the eyes. "The psychiatrist told me today that if you think something odd happened between you and your father, if you sense something, it's almost as though it did happen. I don't know why I'm getting more and more uncomfortable yet more and more fascinated with this business. I can't believe Sol ever did anything to me. He wouldn't. But Matthew, something's gnawing at me, something is very disturbing to me. Whole layers of stuff I can't get to. Can't remember."

"It's hard to have your little girl turn from a duckling into a swan. A sexual swan." Matthew touched her forehead. "I know. I admit it. It was hard when my daughter matured. Overnight she had a woman's body."

"Somehow it seems that it would be easier to deal with if I knew for sure, if I actually remembered that something did happen, instead of all this sensing, all this wondering."

"It's probably very unlikely something happened," he said.

"Maybe. I don't know, I have such a persistent sense of it. Nothing specific. But even if it's a hand on a breast at puberty, I sense some kind of violation."

Matthew was nibbling at her breast. Slowly, deliberately, the tongue made figure-eights on the left then the right nipple. He was getting to know her. It was the only thing that could get her to stop talking.

They lay there, their bodies wet, grateful for the exertion. Every time Naomi felt this complete with Matthew, she felt very nervous. As though she were losing something. That some little piece of herself was disappearing into his bloodstream, that because of his semen flowing into her, somehow a piece of her soul would be canceled out. She hadn't fallen in love in so long that . . . no, she had never been in love, let's put it that way, she decided to be honest for once in her life.

She lay there, thinking how she had fought to be where she is. Before Matthew. How not being encumbered emotionally, no matter how she thought she yearned for it, had enabled her to be free. Hank didn't count. That was to get out of the house, to get her father off her back. Hank had wanted a real corporate wife, to host dinner parties and wait on him in front of the firm's president. He wanted an appendage, someone in whose eyes he could admire his own reflection.

All her women friends kept saying they were going to adopt children on their own because there were no men around who were interesting enough to father them. One editor at the magazine had been celibate for a year. It just wasn't worth it. Men couldn't make commitments and they seemed intimidated by women's new power.

Except for Matthew Johnson. He barely noticed Naomi's power. Dyan Cannon, that great oracle, had written somewhere that two incompletes don't make a complete. That had made enormous sense to Naomi; and so, truthfully, her relationships had been only adventures. And so she had seen the inside of the most extravagant hotel rooms all over the world.

The general in Beirut had kept his gun by his bed when she stayed beyond curfew and had to sleep in his villa. They had made love all night and he couldn't believe he could be that passionate with someone other than his wife. He had confided in her, this career officer, that his son was a pacifist. He had been a nice man and they had met in Washington for a weekend once when he wasn't in some war someplace, to see what they could see. They had gone to the movies in the afternoon and had a lot to drink.

Then there was the Southern senator who, after months of cajoling, had entertained her at his family's plantation. They actually drank mint juleps on the veranda, served by a black man in a white coat. She had liked his house, his green lawn, but not his politics.

Adventures. Moments in time. Having nothing to do with previous moments in time.

That's the way she had always kept things, to protect herself from letting anything get in the way of achieving her goal.

Of achieving what? Of being Oriana Fallaci, of being able to tell Mr. Kissinger where to get off? Of getting President Thieu's telephone number and sharing it with the world? By the way, whatever did happen to President Thieu? Naomi could write *and* take photos. Naomi could be Margaret Bourke-White and Fallaci all at the same time.

"Thinking about us, pretty lady?"

Looking like a cow in a pasture having only the strength to brush away a few flies with his tail, eyes benign and utterly content, Matthew kissed her hand. Catching her in thought.

"I was just thinking." Matthew took a long stretch. Naomi knew a monologue was coming. "When I was twenty years old," he began, "I was a line company first sergeant in charge of two hundred of the best soldiers in the army. I took my beautiful new wife on a honeymoon and fucked ten times within as many hours, consumed an enormous crazy breakfast: a quart of milk and a banana split, four rashers of bacon, four eggs, a stack of hotcakes, a bowl of fresh strawberries, and a slice of watermelon. Then I drove six hundred miles and fucked five more times."

Naomi looked at him incredulously.

"Matthew, you and I just made love."

"Right, I was just wondering if I will ever be impotent with you. Disappointment and exaggerated expectation can do it for me. For some strange reason I am at ease with you. You are loving and you are an adversary. And somehow I like that."

"Which wife was that?"

"First. The mother of my kids. Hey, my daughter just made me a grandfather last month. Got married too young like me. Anyway, my wife thought that ten times a day was how the marriage was going to be and was charmingly concerned. Yet my sweet love, when I was turned down for a direct commission to first lieutenant, I suffered impotence that very day and have, off and on since in similar circumstances."

Naomi smoothed Matthew's cheek. It was warm. She wanted to retract her thoughts of herself. Why was she always thinking of herself? Her head whirled with thoughts of Naomi.

Tell me Naomi, Sol said in her head, in all innocence, in all cruelty, Sol said in her head, sitting at the table the three of them in that giant dining room, the candlelight flickering on all their faces, waiting for the dessert and coffee. Tell me Naomi, he had said, looking from one to the other, mother to daughter, daughter to mother, tell me how does it make you feel, psychologically speaking, I mean, how does it make you feel when you know your father loves your mother so much?

Tell me honeylamb, tell old Sol who wooed and petted and loved you to distraction when you were little, but no matter what, on Sunday mornings worshipped only Esther who sat on the throne. Only Esther, who always had the last word. His answer always, ask your mother, that's her department. Love 'em, and leave 'em. Sol baby could only go so far.

Sweet sixteen and already been . . .

Sweetie pie, let's get the best table at Sardi's. Vincent thinks I'm here with one of my chippies, Vincent thinks you're one of my girls, well let's just let him think so; not everyone can walk into a restaurant and have everyone turn around and the person they are looking at is his date, his darling . . .

"For me," Matthew continued, "when I've been impotent it's been when some overwhelming insecurity takes over my whole mind and body. So, my dear, what I'm saying is that good sex depends on the merging of mind and body. As in what just occurred on these premises only moments ago. It depends upon the acceptance of another as is and love for another as is."

"Matthew."

"I know. I do go on. Why, I do not know. Why, I cannot for the life of me fathom, but there are great wells of tears inside me for you. There is always a tristesse of sorts after coming, a little death, but a good tristesse. It is as it should be. Happiness is not merely the lack of unhappiness in our lives. Allow me. I want you to know I care for you. I care for you more, in some ways, than you care for yourself. You are better than you think you are. Believe me."

"Matthew . . ."

"Just one more thing. People who read my books do not know what to do with my sense of reality. I know that one of the powers of my work is that I can deal with the reality of which I write without any self-consciousness, I call it as I have seen it. I went to school with a kid who had an affair with our best friend's mother when he was thirteen. For three years. I knew another guy who had sex with his mother from when he was eleven till about thirteen. True. He always distrusted the middle class as much as I. Said all those dudes spend their time on the couch talking about the fantasy of screwing their mothers, whereas he did it. I've written about both these kinds of realities.

"But they mistake, these people who are offended by my work. I am a moralist, a romanticist, not a sentimentalist, more than less freed from conventional Judeo-Christian guilt and associated bullshit . . ."

"Matthew. Your pomposity is unforgivable. You are the most ponderous man I have ever met. Matthew . . ."

He had even tired himself. He was dozing. They lay there till dusk, bathed in the plethora of his words. The bond between them thickening; this bond, this fearsome thing.

23

Matthew left before 6:00 A.M. The ducks had awakened him, their guttural chatter an unfriendly reminder that he had to return to his perch at the top of the elevator at the top of the hill and get to work.

"Be careful that you do not begin to embrace the symptoms of that which you are investigating," the note read, pinned to a dish towel in the kitchen. "I worry that you are engaged in something vaguely reminiscent of a college freshman encountering psychology or a medical student in his first semester. Every girl feels a strong sexual attachment for her father, and vice versa. When my daughter began to get a brick shithouse of a body I thought God would strike me blind. I had to become acquainted with and learn to deal with my feelings. And I lived. I got over it. We're fine friends. Be careful you are not building mountains in your zeal to get a good story, to get to the bottom of all this tawdry stuff. . . . I will talk to you after I get some pages done. Pretty lady. You looked like Pocahontas all wrapped in sleep this morning. Be well, my love."

Naomi took the note, crumpled it into a tight ball and flung it across the room into a basket.

"Son of a bitch. Condescending, patronizing son of a bitch." If only she could remember. If only her childhood was not vague pictures verified by endless photographs, faithfully, painstakingly pasted into her father's albums, preserving every rite of passage, every moment that could be interpreted as meaningful. It was as though they were her life, those pictures, and the little girl in the flesh had been replaced by that little girl with the long braids and wistful look staring at the camera, that little girl with no teeth hugging her daddy on the beach and in the bathtub and roughhousing on the bed. That little girl had nothing to do with Naomi Lazurus Loeffler, thirty-five. This person here now. William Maxwell had written that, truly, we remember only the story of the memory, and not necessarily the memory itself. Naomi wondered if we truly ever remember anything the way it really was?

But memory plays tricks on you. There had been things Naomi sensed happened, recalled with such vivid feeling that the emotion of the memory, if not necessarily the accuracy of the facts, could still be searing. When she was about ten they were visiting Grandma and Grandpa Frank. The scene in her mind's eye of Grandpa chasing Grandma Nettie up the stairs with a butcher knife is very clear. Did someone tell her about it? Did she imagine it? But in her child's head she saw the fear in Nettie's eyes, the daring him to come closer, the desperation in her grandfather's gaze. Yet she knew Maurice Frank idolized Nettie.

Esther said it never happened, and was appalled that Naomi would conjure such a barbaric scene. Esther and Sol were continually questioning Naomi's remembrances so after a while their "you aways make up stories," and "stop imagining things that never happened," made her start keeping a lot of those things, true or dreamed, to herself. After a while she began to doubt the veracity of her own spirit. It's not that they actually accused her of lying, but Big Daddy's invective of "mendacity" did cross Sol's lips once or twice. No offense meant, he cautioned, it's just that his remembrance of Naomi's past did not quite coincide with hers.

But, Naomi thought as she dressed quickly for her morning interview, but, I remember almost nothing. Nothing that adds up, that makes any important sense. She tried hard to let her mind float as she drove the freeway, tried hard to remember who that little girl was. But it was a void, her memory bank. Account closed.

The smog was heavy in Altadena as Naomi drove into Sally Stewart's driveway. Pockets of it lay like smoke three days after a fire, between the mountains and the highway. It seemed an old town, old money, old houses, but there was a cultivated charm about it. It seemed substantial, certain to stay put for a while.

Naomi did not know what to expect after she rang the bell. On the phone Sally Stewart had answered sweetly, the singsong tones antithetical to the salutation, "Survivors Anonymous." Sally, an incest victim, had started the organization several years ago.

The survivor opened the door. She was a tiny woman, assuredly not even five feet tall, about thirty-five years old, with curlers in her hair. She was carefully made up. Her teeth were very white, protuberant, almost too perfect. A suburban housewife.

As the door opened the bell was still ringing with strains of "L'Arlesienne Suite." It was obvious someone collected clocks. The hall and the living room through which they walked were filled with clocks hanging on the walls and standing in corners. There were plastic trees and a gray shag rug. Sally offered Naomi a seat in her den-office.

Sally was friendly, a bit detached, but relaxed. She gave Naomi a cup of coffee, said she did not mind the tape recorder.

Softly: "Have you been able to forgive your father, Sally?"

"Forgive?" She started taking the curlers out of her hair. "Forgiving implies accepting. And with forgiving comes making your own amends. Look, you know, I can't afford to be resentful. I've got to keep it simple. I talk about it all the time in the group. I flush it out, I work it out, knead it, you know, like a heavy massage. I talk about it and talk about it, in detail. You've got to dump the guilt. You have to admit that yes there was pleasure. You have to admit that you think you initiated it, that a lot of it may have been your fault."

Sally leaned back in her chair and stared out the window as she talked. Sounds of children playing on the street outside were muted, muffled. Naomi could see the woman next door hanging out her wash. Hanging out her wash. She hadn't seen anyone do that since two years ago in Italy when the courtyards of apartment buildings seemed to flutter with the flags of all nations, shirts of all residents who didn't own a dryer, who wouldn't think of putting their clothes into some electrically heated oven instead of the sweetness and freshness of the noon-day sun. Naomi was comforted by the prosaic act, warmed by the mundane movement of the woman taking the clothespins out of her mouth and pinning the shirts and sheets onto the white rope stretched taut in the morning sun.

"It's true for me and it's true for every woman who comes to the meetings," Sally continued. "But we've got to identify the feelings. At the beginning I started out saying 'I don't feel any-thing. I don't feel anything.' And then slowly you begin to see. Sure some of us enjoyed it, being held. Christ, it was the only damn place we'd ever felt love. And it was all mixed up, the rage, and the anger and the sex and the love. Sure. It's not so easy. You got to be very honest with yourself. And that's hard. A lot of women collapse. Just fall apart. They can't take it. They can't take what they hear themselves saying.

"And you know what?" Her voice became louder for the first time. "We're all the same. The stories might be different but once we get under a few layers and identify who we are, there we are. Self-destructive behavior like you wouldn't believe. Psychosomatic illnesses, an inability to trust, an inability to suc-ceed. Christ, you get so close to succeeding and then whammo, you remind yourself, hey, don't you remember, that's not your script. You're no good. You're shit, remember? All you're good for is bed, you know?

"And then what happens, and what we hope for in the group is that we decide that we want to change. Some of us need private therapy. We find that it is impossible to let go of our parents. We do psychodrama, confront the father, the mythical father, the imaginary father, played by another girl. We write letters we never mail. I've written hundreds of pages to my father. Hundreds. The point is to get on the road to change our lives. We have to do that for ourselves, for each other. We trust each other. We know when we're in those rooms we're not alone. That we have each other, and that each and every one of us understands."

She had finished taking the curlers out of her hair, and now took a brush out and started brushing. Very politely, apologiz-ing, "Excuse me. I just washed my hair, didn't have a chance to go to the beauty parlor this week." Her blue eyes shone under the light purple shadow. Naomi noticed the cleft in her chin.

"That's okay. Sally, why do you think you survived. What gave you the strength to go on?"

"It's hard to explain. Especially to a stranger." She hesitated. "You see, I had to find love inside me. After all the shit I've been through, I had to unleash all those feelings. I mean stuff like when I was nine years old I got my period, in a foster home, and this woman, this foster mother French-kissed me when I got my period. Sick, right? I got messed up so early.

"Early on, sex became a weapon for me. I learned to use it as a weapon. I learned really early that if you learn to control the muscle you use when you go to the bathroom, you could develop a technique in sex. I went to psychiatrists and they never helped me. I manipulated them. I went to bed with them.

"It wasn't till finally I got to Alcoholics Anonymous, and finally stopped drinking, and realized why I was drinking in the first place, that I got help. It wasn't until I could talk about my past with people who'd been through the same things, who wouldn't sit in judgment of me, who knew. It wasn't till psychodrama when I allowed myself to relive all those bodies and all those years, it wasn't until I finally stopped stuffing it down that I allowed myself to feel. In all the therapy I had, I'd never cried. Never. But one time in the women's group I started to cry and scream and yell and holler and carry on, and I couldn't stop. They couldn't stop me. It went on and on. All that pain and all that hurt finally came out. Turned it around for me. My survival has to do with not stuffing the shit anymore."

Naomi's eyes were wet with tears.

"Look, I didn't want to make you cry. It's all right. That goes on in the group all the time. I've got women coming in from all over the city from Long Beach to Palos Verdes, all over. I don't advertise, just handbills and a phone number. The phone doesn't stop ringing. So many women are getting the courage to talk about it, to let go of that giant scream like the one I carried around in me for so long.

"I mean I'm all right now, you know. Happily married, my kids from my first husband are teenagers now, my husband adopted them. He adores them.

"But you know, I'll admit something to you, if I wake up in the middle of the night and see that my husband, God love him, much as I adore him, if I see that he's not there lying next to me,

I get up like a bat out of hell and shoot into my daughter's room. Just to check that he's not in there. Automatic, you know? Second nature, I guess."

The water came hard out of the shower nozzle. Hot. Naomi welcomed the bristling sting of it as it splattered over her. Her stall shower had green tiles and a little seat in the corner where the soap and shampoo rested. She could sit on it if she wanted to rest, but there was, of course, no resting in the shower, as the water belted down on her, hard.

Moments later Matthew joined her, noiselessly. He took her ears in his big hands and bent her head back and gently kissed her on the mouth, her wet hair, her forehead. She put her arms around his big self, and just made it, barely clasping her hands behind him.

She felt her breasts flatten against him, dripping, and at the same time his looseness tighten and harden against her at the top of his legs, pressing into her. They stood this way, no words, for a time, holding, wet, the water washing them away until Matthew placed her back against the green tile wall of the shower, took the soap off the little seat in the corner and began soaping her. He made a lather with his hands and began at the nape of her heck; kneading her slowly in the great hollows before the clavicle and under the ears. He made great soapy circles out of his hands as he slowly massaged her breasts, caressing, making bubbles of friction on the nipples. Her knees grew weak, her eyes closed. His hands washed the indentation deep into her waist, smoothing lightly the pubic bones, the long flanks of bone and flesh.

When he got to her mound, the long curly hair straightened by the wetness, he softly began to massage the swelling, moving slowly from belly to mound, mound to belly. The gesture was hypnotic, the circles a ritual of roundness. The tummy was a safe place, a safe house, the below part was not a safe place. Leaning back against the green tile Naomi felt her eyes opening, the water making splashes into her eyes as though her lashes were washing rain away, the tummy part felt like the inside of her mouth, soft and mysterious, secret and safe, warm and moist.

There are places in there, don't go down into that part, the part where the hair is coming, that's the new part, the part you're not supposed to see, the part you're not supposed to wash, the part where all the new hair so soft so fine so different from the hair on my head is coming, like the new fine threads under my arms; not down there it's clean, I washed there, I always wash there, Daddy, I've done that, no more there that's not a safe place no no not there Dad . . .

"NO." Naomi began to shake and push Matthew away. Her eyes were open now, her hair stringy wet. She ceased to appear the mermaid delightfully moistened by the sea. She was transformed; a Medusa of the waves, a harridan of the green tiles.

"Sweetheart, what? What? It's me. It's Matthew. It's all right, Naomi."

Naomi began weeping, crying uncontrollably. She could not find her breath. The water was getting in her eyes and ears as she struggled to find the door of the stall shower. The green tile seemed to her the bottom of the ocean floor.

"What is it? Sweetheart . . ." Matthew was holding her, helping her stumble out of the shower onto firm ground, onto a truly safe place.

He lay her on the bed and covered her with an oversize towel. He dried her body, avoiding her secret place. He waited until her sobs subsided, until she could tell him what was the matter.

New York

24

"I didn't just fold up my tent like an Arab. That's a bad metaphor anyway in view of my ethnic persuasion. Helene called me up in the middle of the night and said grab the next plane and I did. I left you a note, I left you four thousand Xs at the bottom of the page, I left you a bottle of champagne and gave you my precious copy of Anne Sexton to read."

"I don't like melancholy Catholic musings."

"My you're dyspeptic."

Naomi was lying naked, sprawled on her own bed in her own apartment three thousand miles away from Venice and Matthew, three thousand miles away from the Hollywood elevator that looked like the Tower of Pisa. By some fortuitous stroke of luck the girl with whom she had made the apartment switch was out of town for four days and she had her place to herself.

"I am not dyspeptic. I am not used to my ladies taking off like a thief in the night. I was truly worried about you, Naomi, and then I wake up and you're not even here for Christ's sake. How long are you staying in New York?"

"Not long." Naomi wound herself tightly into a ball, the phone wire between her legs. "I have to see Helene this afternoon and decide on some strategy with this story. Suddenly she wants to talk in person about it. I'm going to have dinner with her. Then some family stuff and I should be back at the end of the week. And what is this 'my lady' business? This is my work, this is the way I do it. I come and go. I fly around all over the place."

Silence. He didn't want her to be here. He wanted her to be there, with him. She was disturbing his train of thought. She was interrupting his work. She should stay put.

But for Naomi there was some relief being away. She was getting too vulnerable with this man. She was losing her cool and that was dangerous, impossible. She would have none of it, she would not have a man creep inside her no matter how charming, no matter how loving he was. He'll be taking off pretty soon anyway, she figured, him and his ladies, him and his zillions of ladies.

"Are you all right, Naomi?"

"Of course I'm all right . . . oh you mean last night, about the shower. I'm sorry. I'm sorry if I frightened you. I don't know what that's all about, I have to sort it out, Matthew. I can't talk about it yet until I do."

"Don't move away, kiddo."

"Who's moving?" There was a catch in her voice. He had the disgusting habit of always knowing what she was thinking. Of always second-guessing her. They had never talked about it but somewhere she knew that he knew that she would consider leaving him before he had the chance to abandon her. What a bore. The battle between the sexes, a crashing bore. She will go back to her work, back to her incest, back . . .

"You've gotten under my skin, skinny." Pause. "So I did what you told me. I canceled your paper, notified your service, put out the garbage. Followed your letter of instruction to the, if not quite *T*, to the *L* at least. *L* is for love, pretty lady. I'm going to work and unplug. I'll call you, don't call me. Ciao."

And he was gone. Gone three thousand miles away. Gone away into the wires into the telephone poles into the bodies of the birds sitting on the telephone poles in Oklahoma and in Wyoming sweltering in the desert sun sitting there on those poles. She lay on the bed. Her arms around her own body. Hugging herself. The man is goddamn moving himself right in.

There were only about twelve tables in the restaurant. It was in the east Eighties and Helene said it was her favorite spot and would Naomi please meet her there, canceling their late afternoon appointment in the office. Helene had sounded tired, terse on the phone.

She rushed in, forty-five minutes late. Naomi was on her second Scotch, ninth carrot, seventh black olive, third radish. Helene looked harried, but handsome. Always handsome. Always with a hat. God, Naomi wished she could wear hats. But she couldn't wear them with panache. On her, hats just sat there. On Helene the profile came alive with sensuality and mystery the minute some felt or straw or velvet hat appeared on her head. One thought of the Orient Express or a tryst in Marrakesh. It wasn't fair.

Not that Naomi was complaining. Since Esther was so chic and so perfect and so put together both Naomi and Becky had always had trouble even meeting standard requirements set by the *Hobo News*, dressing appropriately either for the supermarket or for Princess Grace's New Year's Eve extravaganza. But Naomi, fortunately, had learned to know her body. That long lanky thing that could wear anything, as long as the cut was trim, had a decent flow, and somewhere, somehow, a sense of humor. It was here she excelled. There was always a suspender or a boot, a scarf or a lapel that relaxed the look. Made her laugh. She liked that about herself and her taste.

Becky of course had no chic whatsoever. Elegance eluded her. Since her bulk took precedence over all else, Becky sadly was doomed to lack style. She courted it, yes, yearned for it, absolutely. But as happens sometimes when the will is weaker than the pain, the casual, the easy, yes, the sloppy . . . had taken over.

"Sorry I'm late." Helene bent down to have her cheek kissed. Who else does that? Esther, of course. Naomi was doomed to spend her life with ladies who lunch, who never put out. Figuratively, of course. Helene sank down in the chair opposite Naomi, her briefcase and bags dropped on the chair between them. She exuded the scent of Opium, strong and heavy. Her Italian suit was cut with flawless grace and around her neck lay a gray fox boa. She was right out of Central Casting.

"I want a martini. An old-fashioned stiff drink. You wouldn't believe my day. Let me look at you." She sat back, undid the boa, threw it on the chair next to her. Squinted. "Good. You really look good. That southern exposure must hit the spot. Or is it something else?"

Naomi blushed. She never blushed. She was too old, too

jaded, too been-around to blush. But she felt the heat creep up under her ears to the tip of her head.

"I'll have another Scotch," she said to the waiter as he brought Helene's martini.

"I've got to catch up. I'll have another, please," Helene said as she sipped gingerly and then gulped the rest of her glass. "I haven't had a martini in ages but all day for some reason the thought of one in a chilled glass with a twist of lemon has been haunting me. Oh . . . before I forget . . . I've got a batch of stuff I've been saving for you." She rummaged around in her brief-case and came out with a thick file.

"Was there anything specific you wanted to talk about, or just about where the piece is going generally?"

"Touch base. It's really important for me to touch base with you. I want to get all this material together for the June issue. That gives you maybe another month to put it all together."

"That's okay."

"From what you told me on the phone you're getting some good stuff."

"Really."

"Well, actually you probably could wrap it up on the coast and work out of New York now."

Naomi felt a chill.

"I mean it doesn't really make any difference where you write, does it?" Helene said as she perused the menu the waiter had handed to her.

"I know what I want, I always have the same thing; four hundred calories and tastes like a thousand." Helene addressed the waiter, "I'll have the chicken and a salad. But look, I want to drink for a while, serve it in about half an hour, okay? Naomi, order the chicken. They do it like nobody else in town."

"No, I'll have the trout, please. Thank you." Nobody, but nobody, even a boss of sorts, was going to order for her. She hated being ordered for. Matthew sneaks it in. Before she realizes her dinner is in front of her and she is enjoying it. Matthew. Matthew Johnson. He would not like Helene.

"Well, I mean there really isn't any reason for you to stay out there, is there?"

"I've made some good contacts. There are some people out there who are very sophisticated in this area. I think I'll exhaust what I've started. I've got an apartment exchange anyway and it's not costing me anything."

Helene looked hard at her. She was beginning to feel what she wanted to feel. Woozy and loose, the tension beginning slowly to ooze out of her.

"Who'd you meet?"

"What are you talking about? Honestly Helene, you do tend to simplify . . ."

"I know you. There's something different about you. Don't tell me the hard, lean, independent, there's-nobody-interesting-out-there Naomi Lazurus Loeffler has met the last of a vanishing breed, a real man?"

Naomi laughed a bit too loudly. "I don't know what you're getting at. You know that if I'd met someone I'd tell you."

"You would certainly not. I've never met anyone as private as you about your private life. Unlike other people, unlike people like me who seem to have a need to unburden themselves and their love life to every old lady with glasses and pearl earrings sitting alongside them on every crosstown bus." She did not skip a beat. "Think you'll ever get married again?"

Naomi looked startled.

"What may I ask is so weird about that question?" Helene said.

"It was the 'again.' Somehow I always forget that I was married at all. I mean, I really should have given the presents back, all those candlesticks and fruit bowls. It didn't even last two years and it was really over in a couple of months. I mean it wasn't like a marriage, whatever that is."

"How old are you?"

"What is this Helene, the third degree? What's going on with you?"

Helene leaned forward. She took off her blue tinted glasses.

"I've been thinking a lot lately. I've been running so fast that I never have time to take stock. My grandmother used to tell me to sit in a room quietly. Take stock. Get perspective. Mine eludes me, my perspective is like a flock of birds floating up a chimney."

"And . . ." Naomi was feeling her drinks too. She always liked Helene better after a few drinks.

"And, I'm going to be thirty-nine next week. Thirty-fucking-nine years old which is one fucking year away from being forty."

"And . . ."

"Stop with the *and* every minute." Sharp. "Sorry, you're interrupting my train of thought. And, I mean where am I?" Helene was on a roll. "I've gotten exactly what I wanted. I wanted to be a head honcho, right? The most important woman editor in New York. That's what I wanted and that's what I got. When Andy died I decided that there was no point in even trying to love a man again, so I took all that energy and all that sex in me and threw it into getting to be the best. I worked my ass off and here I am. And you know what . . . I love it. I love where I am. I love being successful. I love that maitre d' over there scraping and carrying on when I come into a room, and I love that they bring the phone to the table when my office calls or that lady senator from Kansas, what's her name Alf Landon's daughter, Kassenbaum, calls and has to talk to me about the ERA and that Eleanor Holmes Norton wants me to sit next to her on the dais at a big women's powwow. You know what, I love it. I love the power and I love the feeling that maybe we could get something done, that women could maybe move mountains . . ."

Her fingers were long and thin. Beautifully cared for. Calcium. Helene must have great fountains of calcium deposits flowing all over her body, Naomi decided. Her life was orchestrated and organized, choreographed to perfection.

"But the point is that I'm going to be thirty-nine, and then forty. And I do not share my life with anyone. I have had so many lovers I can't remember. It's not that I am lonely, that's not what I am talking about. I have zillions of friends, I never sit home, there is always a literary cocktail party to go to or a political rally, people call me up all the time. It's just that there's a hole, Naomi. Something is missing and I'm never going to find out what it is because I'm not willing to give up one minute of what I've got to find out what it is. I will not relinquish one thing."

Naomi realized that she had flown three thousand miles to New York because Helene wanted to talk about getting old. That Helene wanted a man, that Helene was going to say she was getting too old to have a baby. That was next. That Helene called her because she knew she would understand, because as much as she hated to admit it she was just like Helene Stanley in a lot of ways.

The maitre d' put the food in front of them, but neither woman touched it. Helene ordered a bottle of very expensive wine. The waiters hovered solicitously; a fire appeared in the small fireplace carved out of one brick wall.

Time stopped. Naomi smoothed the sides of the round belly of the wine glass, the coolness a grateful moment at the table, warm from the candlelight. It was as though Helene understood somehow that the intimacy had to be choreographed, was dependent on the wine and the yellow light, the womblike heat of the restaurant; as though the stage had to be set for the closeness to happen.

"I just finished a course at the New School," Helene reported.

"On what?"

"Emotional Conflicts of the Career Woman."

"You? What for?"

"I don't know. I've been edgy lately. I don't know, some kind of free-floating anxiety brought on, I'm sure, by the birthday. By the fact that I'm going to be forty and I don't think I've come to terms with the 'is this all there is?' syndrome."

"Did the course help?"

"I don't know. It clarified a few things, made me feel a little more comfortable in my own skin. Some women there, top lawyers and executives, talked about feeling guilty about neglecting their kids and their husbands; others felt they'd been sold a bill of goods because success wasn't what it's all cracked up to be. Lonely at the top and all that bullshit."

"Luckily that doesn't affect either of us, right?" Naomi was more than half facetious.

"Wrong. Naomi, I get this image of myself in ten years as a fifty-year-old woman, no longer beautiful. Handsome, they will say, and they will mean it. I'll grant them that. And this handsome fifty-year-old woman with brown spots on her hands will be having an affair with her twenty-two-year-old male secretary who wants to sleep his way to the top.

"Can you believe this? Can you believe I am talking like this? I've got it made and I don't understand what's happened in the world. Betty Friedan was right all the way down the line. I believed everything she said, I got out of the kitchen and into the frying pan, and so except for my group therapy once a week I rarely get a chance to really talk to anyone. I wheel and I deal and I absolutely love it. But Naomi, I want it all."

Helene leaned forward conspiratorially. "I even want the baby part, there is still this ridiculous fantasy part of me that still thinks, well, maybe it isn't too late after all; maybe I could chuck it all and find the great substantial guy who's as smart as I am, who makes as much money as I do, and I would get a Swedish girl to come live in who would get up with the baby in the middle of the night . . ."

Helene took a long swallow of her wine. "Naomi, what am I talking about?"

"You're talking about having everything. And you can't. None of us can. Maybe those super-duper women having the big jobs and making the great dinners and giving the boys dolls and the girls trucks . . ."

"Don't make fun of that, we ran a whole issue on that."

"I know. I read the magazine. I'm as crazy as you are and only a few years younger than you. But for me it was all right when I was certain there were absolutely no real men out there. When I was convinced that he didn't exist, the loving animal, the secure, nonthreatened, funny, loving man. But the scary part is that there is a possibility that he really does exist after all. And what do you do with that kettle of fish? That's another can of worms, isn't it?" She looked seriously at Helene as though she had just composed the Articles of Confederation, and then they both burst into giggles at the ridiculousness of the mixed metaphor.

"How about another bottle?" Helene needed this. She did not want it to end.

"I couldn't, I want to jog in the park early in the morning, and tend to a bunch of . . . "

"Come on, un demi, that's a glass and a half."

"You didn't eat a thing, Helene."

"I did so. It wasn't as good as usual. Come on, it's on the expense account. The wine list here is the best, I'll get a really good bottle of Haut Brion. I'm sure they have it."

"That's almost a hundred dollars a bottle."

"Something like that."

"I'm going to throw up."

"You're not going to throw up. Don't be vulgar." She motioned for the waiter. Pointed to a number on the wine list. "Would you adopt a baby? Bea Andrews, head of the story department at Warner Brothers, quit her job and is adopting a three-year-old."

"No."

"Well, she didn't exactly quit, she's working three days a week and the rest from home. They made some kind of arrangement with her that was good for them and good for the social worker. You know what else the course at the New School said . . . God, you'd think they'd start calling it the Old School by now, it hasn't been new in ages."

"What?"

The waiter flourished a new bottle in front of Helene who went through the shenanigans of looking at the label, sniffing the cork, sipping and nodding her head. Naomi had to go to the bathroom.

"Now they're seeing the children of career women in psychiatrist's offices, and these kids are saying that they're mad at their mothers because they're away working. They don't get mad at their fathers, because society expects them to be away earning the bacon, shooting the wolves. You know? And the husbands, they feel they're being neglected too, since, in this same society that we've already referred to, he's been taught that women will continually nurture you, whether it be your secretary, your mother, or your wife."

"So?"

"So, it's all pretty fucked. You know? I mean career women, many of them really expect their children to grow up fast. Like after about two days, you know? They want the children to be more like themselves, resourceful, independent. And frankly, between you and me, what two-day-old is going to stand for that?"

"So true. So what's the answer? That we shouldn't have children at all?"

"I was going to ask you. Maybe we're better off with no men."

"What about all your men? You always have scads."

129

"Scads. No such word, look it up."

"Helene, what about Allen, the married one, and Billy, the one you met jogging in the park, and that dentist in Greenwich."

"Blowing in the wind. You see, I talk. It is necessary for those who really know and love me to see through my big talk. I talk."

The tone abruptly changed. Suddenly Helene was editor-in-chief again.

"Naomi, this incest and abuse story is very important to me. In my own life there's still a lot of unfinished business between me and my own father."

Naomi sat up, listening very carefully.

Helene twirled the stem of her glass as she spoke. "My father was this big sexy man who was wildly seductive with me, and he played me and my mother off against each other all the time. Shit, I don't think he knew what he was doing, or maybe he did. All I know is that he was very attentive to me physically until I hit puberty, and then whammo, curfews and questions and strictness and he would push me away when I would want to hug and kiss him. Poor guy didn't know what hit him once I grew tits and ass . . . "

"I know."

Helene became very animated. "Did I ever tell you that I have total recall?"

"Many times."

"Right, well do you know that I can remember when I was about two years old and my father was bouncing me on his foot and his toes were right at my vagina and I remember enjoying the feeling. And you know what else I remember?"

"What?"

"I have a vague sense that he knew that I was enjoying it and why, and that he kept on doing it exactly for that reason."

"A lot of women I interviewed said the same thing. Were you an only child?" Naomi leaned forward.

"And baby makes three. Three. That's what we were, a ménage à trois. I swear I was brought up to be the other woman."

Naomi lit a cigarette. The words repeated in her head. Brought up to be the other woman.

Suddenly Helene's voice was a whisper. Naomi could barely hear her as she watched her lips move. Naomi was caught up in her own thoughts.

This is your room Naomi, I know you hate to walk up three flights but it was indeed charming, this old attic of a room, and Neil put her bag down and gave her fresh towels. Neil's wife, the lady he was sleeping with when he was not sleeping with Naomi, was downstairs cooking dinner for them and feeding Neil and Laura's six-year-old little boy, and Naomi was of course in the guest room being the guest. You will love Laura, you will find her interesting, maybe you can do a story on her, her work is being exhibited in a few months at the National Gallery. I know you two will like each other a lot. He put a glass of chilled white wine on the night table next to the bed and Naomi wondered what she was doing here. How did she get there in her lover's house in Georgetown, with a little garden out back and three floors and narrow staircases. On the second floor, in the room directly below hers as a matter of fact, they slept together, Neil and Laura, when of course Neil wasn't sleeping with Naomi.

Laura turned out to be all right and yes Naomi did like her, and the little boy turned out to be charming and well behaved, and they all had dinner, and Naomi took a few pictures of Laura and her work, which was good; strong massive pieces that looked as though they had been welded by a large six-foot-two man. Laura was not quite five feet tall but she had big hands and long blond hair and the hint of a white blond mustache.

In the third floor attic guest room, Naomi was reading in bed. She sipped her wine, listening to the muffled voices in the room below, Neil going into the hall to go to the bathroom, Laura moving across the hall to see if the boy needed anything. And the outsider, interloper, intruder, third party, other woman, lay upstairs feeling a feeling that was vaguely familiar. She may as well be sleeping in the middle of their big bed with them, she may as well say move over Neil, shove over Laura, here I come, the other woman has arrived to make this complete, to come full circle to fulfill the familiarity of this.

Naomi left very early the next morning; pleading assignment, pleading work. Neil was a freethinker and couldn't understand why Naomi never returned his calls or came back to his house. But even thick-headed Naomi Lazurus Loeffler could figure out the symbolism of that Washington weekend, in a rare epiphany realizing that being the other woman was thankless, boring, and too gnawingly familiar to be comfortable.

Helene crossed her legs and kicked Naomi under the table.

"Well, you probably can't identify with that, but my daddy sure did a number on me, I'll tell you that." Helene poured cream in her coffee. "What do you say Naomi, one cognac before we go and we'll call it a night? Come on, it'll help you get to your deadline. Six weeks. I want to wrap the whole thing up in six weeks."

There was silence at the table. Naomi was deep in thought. Helene was not quite talked out yet.

"What do you think? Ten years. At fifty what will I be? An aging editor-in-chief with gray pubic hair and a lust for twenty-year-olds? Childless? Husbandless? Or at peace with myself, with a job well done, having wielded my power, made my mark. What do you think?"

25

Woodpeckers were playing the "Anvil Chorus" on the telephone pole outside her window and five thousand chickadees were chirping in great annoyance as their perch was being made more and more precarious by the moment. Naomi turned over and put the pillow over her head; it sounded closer and closer and she was sure the pole would topple over at any moment now.

"For Christ's sake open the door."

Woodpeckers don't talk.

She bolted up in bed. That voice coming through the door sounded very familiar.

Naomi threw on a robe, and peered into the little peephole eye high in the front door. Another eye, equally eye high, was staring back at her. That eye was basically blue, but it looked also like the red eye special.

Matthew.

Naomi unbolted the four locks, and the police lock. It took about four minutes. Her heart was beating very fast.

"What are you doing here? What a great treat!" She threw her arms around him.

He hugged her, stumbled into the kitchen. "I just saw the most beautiful sunrise. Now I need a cup of coffee, an aspirin, and a bed. Then we'll talk."

She quickly boiled some water. She was utterly delighted to see him. Unnerved, surprised. But delighted.

"What are you doing this morning?" Matthew mumbled.

"Well, I was going to jog and see if my parents are home yet, and my sis . . . "

"Forget it. Come to sleep with me. I couldn't sleep a minute on that red eye, and I've got to get an hour's sleep or die. I'm turning around and going back home tomorrow. Just felt like pressing the flesh."

"Woodpeckers . . . "

"What? Isn't that water boiled yet? Give me a kiss and let's lie down."

In ten minutes he was asleep. Naomi had to take off his cowboy boots and his socks. At least he had undone his own belt and unzipped his fly before he collapsed.

She lay back, curled like a sleeping snail deep in the middle of Matthew's arms.

26

"I can't hear you, talk louder, dear. This is a terrible connection."

The phone had jolted Naomi out of a deep sleep. It was Sunday morning, the next day. They had stayed in the apartment all weekend. Matthew would be leaving soon.

"Mother, what time is it?"

"I don't know there. Here it's noon. I've just made three attempts to get through to you. I screamed at the service. You should never leave word for them not to wake you, something terrible could always happen. There is always an emergency. What's happening?"

Naomi sat up in bed, pulling the cover over her breasts.

"Mother, what do you mean, what's happening? Mother, you just left four days ago. How is Bahama? Or is that plural. Bahamas?"

"Four days and we haven't heard one word from you. We have no news from home."

"Mother, what's the weather like?"

"Don't change the subject, your father is furious. You know how he can't bear not to know what's going on."

"Mother, what the hell could have happened in four days?" Naomi took a deep breath. "Are you getting any sun?"

"I'm putting your father on."

"Mother . . . "

Matthew sat up, rubbing the sleep out of his eyes. "This is like the George Jessel joke, that's got to be your mother. You've only mentioned her name ten times."

Naomi put her hand over the receiver. "Shush."

"Hi Dad. What's doing?"

Naomi held the phone away from her ear as her father's voice punctuated the air. "Not one word from you I've heard."

"There really hasn't been anything to write, Dad. Look, is there anything else you wanted to say?"

"Have you checked in on Rebecca? When we left she was not in such good shape."

"I talked to her a few days ago."

"She was low, real low," Sol said. Then, seductively, the tone abruptly changing. "So how's my baby girl?"

"Fine Dad, just fine. Did a fascinating interview the other day." She looked over at Matthew's back, freckled, dappled with scars.

"With who? I've just made up my mind about something, wanted to tell you. Your mother and I are going to be married forty years soon. You know . . . "

"I know Da . . . "

"And we really want to do a terrific thing for ourselves, for the whole family, so everybody will always know that Esther and Sol lasted all these years and are still madly in love. So what I want to do is . . . "

"Dad, you told me all about the party before you le . . . "

"Don't interrupt, Naomi, you are always talking when I'm talking. When will you ever learn to let your father talk?"

"Dad, I wasn't interrupting, I just said . . . "

"Let me finish."

"Finish."

Matthew was watching Naomi carefully.

"You take the joy out." Sol was yelling.

"Finish, Dad. For God's sake, you're paying for this call."

"What's that got to do with it? You sure you're all right? You sound oddball to me."

"Dad, please. What is it you want to say?"

"Don't rush me. I want you to start making up a guest list, any of your famous friends you want to invite is fine with me. We're going to do it at the Pierre."

Naomi held the phone away from her ear.

Minutes later when she put it back he was still talking.

"And we want your total cooperation in this. It is a family venture, a way to share with everyone that is near and dear that marriage can be beautiful, if you're as lucky as I have been in my life. Your mother is as beautiful today as she was the . . . "

"Day you married her. I know, Dad."

"Don't make fun, don't you dare make fun. Do I say a word about your life-style? Didn't I permit you to marry that Henry Loeffler? He didn't even know better than to put the butter knife with the butter still on it right smack into the jam jar."

"I thought you forgave him for that. You certainly do bear grud . . ."

"You certainly are the smart one across the miles. So I'm getting off. You should go over to your sister's apartment and make sure she's not eating. You should bang down the door if necessary, that girl's going to kill herself."

Naomi, very agitated, held the wire and kept twisting it around her finger.

Matthew gently pushed her finger away.

"Look Dad," Naomi said with a deep sigh, "I'm glad you called and I hope you're having a good time. I'll get in touch with Becky and see how she is, I promise."

"She's having trouble with the maid." Esther had apparently been on an extension phone. "I just hope there's someone with Janie all the time."

"I thought you'd gotten off the phone, Mother." Naomi heard the archness in her own voice.

Matthew lay back on the pillow; his hands folded behind his head, eyes staring at the ceiling.

"Okay you two, now don't start. Naomi, your mother is your best friend. She is the most unselfish person I know. Do you know that she isn't buying only things for herself on this trip? Do you know that she is always urging me to buy for you, even though it means she's not getting all she wanted?"

Naomi pushed the phone away from her ear again. From afar, she spoke into the phone.

"Dad, I've really got to go. I'm glad you called. Now that we've spoken I don't have to write, right?"

"Wrong. We're going to be away another ten days and I'm

expecting at least one letter. Come on, give your old father a break. All right, love?"

Exhausted, Naomi shut her eyes.

"Okay, Dad."

"What else is new?"

"Nothing."

"What about that disgusting business, the child porno thing you're working on?"

"It's coming. As a matter of fact, someone may want me to do a book on it, which is something I . . ."

"Don't forget to check on Rebecca. She must be up to two hundred by now, ready to enter the heavyweights, ready to take on old Ali himself."

"Dad . . . that's crue . . ."

"Such a gorgeous punim on that one and buns as big as a house."

Matthew was kissing her behind her ear.

"I've got to go, Dad."

"This is a crazy place to come to, warm, but not much night life. Didn't we take you here once?"

"Me and Becky years ago. Years and years. Barbara Hutton was there with a long gray braid down her back."

"Well, I don't remember that. I remember you had a plum bathing suit and some Italian guy you went out with told you you had legs as long as the Tower of Pisa."

"What a thing to remember, I don't remember that. What . . ."

"Naomi, don't forget to go over to Becky's and make sure she doesn't leave Janie alone." Another country was heard from again.

"Mother, you mentioned that. I thought you had gotten off the phone. How come I never know if I'm speaking to one of you or a group of you."

"Your father hasn't been feeling well, you know."

"Dad, what's the matter?"

"Oh, nothing, just old age. We're getting to be two old cockers, ready for the porch. That's all I want to do, take off my shoes and sit on the porch. Well, nice talking to you, old girl. Take care of your sister and write us all the news."

"Okay, Dad. Be well, and thanks, thanks for calling."

"Okay. Esther, talk but a minute, this costs a fortune."

"Look Naomi, I don't want to bother you with my things, you've got enough in your mind, problems of your own; I know that."

"Mother . . ."

"It's just that sometimes I get so lonesome. I adore your father, but I'm the only one around and I get the brunt of whatever pain he's in." She was struggling for the words. "And, I don't know, there just isn't anyone for me, just for me to talk to. You're always so busy and Becky's always in some sort of trouble. There's never anybody just for me."

"Mom. I . . ."

"I just don't feel that you love me. Tell me. I can take it. I can live with it, if it's true."

Naomi shut her eyes.

"I love you, Mom."

Naomi hung up the phone. She turned over and lay her head on Matthew's chest.

"I got to go, girl," he said into her hair. "Got to be on my way."

He started humming, "free at last," as he gently removed himself from under her, and struggled up out of the bed.

She put her feet on his back. They were imploring him, in their own way, to stay.

"Just like a man, into one-night stands." A joke, but there was an edge to her voice.

27

Becky had bulimia. That was the word for it. Naomi looked it up. Continual hunger. And Naomi could go days without eating. For Becky, as long as there were laxatives to help make room for one more, a corner could always be found for more cheesecake, more pizza, more pasta. Like Oliver Twist she insisted on "more." Several years ago Naomi had seen *Le Grand Bouffe*, a movie about a group of Frenchmen who decided to eat themselves to death. Her sister's face had superimposed itself over every character; Becky's fullness replacing the startling image, for example, of a Rubensesque maid whose bare buttocks formed a swollen valentine, sitting right there in the middle of a mountainous wheel of cheese.

Naomi was convinced that the obsession with more that controlled her sister touched her as well. She wasn't quite sure how, but she knew somewhere that there would never be enough. No matter what. Enough chocolate, enough cashmere, enough cars, enough wine, enough sex. Enough something. Becky drowned in food. Naomi gorged on work.

"They gave us everything, but they gave us nothing," Becky said to Naomi as she lay on her back in front of the fire in her apartment. She was throwing unsalted cashews high into the air and catching them in her mouth.

"They can't be slimming if you eat a million of them."

"They're unsalted."

Becky kept missing and lay in a bed of curled cashews cascading around her. There were about a dozen little empty boxes of raisins on the floor and one small wedge of banana bread on a plate. There were three apple cores and the skin from some Jarlsberg cheese on another plate. One small sliver of Greenberg's super chocolate cake sat in lonely splendor on a white Wedgewood dish. Becky kept picking at it.

"Want something to eat?"

It was the last thing Naomi wanted to do.

"Becky, what about Pritikin?"

"What about him? I can't afford it; who am I going to leave Janie with if I go to California? Mother certainly can't handle her, and I certainly don't like the idea of all that fiber making its way into my system. So I got rid of that idea."

"Beck, you've got to lose some weight."

"Look, shut up, will you. Just shut up. If you're going to get at me like they do just don't come over. You know? I'm all right. I'm not sleeping with anyone at the moment, so it doesn't matter, no one sees me but me and I don't bother me in the least. I'll end up having less wrinkles than you any time. Do you know that people with full faces rarely get wrinkled, while people of your persuasion usually shrivel up like a prune?"

"Charming."

"Naomi, I know you mean well. I give you that. But I'm all right. I'm just a little scared about a few things now. You know. I can't go looking for a job because I don't have any clothes and I don't have any clothes because I can't bear the thought of a three-way mirror in a store or some snoopy saleslady just standing there in back of the curtain hissing, 'How does it fit dear?' So I can't get a job. You see. And I can't just go be a typist or something, it's beneath me. I can't do that with all my education and I can't go back to school to finish that degree because I'm not interested in school guidance anymore. Small potatoes; I want to make a killing, I want to score on the stock market, or invest in land in Paraguay."

"Paraguay?"

"Some country like that. I was reading about where they're welcoming foreign investments."

"You don't have anything to invest with."

"That's exactly my point. I mean they bought us toys and

clothes, but they never gave us a trust fund, never gave us a future."

"Get a job. This is too boring for words. Make your own future."

"I don't have a talent like you. I am not aggressive or competitive. I'm not the great feminist you are."

"What the hell does feminism have to do with it? I want to succeed."

"So you identified with him and I identified with her. It's really all very simple."

"Freudian bullshit. You'd think that with all the courses you take at the New School something other than Freudian bullshit would sink in."

"I'm telling you they gave us everything, and they gave us nothing."

"Becky, I'm a busy person. Places to go, people to meet, things to do. I did not come over here to hear you blame them for everything that ever went wrong in your life."

Naomi got up abruptly.

"I came here to see Janie too, Becky. You said she would be home."

"I forgot. So I forgot. You're beginning to sound like Mom. No self-righteousness today," Becky continued. "Please, sister dear. I don't have a talent, I'm not trained for anything like you are. I've had a lot of bad breaks. Everything's gone wrong in my life. Harvey ran out on me with a girl who weighs two pounds, who happened to be my best friend in the world. I came within three credits of my masters and got sick . . . "

"Go back to school. Finish. Look, I can't hear more of this. I'm getting a pain in my stomach."

"You want a tranquilizer?"

Naomi wanted to cry. That person used to be a tow-headed little girl with tight curls ringing her head that got sweetly damp when she perspired. She used to be a little girl Naomi would take care of: pour tea for into miniature cups at tea parties, place furniture for in the antique doll house. She used to be a person to giggle with and protect when Daddy got angry. When he would scream and yell and Becky would run and lock herself in the closet, Naomi would stand her ground, but the trigger pain, that stomach slash, would rivet her to the spot.

When it was over Naomi would rush to the closet and cajole her little sister out of there, coo to her, plead with her that the hurricane had passed and that the peaceful daddy, the good daddy would return with Tootsie Rolls in his pockets and games on his lap. Don't worry little sister, I will take care of you. I will protect you from the Park Avenue monster, the urban dragon whose breath of fire will kill us all, just like the old Halloween debbil if you don't watch out.

"Tranquilizer. Do you want to make your stomach tranquil?" Becky repeated.

"You take too many tranquilizers," Naomi said.

"And you don't." Becky looked hard at her sister.

"I try not to," Naomi answered quickly.

"Self-righteousness, thy name is you know who. Say what you will, that pill I take cures the Lazurus syndrome. We've all got it, the Lazurus belly, at the first sign of confrontation the bell goes off and the Lazurus syndrome strikes back."

"I've got to go."

"Don't. I had the most revolting day yesterday. That's why I stayed in all day today."

Naomi looked up. She did worry about her sister. They used to be so close.

"What happened?"

"Well, I think I'm becoming a shopping bag lady sans shopping bag. You know what I mean? I mean, it's kind of as though things are unraveling a little bit.

"I just find myself giving up before I even start. You know? I can't seem to do anything right. I mean yesterday, for example, I broke the third pocketbook this week. The zipper, I broke three pocketbook zippers in one week, and even Janie said why don't you get a checkbook with a cover on it for your checks, like her friend's mother. I mean she was rummaging around for some change in my pocketbook and I was really embarrassed. I yelled at her because I was ashamed. The inside of my pocketbook looks like one of the shopping bag ladies' bags only theirs is probably neater. There are old tampaxes that have parted company with their containers and old eyebrow pencils whose tops have come off and old Master Charge receipts and unopened bills and papers, important papers . . ."

"And . . ."

"I'm getting to it. So when the zipper broke I went into a Kitty Kelly or Susie Simpson, one of those cheap shoe stores, and figured I'd throw out the broken bag and get a new one. So I opened my wallet vaguely remembering that one of my charge-card people had written me they were closing me out until I paid. I couldn't remember which one. I didn't have any money for bills this month so I didn't pay it. And then I remembered it after the lady had written me up, gotten my signature, looked me up in the little yellow book with the tiny numbers all listed in a row, called the home office or wherever it is they have that great tablet in the sky that says you can't use the magic card anymore. By this time I had transferred all my stuff into the new bag; the wallet and the torn tampaxes and the eyebrow pencils without tops and the checks floating around and the unopened bills and I was just about to zip up and be on my way when she said, 'No way.' So Naomi, I leaned against the Kitty Kelly counter and I started crying, like a blithering baby. What difference does it make if my father can buy the store? They know from nothing. It was like being fourteen in Miss Kraft's geometry class when I couldn't do it and couldn't understand it and I would just sit there and feel stupid.

"Which is what I did in Kitty Kelly. Felt stupid. Gave them another credit card and walked out."

"And . . ."

"And nothing, that's the story."

Becky retrenched a bit. She couldn't bear the pity in her sister's eyes. She tossed her head. Forced a laugh.

"I don't know why I told that dumb story. I'll be fine tomorrow. And I'll call your friend, the stockbroker, I will, I keep putting it off. But tomorrow's the day. Early. I'm trying not to sleep so late anymore."

A deep breath.

"So what's with you? I have been going on and on about myself. How long are you staying?"

"Just a few days."

"How's the child abuse thing going?"

"Good. Just fine."

"Must be awful, when you can't even trust your own parents. How can anyone hurt a child, I can't imagine it. Remember how Dad used to play with us, roughhouse on the bed, and hold us so tight that sometimes I would turn blue until he'd let go. I hated that. You know. I used to feel I could never get out. He was a big strong man and I was so little and I would always be squiggling away. He does that to Janie sometimes and it gets me very nervous. But that's hardly abusive, is it? He just adores us all to distraction. Maybe not a million dollars worth, but he does adore us."

Abusive, what's abusive? the words sang in Naomi's head. "*A* you're adorable, *B* you're so beautiful."

Becky began arranging the silk flowers resting on the coffee table.

"You sure you don't want some tea and crumpets or something?"

"I can't. I don't even know what a crumpet looks like." Naomi didn't know what to say. "When's Janie coming back?"

"She's sleeping at her father's."

"So why don't you get a friend and go to a movie or something."

Becky kept taking the red silk flower out of the vase and moving it next to the gray one. The peach one.

"Not important. I think the folks are coming home tomorrow."

"So soon?"

"They've been away ten days. Mom says she wants to rearrange my living room. It really isn't right, you know, it never has been."

"I've got to go."

Naomi leaned over and kissed her sister's cheek. It felt almost too soft, yielding. She smelled of baby powder. Naomi felt the exaggerated roundness of her arms. Popeye the Sailor Man, pillowed arms full of down.

Little sister. The little sister.

28

The apartment was very empty.

There was a long obscene message from Matthew on her machine, wishing her well and wishing every part of her body well, which he would appreciate if she would please bring back to California in a day or two. There was also a message from Maria, who was subleasing, saying that she would be back in town in two days and would Naomi be out of the apartment.

Naomi ran a hot bath and almost dozed off in it before she pulled herself out and into her bed. She fell asleep to David Susskind interviewing four transsexuals whose names Naomi jotted down on the pad on the night table, for a future story.

The television was still on when the phone jangled her out of a heavy sleep. The light from the set and its great hum jarred her awake at the same time as the phone rang insistently.

"Naomi, wake up."

"Who is this?"

"Mother. Something's happened to your father."

Naomi bolted up. She was wide awake.

"Where are you?"

"Emergency Room, Mount Sinai. Thank God you're in town."

"What entrance?"

"I don't know. I don't know what street I'm on. We were getting off the plane, Naomi. We decided to come home a few days early, and we were getting off the plane, just stepping off onto the steps, you know, and he toppled over. He almost fell down all those steps, but the man in back of us caught him."

"Mother . . . "

"They had to get a wheelchair and we had to rush him to the hospital. Luckily, Joseph was there with the car."

"Mother, what exactly is the matter with him?"

"I don't know Naomi, they don't know yet. Come down, up, I don't know what street I'm on. I called Becky."

Then she clicked off. There was silence in the phone. Naomi dressed quickly, there was no time for thought, no musing. In a few minutes she was out of the apartment, had hailed a cab and was on her way to the hospital.

It was two in the morning, the driver told Naomi after she had asked him. He was a jovial black man who wanted to talk. It was lonely on those streets at this time of the morning and he wanted to talk. It did not matter that she didn't respond. He told her that in four years he was going to retire and go back to North Carolina and raise rabbits on a farm he bought. At fifty-eight he was a great-grandfather. He married at seventeen and he handed the pictures of the great-grandchildren back so Naomi could see them. The faces were blurred, but they were smiling and their eyes bright. Married forty-one years and he still adores his wife. She has a glandular condition and weighs 550 pounds. It doesn't matter. Lady, he says, if that woman died tomorrow I would die the next day. That's the way it is. He got out of the cab and opened the door for her in front of the hospital at two in the morning. She gave him a dollar tip, and touched his arm. Five hundred and fifty pounds.

The rest of the night was a dream, and as if she were in a trance Naomi moved through it. They wouldn't let the two of them into the emergency room at the same time so she went in when her mother walked out. It could be a heart attack, or an embolism, they told her. They couldn't tell yet. Sol was ashen. He had the gray pallor that Naomi had seen in hospitals in Vietnam, in VA hospitals. A fearsome color that gray. He was lying down and suddenly the lines had been totally erased from his face, smoothed out, ironed.

Naomi kissed Sol. He felt damp, his eyes looked like a frightened cow. He always did have cow eyes, deep and brown. Very round. She had his eyes. Naomi had her father's eyes. She held his hand, in between the round knobs of the cardiogram hooked up to different surfaces of his body. Suddenly the round eyes became rounder, the pain slashed at him. Sol began to throw up. The doctors and nurses shooed Naomi out of there.

The important thing it seemed at that moment was to make her mother all right. Naomi took it upon herself. She and Esther went to the office and had Sol officially admitted to the hospital. Esther, organized as ever, had the appropriate cards and insurance information the officious young man in the little cubicle wanted. Naomi took Esther's arm and helped her into the elevator where they went into intensive care on the fifth floor.

Hospitals were fearsome. Especially intensive care. Here there was moaning, a lot of moaning and a lot of old people, thin and frail. A lot of gray faces in those rooms, as Naomi and Esther walked down the corridor to Sol's room. One old woman kept crying out, "Mommy, Mommy, Mommy."

Father. Dad. Daddy. Lying there, tubes in his nose, in his penis, in his arm. Low on potassium, the nurse said. Poor Sol. Just his luck, he who loved the lushness of the female form, especially one encased in the enticing starchiness of a white nurse's uniform, Sol pulled a gay male nurse. A nice, efficient, slow-humored faegele from Jackson, Mississippi, for Sol.

Sol was cold. He was so cold. He wanted another blanket. His moans were hollow. He didn't want to scream. He looked through the two of them. Where's Becky?

The cardiologist arrived. He pushed Naomi and Esther out so he could examine Sol. Through the open curtain Naomi could see her father's flanks. My father is old, she thought. The doctor seemed to have left his bedside manner at home. But he also seemed to care. He would take no nonsense from Sol and wanted to know exactly what happened.

The roles were reversed. How many times through appendicitis and tonsils, stitches in the knees, stitches in the head, had Daddy been there comforting, standing by the bed? It was her turn to stand by the bed. "Remember," Sol whispered, "the last time I was sick, the time they thought I had stones and Becky came every day to the hospital? Every day she came. And Naomi came," he added, "and wrote *I love you Daddy* on the little blackboard. I saved it and took it home."

He didn't die. An embolism. Probably lodged in the bowel, that's what caused the pain. He was dizzy when he was walking down the steps out of the plane. He was spinning. There was nausea and pain. Something had snapped out of the heart. My father. You are my enemy. My friend. My love. Don't die. I couldn't bear it.

Time, what happened to time? When her tenant returned, Naomi moved into her parents' apartment.

"I don't know how long I'm going to have to stay," Naomi whispered into the phone in the living room as her mother moved slowly about in the next room.

"Are you sure you have to stay?"

"What kind of remark is that?" Naomi bristled. She wished he were here. She wished Matthew Johnson were here next to her. But she would be damned if she would tell him how much she missed him. Instead, she got angry.

"I'll stay as long as I'm needed, and don't you dare make me feel guilty."

"Nobody can make anybody feel guilty, kiddo. I don't have that kind of power. Naomi, I'm real sorry your dad is so sick. It's just that I really miss you."

"He's not out of danger, Matthew."

"I know, love. You come back when you can. You hear? I just have a perverse way of showing that I'm missing you a whole lot."

"Me too," was all she could manage.

During the following days Naomi lived in the world of the hospital and making sure her mother was all right. Becky was somnambulistic during this whole period and was eating more and more under the tension. She admitted to Naomi that late last night she ate an old chocolate bar she had found at the bottom of some drawer somewhere, had found worms in it and kept on eating it anyway. But Naomi could not think about that, she had to deal with her father. And her mother.

149

29

Something had happened. On the fifth day the pain went away. The stomach didn't bother Sol anymore. He was not throwing up but was disoriented. Sol had had a stroke. They finally said the word. He looked at Naomi like a poor lost child. Sol Lazurus. His eyes were not brown anymore. They were no color, gray, shining, oddly empty. There was no past, no future, only an inkling of the present. He smiled like a little boy; "Kiki girl," he murmured to Naomi as though she were two and he were three.

The neurologist finally came. He was a slim man with huge eyes and a humpback. He was very firm. He yelled at her father, insisting he listen to him. Draw a circle, draw a triangle, write your name, what is this? Her father, through his haze, through the clouds in his brain, would not be intimidated by this man. He drew a shaky circle, an impossible triangle. He wrote his name five times until he got some semblance of an identity.

Pick up your arm, now the other. Your left leg, your right one. Where am I touching you? Her father slurred out the answers; some he could do, others would not come. The words would not come. Naomi and her mother sat there, Naomi's arm around Esther's shoulder.

When Sol picked up his right foot his penis showed. Once Naomi had seen it when she was a little girl. He was sitting on the bed changing his shorts and it had frightened her. She had never seen a penis before, not her cousin's, not anybody's.

And now. That man doing a four-year-old's exercise, lifting his foot for the doctor, his penis showing under the short blue and white hospital gown, somehow, some way, was eking out some dignity from this preposterous situation. There was a dignity in the way he wanted to please, to pass the test. So badly. There was suddenly a sweetness to him, a softness.

After the doctor left, Sol kissed Naomi's hand over and over. And he kept asking what time it was, over and over and over; and he would ask Esther how she was. How are you, Mom? Are you all right, Essie?

Oh, it was humiliating and he was very sick and the neurologist said he would have to have a blood thinner, and would have to stay for ten days and there was always a possibility he could get it again. Naomi's father had had a stroke.

And two days later he was almost normal. As though a spring rain had washed the cobwebs from his brain, like some magical thing had happened overnight, Sol became lucid and cantankerous and joking and opinionated. Sol came back. Overnight, a reprieve. They told him he could go home this weekend. Esther almost fainted with relief.

Naomi watched him in his bed, back, to some degree, to the old Sol, and ruefully admitted to herself that she had liked him better when he was the two-year-old. So loving, so innocent, so giving. He had kissed her hand. He was as he may have been to her when she was a small child. If she could only remember. It had seemed somehow that there had been a time when he was all hers.

Two days later Sol went home. There was much fuss and fanfare in the hospital. He was a different man from ten days ago. But alive. He didn't walk well, and his eyes disappeared periodically into a vacant stare. They rolled and they stared. He was not easy to get out of the hospital because he didn't like being in a wheelchair and he didn't like being an invalid. He had great pains in his stomach again. And after they had finally got him out of the hospital and into the car and out of the car and into the elevator and out of the elevator and into his bedroom, he threw up.

Naomi slept in her old room in which she grew up, the room where the walls were filled with photographs of her sleep-away camp bunk and the whole camp, graduation pictures from high school and college, diplomas, prizes, awards.

Her magazine story, Matthew, all paled. Becky, for whom this whole business had proved too much, who, when it was established that Sol was out of danger, took off with Janie without further ado to the Virgin Islands. Naomi couldn't think about that either. It was important that Sol get well, that they all get back to the madness of "family," the bickering and fighting, the ambivalence, the love, and the deadly feeling that she might have to continue to put oceans of miles and emotions between them if she were to survive.

She slept fitfully Sol's first night home, in her old room, and dreamed. She dreamed Sol kept falling down. He couldn't walk a few steps without falling to the ground. In the dream, Sol had only half a head. There was only half of it there. And it was like an apple. She felt it, and it was smooth, and cold. Exactly like the top of an apple. Naomi's own cries woke her.

Throwing on a robe, she walked into the massive living room. Outside it was snowing, the streets wet with the giant flakes. It looked as though it might stick, she thought as she pulled the curtain aside. It was February and they had finally taken away the Christmas trees on the islands in between uptown and downtown on Park Avenue.

Naomi curled up in her father's chair and looked at the grandfather clock against the wall. Three o'clock. It was midnight in Los Angeles. She dialed Matthew's number, still curled in the massive chair, her feet underneath her. He wasn't home. She hadn't talked to him in several days, being so immersed in the drama here. Where was he? She didn't like it that he wasn't home. She didn't like it at all. She wanted him to be where she wanted him to be. She would go soon, now it was Esther's turn to take over. They would be all right. She had taken ten days. Ten days had gone by. Naomi stared out the window as the snow became heavier.

All this Sturm und Drang about Sol, she thought. I mourn the loss of his vitality, the emergence of this old man. There are folds under his neck, the cock of the walk has become a cock without a coxcomb. I see him opposite me in the kitchen. Sunday morning, making breakfast for my mother. I do not exist when it comes to her. He has laid out the tray the night before.

The cup and the saucer, the pot rinsed with hot water to be filled with steaming coffee in the morning. A dish for the cottage cheese. A dish for the toast. The good dishes. Esther likes that. A place for the jar of jam. On Sunday morning we chat, I in my nightdress and he in his cap, and I feel old and ugly because he is taking breakfast for the ten thousandth time this Sunday morning to his bride.

More Sundays? Will there be more Sundays for Sol? He will probably fool us all and walk and talk and make breakfast for Esther a thousand more times.

On Sunday mornings, the Queen would accept her breakfast graciously, turn her cool smooth cold-creamed cheek to be kissed, and sometimes I would sit on the bed between the book and travel sections of the *Times* and he would be wearing the silk bathrobe, sometimes embellished by an ascot; not quite playboy not quite cowboy, an attempt at the debonair.

He used to be so formidable, he used to have black hair, such curly black hair on his chest and arms, how it frightened me, attracted me, intimidated me, that hair, on his chest, on the arms. He used to tower, he used to bellow, he used to lose his temper for days and never find it again, he used to listen in on my phone calls, he used to open my mail, he used to love me, how he used to love me, he used to call me his little princess his favorite girl, his baby girl, he used to say I had the best legs in town, he used to say I was beautiful, he used to say I was too thin, he used to come back from a trip and show me pictures of half-naked girls with his arms around them, he used to drop names, he used to tell me stories about Winken, Blinken, and Nod, he used to be my daddy, he used to be so proud of me when I was a little girl, but then I grew up and he used to not know what to do with that. Oh my God, how I loved him when he was my daddy.

30

Something was making her crazy.

Naomi called Matthew every half hour. She let the obsession creep inside, get a foothold, and take over. She had no warning, the power of it swept her away. She had gone back into her room, tried to read, took a shower. She listened to an all-night program featuring a forensic pathologist who talked about the cast of characters in the Kennedy assassination, and through intermittent dozings she heard the names Oswald, Ruby, Dallas.

In between fitful wakings, now every five minutes, she called his number. It was 4:00, 5:00, 6:00 A.M. in New York, now 3:00 in Hollywood on top of Matthew's hill. Was the elevator stuck between boulders, was he making love to some lady less neurotic than she on the floor of the elevator with the black iron-grate door between them and the stars?

She conjured the most lascivious poses, his mouth on the elevator woman's breasts, bountiful, full, nipples spread the length of them, his face deep down between her legs kissing the softness there. The pain was so sweet, so sharp Naomi could not bear it. She was sure she could not exist until the next moment, she could not get through the minutes. She lay on the bed, looking at the ceiling, dialed the phone. The tyranny of that damn phone. She railed at herself for letting the obsession slither into her stomach like a tapeworm eating away at the resources that kept her sane. She put her hands over her face, ran her fingers through her hair. I will not be betrayed, she thought, "I will not be betrayed," she said softly and then shouted. "Just keep away," she said to all those ladies out there, "keep out, for better or worse he is mine, keep off." He is off-limits. Keep out. Private property.

It was 7:00 A.M. Los Angeles time and that meant he had stayed out all night. Did she make breakfast for him in the morning, the lady in the elevator? Did he pat her behind as she got up to go to the bathroom, is that the way it was? Did she squeeze fresh orange juice for him, and give him a monogrammed towel for his shower?

Naomi railed at herself. She berated the woman in the mirror who was weak and had so little self-esteem and so little confidence all of a sudden. Where was the Naomi Lazurus Loeffler of old? Miss Wonderful?

Finally he answered. Naomi had not slept all night.

"When you comin' back Red Ryder?" he said sleepily, as casually as though he had been tucked in his bed all night. As casually as though he had no idea that she was sick with jealousy about this man to whom she was not committed, against whom she was protecting herself all over the place from getting involved. His life was his life. Everybody knows fidelity is as out of date as spats and bustles.

"Probably about a day more. I think it's all right for me to leave. So how you doing?" Casual, real casual.

"Great, babe. It's a little early to be calling, isn't it? I'm not really up to my usual brilliant palaver. How's your pop?"

"Better. Coming along. How's everything?" She will be suave, she will be cool. She will not let on. "Where were you last night?"

"Last night. What was last night? Oh, down the lane. I worked late then had a few beers with the group that rents the Theda Bara house down the lane a bit."

He sounded so innocent, there were no traces of perfume coming through the phone; Naomi listened very carefully and could not detect the stifled sounds of Lady Lorelei zooming down under the covers at the sound of the phone. She would have to take his word for it. Let it suffice, whatever lie he was telling, whatever cool exterior he was attempting. She would have to let it lie.

"I called at different times and you weren't there."

Silence. Now both feet swathed in silken spike heels were firmly entrenched in her mouth.

"I know I wasn't. Naomi. You sound strange, babe. I know you've been having a rough time there. Look, I'll meet you at the plane. When you comin' home?"

Naomi was near tears. The tension of the past days was getting to her and she was losing control. The one thing she hated to do.

"Matthew . . . I'll call you when I make the reservation. Tomorrow most probably, but don't bother, my car's at the airport, and I only live a minute from there. I'll call. It's good to hear your voice."

She hung up, leaving a very confused Matthew Johnson holding his phone.

Los Angeles

31

The air was almost soft as Naomi stepped into her car at LAX. She was grateful for the air; even though it was not hot, the chill was gone. The rawness of New York winter juxtaposed with the rawness of her feelings had been just about all she could handle. It was hard to leave. Her mother had been grateful for Naomi's help in her way. But Naomi was relieved to be in California. She was relieved to see the mountains and yearned to see the ocean, bleak as it was in winter, dark and mysterious beyond the empty beach.

Driving back to the apartment a sign assaulted Naomi from the top of a building. "Our resident psychiatrist wears an apron in the Ding-Dong bar." She had forgotten the epigrammatic messages sprinkled across the freeways and billboards of L.A. "We push our tush for you," the sign said on Lincoln Boulevard, advertising something called, serenely, The Holistic Car Wash.

Naomi was anxious as she drove into the driveway of her apartment. Matthew was on her mind. And the very same Matthew was sitting in her living room reading when she walked in.

She hugged him. They didn't kiss. Only held each other. Matthew took her bag out of her hand, unbuttoned her coat, unbuttoned her blouse and took her hand, leading her into the bedroom. He removed her boots, her slacks. She lay there in her underwear, suddenly shy. As though it were a first time. Matthew stood over her as he undressed, looking down at her.

There were no words. Only his greeting, "Missed you, kiddo," as he lay down beside her.

Later, they sat on cushions on the floor, drinking white wine and nibbling croissants Naomi had found in the freezer. If she breathed it would go away, this feeling, if she whispered his name it would disappear. All the pain of the last ten days melted away. Why was it so hard to savor such happiness, such pleasure? Matthew had no trouble at all, since each moment for him was the moment in which he was involved. Naomi attributed her inability to sustain joy to her Jewish heart, her being afflicted with the Woody Allen disease of Anhedonia. Matthew scoffed and snorted at the middle-classness of it all. It had nothing to do with reality. The poor and the working class do not have the luxury of Anhedonia. Happiness is the pursuit of it. Everybody knows that.

"Did you feel the earth move?"

He buttered the warm croissant, watching the yellow melt into the velvet insides.

"What chutzpah! What ego! It was terrific but I wouldn't quite say that the earth . . ."

"You've just been through an earthquake and didn't even know it."

"What are you talking about?"

"Turn on the radio, you'll see. I would call it a five point on the Peter Meter myself. I watched the flowers in the vase on the table shake over your shoulder during the throes of your passion."

"Matthew . . ."

"It's true. You were too carried away to notice. Look at the canal, the water is still sloshing around." He struggled up out of bed. "I'm glad you're back, Naomi. I'm really glad your dad's going to be all right. Hey, give us a kiss, I have to go."

"Go, go where?" To whom, she meant.

"To work. I've got to go back to work, but let's spend the weekend together."

"I just got back, for God's sake." She was furious.

"So you did. But you know how you are when you're in the middle of a project. Well, I'm into my new book finally. And there is a feeling of fear. I always feel this, even after all this time, all these books. I always feel that someone is going to come along with an official order and make me stop it any day now. 'Back to the oil fields and ships and railroads with you boy, you've gotten away with this shit long enough.' I've missed you but it's something I must follow through now that I finally started to work."

"I thought . . ."

"Can't. This weekend we'll do something wonderful. Drive to Santa Barbara maybe and ride motorcycles into the hills. What do you say? I'd love to feel your arms around my waist, bumping along."

"I just got home."

"I explained I want to work. My love, don't be a pain in the ass like some of your fellow sisters have a tendency to be."

"And just what does that mean, after we have just made love, after I just returned from being away?"

"You know exactly what that means. It means women are so busy being quote free and independent unquote that they forget what a relationship is all about and what it means to care about someone and be with them, really be with them."

"May I be so bold, so gauche as to remind you that you happen to be the one who's leaving?" Naomi refused to be overwhelmed by this onslaught.

"You're a Jewish princess. It's okay, I accept it. I don't like it too much, but it comes with the territory. But it sure is a funny combination, your princesshood and your insistence on being so free; somewhere along the line you lost sight of what it is you want in the first place."

"If you ask me, this sounds like mucho macho meanderings." Naomi took a sip of her wine.

"Nobody asked you. And I happen not to be some kind of macho schmuck. And anyone who thinks so is full of shit."

"Is that so?"

"That's so. Look, Miss Lazurus Loeffler. I like your brain. You're smart. And there is a softness under the veneer, under that running-around, crazy, driving wind of you. I accept that. I like that. That craziness, it's okay. But then my love, so do *you* have to accept that my work is tantamount to breathing to me. And at the moment that's what I have to do."

"Me too. Just remember that." Naomi shouted to get a word in edgewise.

"I've been with many many women and have married three, sired two kids who miraculously turned out not bad."

"So what. I thought you married twice."

"There was one brief one at sixteen that has eluded the biographers." He tossed that one off.

"I think you are one poor risk as a mate person if you ask me," Naomi shouted.

"Wrong. All my life I have longed to love and be loved by someone who can enjoy me and what I do and whom I enjoy. I now feel it possible with you. I am sure you can move importantly into my life without diminishing yourself. My last liaison couldn't and she was very hard to let go of. The sex was good. Very good."

Matthew noticed Naomi wince.

"Quiet, girl. Has nothing to do with you. Long before you. There have been others before you. Just like there have been others before me. You must understand that I am forty-five years old and sex has been obsessive at times in my life, but I know now finally that even when it is beautiful and superlative it must be, of course, something else too. The trouble most people have with sex is that they can't understand the something else too. Lust hardly touches me anymore, outside of a loving relationship, even in fantasy. It has come to that."

He was delivering this soliloquy standing, one shoe off, one shoe on.

"Matthew, sit down, take a minute for God's sake. You are such a pontificator."

"No, this is important." He struggled with the sock and shoe while he stood. "My last lady was a sentimentalist not a romantic, a scientist not a historian, a doer rather than an experiencer, a pragmatist rather than a dreamer. There was no future in it.

"With you, pretty lady, there is always an awareness of the possible endless conversations among us all, you and me, and my closest friends. The people I cherish and want to share.

"I have to go. I will see you in a few days. I'll come to dinner in three days. Use the cookbook. I'd love fish."

He blew a kiss, and was gone.

Naomi threw a shoe at the door. It didn't matter what he said. She was sure he was off to see another woman.

32

Several days later, he wore his beige jacket. With the blue shirt. He knew that the blue shirt made his eyes shine, reflecting the sky. He had left her that morning at breakfast with a lingering kiss, his lips ballooning over hers. His hand had gone into her robe touching the flesh around her nipple. And just who was he going to see this morning in his beige jacket and blue shirt? The man did not engender trust in the heart of this untrusting soul.

Last night he had been an hour late for dinner. She had run to the window so many times wanting to see the beige of his car, beige seemed to be in this year, the year of the beige.

Where was he at that hour? She was sure he was swimming at his health club, playing footsie with some floosie in the Jacuzzi. Or perhaps lying back on a long lounge, book over his stomach soaking up the sun, enjoying the banter and secret eyes, the "lay me" look of some girl, some nubile creature whose breasts would swing and sway, whose belly and hips flowed smoothly out from the tiniest of suits.

The clock had clicked away and the beige man in the beige car did not arrive in the driveway. She had finished making the salad, prepared the fish for broiling. Everything was ready.

I would leave him, she thought, if I could stand the thought of his holding someone else. I would leave him, she thought, at the mere sight of those ladies' names in his blue formerly bachelor phone book resting by the telephone in his house in the sky, high on the hill. The little blue book has names like Melody and Holly, Suki and Bunny, Hollywood names, cutesie names, tight-ass-come-hither names, loose-limbed-ladies-of-lust names.

If those names in his childish scrawl didn't give her the locusts, the fluttering beasties in her stomach, she didn't know what would.

And then there he was at the door. Hello, as blithe as ever, as carefree as could be in his beige and blue. He looked tired and sweaty. Hard, hard day.

Bullshit. She had sniffed him when he arrived. Smart wily bird that she is, she had sniffed for Norell or Charlie settled into his throat. She sniffed for the skin scent of the girls. If it was there she'd find it, never fear.

Hello. I've made a big salad, prepared the fish. She bade the locusts adieu for the moment. And they fluttered out through her vagina, the beating of their wings hesitating around her belly button. He had arrived. She sniffed once more. No traces, so far.

It was new for her. This making someone happy. Men had wined and dined her, preludes to bed, so she had never had to buy presents for them or cook for them or put the candles on the table or wear something that would be soft and sensual to the touch for them.

But she did. Dinner was all muted light and Mozart on the stereo (which Matthew changed to Willie Nelson), and although it was simple, it was tasteful and good. She had two wines and champagne to start. Naturally, something in her fought it all the while, but for moments, long moments, Naomi felt comfortable and right. Making him happy. That's all it was. And it seemed so simple.

"Someone wants to make a film of *Trager*. Offered me a lot of money."

"Did you accept the offer?"

"No way, girl. I'm thinking of making the film myself. Had some drinks with a few guys just now who might be the key to the financing. I don't know. I decided to take the risk and just see what happens, try to do it on my own. Maybe even direct it."

"What do you know about directing?"

"Not one damn thing. But just as much as most of those assholes out there do. You get a good cameraman."

"And that's it?" she said, as sarcastically as she could. "You don't need any experience, any anything, is that right?"

"I know those people in that book better than anyone. I will just have to find a way to do it myself if I can. I want to prove that all the mystery of things that people lay on you is so much bullshit. The mystery of creativity, of science. If one can plan a military campaign involving thousands of men and machinery, one can work out the logistics for a film. I am fucking sick and tired of the mystification of things to satisfy and make exclusive things that are very simple indeed . . . If, of course, genius is available. And it can be fun. So, I'll work on that along with this new book."

Naomi could not get one word in. She had never known anyone she couldn't outtalk.

"Oh God, this new book," he went on. "The whole first chapter is not right. The tone is a bit off. But close, I'm close, kiddo. Feels as if it is about to break loose in a remarkable torrent. I want it to come out steaming, paced like a championship fight."

Naomi moved over to Matthew's chair and placed herself in his lap. "Be quiet for a minute. Just hold me. Let me hold you. You talk so much."

"I know. I love to talk. And I love the feel of you, lady." He smoothed the sheen of the satin shirt Naomi had worn for him. "What have you been up to, kiddo?"

"I went to court today."

He kept rubbing her back. Pulling up the blouse lightly fingering her ribs.

"And how was it?"

"Don't tickle me. Fascinating. Sad. So sad. Saw a couple of incest cases. You don't see much happen, the judge postpones or continues. I saw two kids who came to court from McClaren Hall."

"What's that?"

"It's the protective shelter for abused children. Hardly the best way to handle it, I suppose, but the authorities' hands are tied. They're compelled to take the kids out of the house. There aren't many good foster homes, so they have to put them in this shelter. But get this, the father is released on bail within hours of his arrest, and his kid, the one who he abused, is the one in custody. That system is a merry-go-round."

Her eyes filled with tears. "It's so sad, Matthew, so frustrating. I felt so bad for those little girls I saw. One of them had to spend over a month at McClaren. They just don't know what they get themselves into when they blow the whistle on their fathers. The world comes down around them. The Juvenile Court might take a girl away from her family and then she has to go right back into Criminal Court and stand up there in front of everybody, including her parents, and testify that her daddy is guilty of fucking her. Can you imagine a ten-year-old having to do that? And then the pressures. The mother threatens her, saying the kid's going to be the reason the family's going to go hungry because she's getting rid of the meal ticket. I was in tears the whole time I was in court. Matthew, those poor kids. I don't understand what's happening to me. I've seen much worse. Much much worse, and nothing's affected me like this before."

"Seems to me you've been crying a lot on this project."

"It's making me a little crazy I think. I keep thinking about Sol, and my mother. I can't stop myself from associating. I just feel that veils are falling over my face and being lifted all at the same time."

"That's some ridiculous metaphor."

"Sometimes I have the sense that I was brought up to be the other woman. Helene feels that way too."

"What does that profound statement mean?" Matthew was determined she shouldn't take herself so seriously. "Did you actually think the man was going to throw his wife whom he adored out of his bed and invite you in? I mean, how self-centered can you be, kiddo?"

"I don't know if he ever touched me," Naomi went on, ignoring him. "Maybe he did, maybe he didn't. It almost doesn't even matter."

"Naomi, do you really think something went on?"

"I know that the sexual tension between us still exists in a strange way. At least I'm a big grown-up mature person now and can handle it. But what about the little girl, that person who knew from nothing?"

"Who's that, someone I know? That grown-up person? Do you believe she exists?"

Naomi was about to rush in with platitudes, lies, the usual. For once she kept her mouth shut.

"Well?" Matthew looked straight at her.

"Sometimes. When I'm working, I'm an adult, for certain. But there are memories trapped inside me as though they've been at the bottom of the sea. Like an ancient treasure rotting. My past and my dreams, my childhood. I can't remember any of it. But every now and then I see shadows that are beginning to take shape."

Naomi put her arms around Matthew and kissed him. It was all getting very, very complicated.

"Grown-up," she said. "I'm not so sure there really is such a thing as a grown-up after all."

33

A frenzy had taken hold of Naomi. She canceled the weekend away with Matthew so she could work. She had gotten in touch with an incest victim through Sally Stewart. She would see her tomorrow. Eleanor. No last name. Naomi found herself feeling fragile, alternately irrevocably bound to Matthew, and then the next moment ready to take a plane for Zambia never to return. Sometimes it was too threatening, too much to contemplate, this being connected to someone. The fear of being abandoned by him choked her at times.

The material was increasingly upsetting to her. She worried that her objectivity was wearing away, and she felt strange questionings about her own identity more urgently.

When the woman who lived next door came by one morning to borrow some coffee and told Naomi she was distraught because her little boy's pet lizard had just been eaten up by their cat, Naomi was startled. The woman said she had come into the kitchen and seen the last remaining legs of the lizard slip surreptitiously into the cat's mouth and down the old hatch. After she left, Naomi had screamed at herself in the mirror. You don't know whether to identify with the cat or the lizard, that's why you're so weird inside. Miss Power or Miss Victim. Let's get it all straight. Which one are you?

Matthew was having a hard time with her. She didn't know what to do about that either. Because she found herself being removed, detached, and since they only saw each other rarely now that they were both working so hard, their brief time together was strained.

What had happened? She had had her whole life organized and suddenly it was all coming apart.

At which point, on an impulse, she called New York.

"Hi, Mom, how are you?"

Silence. That usually explained how she was. You have to know that there is never an affirmative answer to that question. Because invariably the silence will come and that of course explains exactly how she is.

"There's no point in talking about it."

So don't talk.

"But things are really not good around here. I do wish you would have the courtesy to call and see how your father is."

"That's what I'm doing. Calling." She put the phone on the pillow on the bed and the other pillow on top of the phone. Let her eat cake. Let her talk into percale.

Naomi picked up the phone again. She had a need to talk about him.

"Mom," she blurted out, "I've met someone. He's a writer, and I think . . ."

" . . . Actually your father's doing remarkably well." Esther was into her own thing. "He's feisty as ever and the doctor said he has made an astounding recovery. All he can think of and care about now is the anniversary party and it's not quite two and a half months away and he is very disappointed in you because you haven't helped at all."

Naomi spoke very slowly. "I believe I told you I was here on a job. I believe I mentioned that to you."

"Yes, you did. But did it ever occur to you that there are priorities in this world and this kind of affair comes around once in a lifetime and we are privileged to be . . ."

Down went the phone again into the down. Naomi pulled the comforter and the sheet over it this time. She took deep breaths and did a little yoga breathing.

" . . . We're not asking for much but I need a good few weeks with you to help me. Jasmine's geting too old to really help me with the planning and I want you to go over the list with me."

"What about Becky?"

Silence.

"So?" She had to get out of there.

"I don't want to talk about it." Her mother was the mysterious provocateur extraordinaire.

"Talk about what?"

"I promised your father I wasn't going to tell you, but I may as well. Rebecca was arrested for shoplifting. The girl has a lot of problems. Maybe your father just wasn't giving her enough money."

Jesus.

"So what's going to happen?"

"Luckily it was a store where Sol knows the chairman of the board and so Becky gave back the merchandise and the store was very nice and they said they wouldn't press charges."

Sol to the rescue. Becky's screaming, look at me, look at me, help me before I drown in my own flesh, and Sol buys the guy off.

"I'm over it now. I was sick. The shame for the family was too much. Now I don't want you to tell a soul. Not a person. We were lucky to have kept it out of the papers."

"Why didn't you tell me?"

"I told you. Your father wanted to settle the thing quietly and quickly. He didn't want any fuss from you. He's out now but you can call back later in an hour when he'll be home."

"I have to go out now. I had wanted to talk to you about a man I . . ."

"Your editor, that attractive tall girl, dear, invite her to the party. Also that movie star, the one you used to go out with."

"I don't see him anymore, since my interview on him came out."

"Invite him anyway. Sol would get such a kick out of it."

"Look Mother, I don't think this is the place to have . . ." Naomi gave up.

"Naomi, you are an independent woman. You fly all over the world, we ask very little of you. This is one night in three hundred sixty-five. Let's make it a happy occasion."

I think I feel the bubonic plague coming on.

"I've got to go, Mother. I'll call Dad later. You say he's feeling all right?"

"I swear, as though he'd never been sick. He's lost some

weight, and looks fit. Don't do anything to disturb him, dear. And thanks for calling, that was very thoughtful of you. How's your life going?"

"What's going to happen to Becky?"

Silence.

"Sol thinks a fat farm will cure everything. I'm inclined to agree with him. She'll probably go to one, maybe in California, pretty soon. You should call her too. You should . . ."

So long. It's been good to know you. Naomi hung up.

Naomi picked up the phone again. She dialed New York again. "Janie, I miss you."

"Me, too. Naomi, I've got two more stories to show you. I'm not showing them to Miss Frankfurt because she'll grade them and I don't want a grade. I want to be a great writer."

Naomi felt better, hearing her voice.

"How's your friend? Is he with you?"

"No, not now," Naomi said.

"When you coming home?"

Home. What's that?

"Pretty soon. There's more to do on this story. How's Mommy?"

"She's okay. Grandma's worried about her. Mom's mad at Grandma 'cause she won't ever babysit. Mom says that's what grandmas should do. Grandma says she can bring me over to their house and Jasmine could take care of me but Mom gets mad." Silence.

"Mmm. That sounds like old times. 'Plus ça change plus c'est la même chose.' "

"Change, that's the only word I recognize."

"I really miss you, sweetie. We're going to have one bangup brunch when I come back. Pancakes and waffles and ice cream and strawberries."

"Come back tomorrow."

"Can't. But soon. Real soon."

"You ever read *Harriet the Spy?*"

"No."

"After I'm a writer I'm going to be a spy. Take notes and sneak pictures through a little baby camera hidden in my necklace."

"Wow. Tootsie, I got to go. I love you."

171

"Me, too. Don't you want to talk to Mom?"

"Is she there?"

"No."

"She didn't leave you alone, did she?"

"Caroline is here."

"Caroline?"

"From next door. She's twelve."

She couldn't worry about that now in the middle of everything.

"Okay, Janie. I'll call soon." She kissed the phone. Got three kisses back. Hung up.

Something was happening to her attention span, Naomi noticed. Something was happening to her patience quotient. She felt as though, like some five o'clock whistle in some factory outside of Pittsburgh, Pennsylvania, she might blow, sky high, one of these days.

34

Naomi was dressing to the "Today Show." Jane Pauley was interviewing Jane Fonda and her father Henry. As she raced from the bedroom to the bathroom to the kitchen, Naomi heard bits and pieces of the interview. She stopped in front of the set, admiring Jane Fonda's clear, intelligent blue eyes. Formidable. She had met her once and had been amazed by how thin and vulnerable she seemed, even though her handshake almost crushed a few bones. Jane was asking Henry if he could have married and lived happily ever after with a woman like Jane. "You mean an activist," Henry said, looking squarely into the interviewer's face. "I think so."

Naomi wanted to hear what Jane said to that one and turned up the sound on the set. "I don't know about living happily," she said. "We could have had a good affair." Half-dressed Naomi sat down to hear the rest of it. Jane admitted that as a child she had been "terrified" by Henry's angry outbursts, confessing that the two still couldn't talk intimately. "A lot of how Dad feels about me I read in the press," she said.

Everybody's got troubles.

Naomi met Eleanor in the square at the Music Center. April had turned the weather warm and for that she was grateful. She had been in California longer than she had anticipated and the city was beginning to take hold, no matter how she fought it. When it was clear, as it was today, and the mountains seemed etched, carved from the sky with a brilliant clarity, there was an

173

unfamiliar peace. There was a serenity in the spaciousness, the curve of the hills. She had had to reeducate herself to look up. In New York she never looked up at the sky, never saw the sun set or rise.

Eleanor worked as a public relations person at one of the firms that publicized the shows in the Music Center complex downtown. She gave Naomi her lunch hour. They sat in front of an imposing Jacques Lipchitz sculpture, and because it was balmy, spring shone on the faces of the lunchtime people sitting and eating their sandwiches.

Eleanor was very nervous. When she saw Naomi's tape recorder she blanched.

"I don't have to use it," Naomi said. "The only reason I have it is as backup to my notes written in the worst handwriting in the world." She quickly put it away in her purse.

"It's just that I don't know you. And it's hard stuff to talk about. Real hard. Can we just walk around?"

"Of course. Of course."

"I don't know, I'd just feel a lot better, you know, until we really get to know each other. I'm in Sally's group and she said you were very nice and easy to talk to, which I'm sure you are, you know? But I don't know, there's just something awfully permanent about a tape recorder."

Naomi liked Eleanor. Under her tortoiseshell glasses were serious green eyes, straightforward. She was neatly dressed in a well-fitting pair of jeans and a trim shirt. Slightly built, Eleanor had beautiful auburn hair, whose red highlights glistened in the sun.

Naomi had to go very slowly.

They walked silently for a while.

"How about lunch?" Naomi stopped short, putting her hand on Eleanor's arm.

"I forgot all about lunch."

"Let's go up to the top of the Music Center. That restaurant with the beautiful view."

"It's so expensive." Still Eleanor sounded interested.

"Expense account."

Moments later the two had a table with a view of the mountains and the sky, houses dotting the hills. Eleanor was more at ease, and Naomi had ordered herself a glass of wine.

Eleanor had a club soda, and toyed with it, stirring the glass, staring deeply into it.

"Ask me some questions. I don't know where to start, you know?" Eleanor smiled. Her smile changed her whole face. In repose the tension tightened the features. When she smiled, years melted away. She looked like a little girl.

"How old are you? That's fairly uncontroversial at your age." Naomi accepted the menus the waiter gave her.

"Thirty-one. Thirty-one years old. I've been in Sally's group for a few months."

"Right." Naomi was determined to be patient. They both ordered the chef's salad. Eleanor leaned forward.

"Look, I'll just tell you the bare facts for a minute. Okay?"

"Great."

Naomi felt that by this time she had heard it all. What was it that Eleanor could tell her that could be so different, so awful?

Eleanor took a deep breath.

"I've been a drunk for eleven years, took a lot of dope. A lot of dope in my day. I've had LSD trips and coke trips, I've shot speed, anything. I've been in detox twenty times. Twenty times I had my stomach pumped. It didn't even bother me the last few times. I tried suicide a couple of times. I was living inside a powder keg. I had a lot I wanted not to remember.

"See," she continued, "I never knew about the incest until two years ago. I'd had a couple of nervous breakdowns, and was in and out of institutions and nobody could find out what was wrong with me. Luckily my family had the money for treatment. Two years ago, under hypnosis I got to it. I remembered. I got to my father having . . ." It was very hard for Eleanor. Her voice was getting softer and softer.

"Your voice is so soft, Eleanor, I'm having trouble hearing."

"Sorry. Sorry. Soft. That's the word he used, my father. A lot. Soft; he used to say my body was soft. See he couldn't with my mother, but he could get a hard on with me because I was soft. He told me. To this day the word gives me strange feelings. I react; the hair stands up on my arms. Soft."

There was more silence. But Eleanor did want to tell it to Naomi.

"It's okay." Naomi touched her hand.

"I know it is. I do."

Eleanor took a deep breath. "I was a daddy's girl. I was the favorite, I loved him more than life itself. My mother didn't exist, nor my sister. I used to cook for my father, make extravagant gourmet meals for him. Beef wellington and chocolate cakes, pastas and coq au vin and chicken kiev. I learned in high school how to be the best cook in the world. For my father. I would be in the kitchen with the apron on when he would come from his office on Sunset Boulevard where all the gang from his big oil conglomerate business would scrape and carry on and look up to this pillar of the community.

"You know? And there I'd be in the kitchen with the apron on whipping up the whipped cream for the gingerbread or whatever. I made my mother fire the maid. You know, we didn't need a maid. I could do it. I would be his cook, his lady, his whore."

"How long did that go on?"

"Years. You know, I just lost track of the time. Let's put it this way. The sun rose and set on that man. And that gorgeous person, that brilliant raconteur, that scion of industry was putting it into his little girl every night for years . . ."

Eleanor began to sound angry. She had barely touched the food that was put in front of her. Her foot was shaking continuously.

"See it's all over now. And I'm killing myself in therapy and Survivors Anonymous to get to the feelings, to talk about it till it goes away, till I can understand it."

"How old were you?"

"Let's put it this way. A cousin of mine just told me recently that she used to see my father put his fingers in my vagina when I was about a year old."

"Jesus." Naomi couldn't stop the word.

"Yeah. Right. And this is the same cousin who my father made suck him off when she was ten. Anyway, under the hypnosis I remembered being fondled and played with and what have you when I was about nine. And then I remembered what I'd been trying to forget. He started having intercourse with me when I was twelve, something like that."

"For how long, Eleanor?"

"Till I was sixteen. Till I had lost thirty-five pounds and

stopped getting my period for three years. Then he stopped. And you want to know why?"

"Why?" She wanted to make Eleanor be all right. She would give anything if Eleanor turned out all right after all this.

"Because he was scared I wouldn't be able to have children. It was important to him that I marry well and have children. Then he got outsmarted and died when I was nineteen. Over and out."

"Did you ever confront him—I guess you never did since you had blocked out the whole experience."

"No way. You didn't fool around with him anyway. He told me no one would ever believe me anyway if I told. No one."

"Did your mother know?"

"Yeah, she knew. She was operating on the biggest denial trip you ever saw. But look, I can't even blame her. She was afraid he would beat her. I remember once when he knocked her against an iron railing, I was so afraid she would die. No, there was nothing she could do. She was one of those women who never came out of her room. For sixteen years, we'd only see her at meals and stuff."

Eleanor was spent. Bad memories.

Naomi was very moved. "I've never really said anything like this. I don't know if it will mean anything to you, I just feel compelled to say it."

She had gotten herself into this for a reason she could not fathom. She could not stop now.

"Eleanor, I've got these vague feelings, this strange floating feeling myself that something happened between me and my father."

"What do you mean?"

"I feel odd talking about it, because there are no facts, no actualities; just feelings. A strangeness. I always thought I was this big strong thing who could take care of everything. But just lately I'm beginning to see how I take anything that hurts and I stash it away into some dark musty corner of my brain. I don't know what happened. I'm just uneasy . . ."

Eleanor put her hand on Naomi's. She kept stroking it. There were tears in her eyes.

"You know what I think?" Eleanor said. "I think that if you

177

feel it, if a father just puts his hand on your breast, or holds you in a certain way and you feel it's not right, then something's wrong. I know I'm right about that. I just know it."

"One more, just one more question. Have you forgiven him? Can you forgive your father?"

Eleanor started to smile. And started to eat.

"No. I've got to forgive myself first. I will. I've got to get out my anger first, instead of putting it on my own back. Like you know, I've been having really bad back trouble these past weeks. I went to the chiropractor, and then to an acupressurist who told me to visualize the pain. You know how they do. And you know what I visualized? I saw big pieces of glass coming out of my back, jagged, sharp. And I visualized my father trying to touch that soft back that he loved so well and getting cut to ribbons from the glass. Just slashed.

"So, no. I haven't forgiven him. But you know. I'm working on it. I'm working on it."

35

"You know what? So what. That's what I say. So what. So what if he fucked you and so what if he didn't, so what if he got a hard on when his sexy little baby pressed up against him for a dance or for a hug. Naomi, so what. Yesterday's news. You're getting nuts from this. And you're making me nuts from it."

The two were paddling the canoe that came with the house. Naomi was feathering the way they taught her in sleep-away camp. Matthew was plunging right in as he taught himself once when he happened to find himself in a canoe.

Naomi splashed him as she thrust the oar into the water with a ferocious stroke. The elaborate feathering got the whole boat wet.

"Watch out how you do that fancy stroking will you, you're getting me soaked."

"You are soaked already. If I'm uncomfortable with this to the degree I seem to be then I have to deal with it. How dare you, how dare you say so what if he did and so what if he didn't. There's a helluva lot of difference, buster."

"Sweetheart, love of my life. Deal with it, flush it out, but do it and be done with it. Will you? I must admit my patience has worn thin on this lugubrious subject of late."

"Is that so. Is that just so? Well, nobody's telling you to hang around and listen to it. This is a whole new ballgame to me. All of it. Including our relationship, by the way, which is not exactly the easiest thing in the world for me. And all this other stuff is just unnerving me."

Matthew was speaking very very quietly.

"I know that. And I think I've been stellar in my understanding. You do tend to overdramatize, and you do go overboard. Now, that can be charming at time, and quite endearing . . . but . . ."

"Don't you dare, don't you dare patronize me, you son of a bitch. I will not be patronized. This is all very real. And goddamn painful for me." Naomi splashed her oar into the water hard, and in so doing lost her equilibrium, footing, aplomb and composure in about two seconds. In a moment they were both in the water.

And this was not water to be in.

Matthew roared with laughter.

"Don't let any of it get in your mouth, it's polluted and there are hundreds of little fish you could swallow," Naomi shouted. "Oh Christ, oh crap. Let's get this thing to shore. Oh crap."

Matthew could not stop laughing. He bellowed so loud that people came outside on their terraces to see what this Viking was doing with seaweed hanging from his beard helping a bean of a girl to shore.

Later, huddled in her robe in front of a fire, sipping a hot toddy, Naomi refused to feel foolish. She insisted it was Matthew's fault they had tipped over, insisted that she was entitled to her obsession. It wasn't hurting anyone but her. Matthew said yes, it was hurting him, because if there was one thing he hated in this world it was being bored, and he was getting very fed up with this tedious topic. To say the least. He had other things on his mind.

"Bored. Did you say you were bored?" Naomi glared at him.

"As a matter of fact . . ."

"Well, that's too damn bad, Johnson. This is my life I'm dealing with here. My past, my hurts. Too bad if it's boring you."

"Naomi."

"What?" She was still sulking.

"You know anything about Indians?"

"Matthew."

"I do. I have studied them for years. I even speak a little Sioux."

"Sioux. So?"

"I don't know, the canoe made me think of Indians."

"Bravo. An extraordinary association."

"Don't be rude."

"I am not rude. I'm chilled and chagrined and confused and angry. I feel angry all the time."

"Then take it out where it belongs. Not on me. Let me get back to the Indians."

"Go on."

"The Sioux had three virtues: courage, without which one can do nothing; generosity, without which one cannot live with anyone; and an original concept of magnanimity, which meant ever striving to be better in spiritual terms, rather than the popular concept of the word which has more of the meaning of gregariousness perhaps."

Naomi was incredulous. At the moment, as in all his conversations, she had no idea where Matthew was leading.

"The Sioux had no word for love, it was just expected. Naomi, they did have a word for lack of love, which meant what we mean when we say insane."

"The point being . . ."

"The point being that there is love here. To lose it would be insane."

Naomi was surprised. The wind disappeared from her sails.

"Matthew . . ."

"Let me finish." He came over to her by the fire and sat down. "I want you to finish your story. I want you to make peace with your parents. You're too old for all this carrying on. I want you to think about you and me."

"I do think about you and me. I don't have to stay in L.A. Why do you think I stay in L.A.? There's lots of incest and child pornography all over the place. I don't have to stay here for the story. There's just a lot of stuff coming down now, and I've never been too good at handling my professional and personal lives at the same time."

"I can see that."

"Matthew, I don't mean it to be that way, it just is. I mean I've never really noticed before how much energy I spend talking about my parents, worrying about what they think, feeling guilty, ungrateful, until I met you. I don't know I just thought everyone was like that, and so what, as long as I could do daring things in my career and take risks with my own life and never think twice about it. So what."

"Because nothing else touched you."

"Rarely."

They both stared into the fire. Somewhere someone was shooting off firecrackers. Somewhere a police helicopter was circling overhead.

Matthew took another tack.

"You know, one thing you've never considered is that if you were in another culture, having sex as a child would not be considered taboo because it had already been accepted in the society."

"Of course I've considered it." Her guard was up.

"For example." Matthew got into his show-off 'I'm going to lay some statistics on you' tone of voice. "In 1929 Malinowsky reported that the children of the Trobriand Islands of Oceania began to indulge in erotic games at the age of four and were enjoying regular intercourse at ten in the case of boys and six in the case of girls."

"Not with their fathers. Incest is an almost universal taboo. I do not happen to be talking about some godforsaken island someplace." Naomi was fighting for control.

"From an anthropological point of view there would never be such a thing as kiddie porn," Matthew lectured. "There are child brides in India and aboriginal Australia, I mean Western society has undergone a revolution in sexual values but has only applied it to adults. It is very possible that kid porn is a manifest demonstration that American children can no longer be insulated from the modern sexual revolution."

"Matthew, that is complete bullshit and has absolutely nothing to do with what I'm dealing with. You sound like those people from the Guyon Society."

"What's that?"

"I can't believe I know something you don't. It's a bona fide organization based on the writings of one René Guyon who proposes that children need sex with tender loving adults to reduce sexual repression which, in their view, causes depression, suicide, assault, and other social problems. I'm surprised you don't push their slogan, 'Sex before eight, before it's too late.' "

"Interesting."

"Interesting!" She exploded. "Is that all you have to say? Interesting? That's like somebody screwing my niece Janie for her own good. Shit. Well, I'll tell you what I think of your anthropological point of view. I think it stinks. That's what I think. I think you trivialize this whole thing. You didn't talk to the women I did who were abused, and you don't know what it's like to be victimized in such a way. You're a man and in spite of all your protestations, you are indeed very macho, and if you want my opinion I think you are incredibly insensitive to this whole business."

He was shouting now.

"I respect your work and I respect what you are trying to do. I am not trivializing the subject at all. I am asking you to take a long look at your overinvolvement in the material. That is what I am trying to do."

"You really don't understand. Do you?"

"It's not that at all. It's just that I am beginning to have more than an inkling of a feeling that you and I are just at a different place at a different time."

Naomi looked up. She did not like the tone of his voice. It was very possible that she had gone too far. Matthew got up off the floor.

"Where are you going? I thought we were going to have dinner."

"Timing. Timing has a lot to do with where people are with each other. Somehow I had thought there was something quite special in our meeting. That we were at similar places. I don't know, Naomi. I can't seem to reach you lately."

"Well that's what happens when I get really absorbed in my work. You're the exact same way for Christ's sake, Matthew. You go off and hibernate for days or play go fish in Mexico in the middle of everything so the muse can light on your forehead. If anyone should understand about all this then you should."

"I do, kiddo." He seemed very serious. "But the difference between us is that I do not obsess."

"What a crock. You set yourself up as Mr. Perfection. Believe me, you're not. He who casts the first . . ."

"I go do what I have to. I do not dwell. I go on about my business. And that is what you are going to have to learn to do. Especially if you are to live with me."

"Well who in hell said I am going to live with you? I never said that. You never even said that. We're just getting to know each other, for Christ's sake."

"I could mean it figuratively or I could mean it literally. It doesn't matter at this point."

"Matthew . . ."

"No, no, no protestations of love, no. The timing is off for the moment. I need a woman, my love. A child I have no need of. I do not want a little girl."

Naomi sat up very straight and used her Oriana Fallaci voice. "I am not a little girl. It is the woman in me that finds your whole attitude repulsive. You are patronizing me and I don't like it one bit, Matthew."

"I am not patronizing you. I wouldn't have stayed around this long if I didn't think there was a woman there, an adored one. But you've got it buried under a lot of stuff, Naomi. You've got to sort a lot of things out, and apparently I'm not able to help you with it. Your daddy's an old man who may have copped a feel once after loving his little darlin' more than he thought he could love anybody. Naomi, there's a lot worse things in this world. You've got to straighten it out with him. With them. I've been through it and I just don't have the patience anymore."

"Well, you keep talking about what you need and what you want. What about what I need and want?" Naomi pulled out a cigarette with a bold gesture, waiting for Matthew to light it.

He ignored her. She lit her own cigarette.

"Kiddo, I thought it was me for a while. You're too preoccupied. If it's not your work, it's your parents. If it's not your parents, it's your self-obsession. No room at the inn, kiddo."

He bent down and wiped away the tears that were involuntarily coming out of Naomi's eyes. He stood over her, playing with his belt buckle.

"This afternoon when you walked into the room in your white bikini, a nice broad hint of dark pubic hair peeped over the top. I wanted to slide the cloth down your thighs and kiss your belly and sex and hug you tight. I find you very beautiful, Naomi, no more my ideal woman than I am your ideal man, but of a quality and power and beauty that my ideal is changed, altered, expanded by knowing you.

"My dear, I would like to take you dancing and teach you the Texas two-step, where you hold close but keep on dancing. And afterwards, our clothes damp with sweat, I would like to go look at the sky and show you the North Star, and take a night swim in a Greek sea or a cold French stream and sleep together naked, a bit drunk, bitten by mosquitoes, tousled, and in love.

"But not now. Not for a while, not till you sort out a lot of unfinished business."

Matthew made a move to go to the door. Naomi made the half-hearted dramatic gesture of throwing herself in front of it with outstretched arms. She was crying. Matthew gently put her arms down at her sides.

"You see what I want," he said, his own eyes moist, looking straight into hers, "if anyone is interested in what I want, I would like to have a child, not be with one. Yes, I would like to have a child with you, Naomi. Someday. Look, I'll see you around, kiddo. We'll talk in a few days."

And he was gone.

She ran out on the terrace and screamed after him.

"And just what does that mean? Have a child? You come back here, Matthew Johnson. Don't you dare leave me cliff-hanging with that one. Oriana Fallaci went in a bumpy truck on a bumpy road when she was pregnant. Matthew!" She screamed into the dark night, his car long gone down the narrow canal street. "Damn you, Matthew Johnson."

185

36

There was nothing else to do. She couldn't stay here any-more. There must be a new war brewing in South America that she could cover. Or a trip down or up the Amazon would be nice. No parents. No men, just alligators and iguanas or what-ever they have there.

Naomi was throwing her clothes into her suitcase. Silks and cashmere, leathers and wool. A jumble. She had telephoned her friend, or possibly her ex-friend Maria at the theater in New York and told her she would be back at her apartment unex-pectedly tomorrow and Maria would have to find another place to stay. She couldn't be nice. She was unable, incapable of doing the nice thing which would have been to let her stay there with her for a few nights until she could make arrangements. But the thought of making small talk, the thought of chit-chatting the night away made her ill. So she lost a friend. She was losing a lot of things.

She was unable to talk to Matthew. He was pompous. Lo-quacious. His last comment had thrown her, and she wasn't in the mood for his elucidating. What on earth was he talking about? A child? The man was forty-five years old. He had two children. Forget about him. What about her?

She was thirty-five years old, thirty-six very soon, and had very nearly given up all hope about a baby. Yes, she had wanted one when she was young. She had smoked a lot of pot when she was in high school, and in college when the offerings were more daring and enticing she had reneged. Always, always sticking to pot because she had never read any studies about the horrendous things pot could do to the fetus. She was always protecting that unknown, mythical unborn fetus. She was always keeping it healthy, wealthy, and wise inside there, so no damage would be done. But now. It didn't seem simple anymore. It might be too late. In the first place, how could she do the things she was good at and have the freedom she wanted if she were encumbered with a baby? Secondly, what kind of mother would she make? As a matter of fact, just being that close to Matthew in the first place terrified her.

Too much. Her head was going too fast. The man was driving her crazy. She would do what she always did. Run. Bury herself in her work. She had enough material now, she would barricade herself in her apartment and write her piece. She would try to forget the big cheese Danish, the Viking with the words coming out of his ears. Whose words buried her, whose arms made her feel safe. She could strangle him when he put on his macho big-shot airs but, through it all, the vulnerability of the man had touched her. The feather of his tenderness proved a sweet balance to the part that loved to pontificate and always be right.

Well, too bad. So be it. He just didn't understand what she was going through and what she was trying to do and how important it was that she make some peace with all this raging around her.

It took her a day to do all the things she had to do. Clean the apartment, finish her affairs in Los Angeles. She had intended to slip away like some barefoot Indian on reconnaissance, but just after she had gotten the mail, she had an uncontrollable urge to say goodbye.

She let the phone ring a long time. Matthew had obviously unplugged it, and he didn't have a service. The phone just rang and rang. Just as well. Then this is the way it would have to be for a while. Naomi just couldn't concentrate on so many things at one time.

She sat waiting for the taxi to come pick her up since, painfully, she had given back her trusty Toyota to the rental man. Naomi sat, surrounded by her bags and boxes. It was the only thing she could think of doing now, this packing up her tent and stealing away. She was Abou Ben Adam, may his tribe increase, she was T. E. Lawrence, she was Peter O'Toole raging across the desert. It was the only way to get out of there.

She opened a package that had come in the mail. It was a paperback book, a collection of poems by Anne Sexton. It was from Eleanor. On the very last page Eleanor had underlined the last several lines of a poem. Naomi read them out loud.

> There was a theft.
> That much I am told.
> I was abandoned.
> That much I know.
> I was forced backward.
> I was forced forward.
> I was passed hand to hand
> like a bowl of fruit.
>
> Each night I am nailed into place
> and I forget who I am.
> Daddy?
> That's another kind of prison.
> It's not the prince at all,
> but my father
> drunkenly bent over my bed,
> circling the abyss like a shark,
> my father thick upon me
> like some sleeping jellyfish.

Poor Eleanor. Poor Anne. Poor Butterfly.

She stood up. But not poor Naomi, she said out loud. Her mouth was tight. Not poor Naomi, she heard herself say as she ran outside to tell the taxi man to stop beeping please and come inside and get her bags.

New York

37

"And then he hit me with the side of his hand when I took so long in getting the money out of my pocket. And it hurt and I couldn't get the money out of my pocket . . ."

Janie could barely get the words out. Her face was streaked with tears, the salty wetness moving in and around her freckles.

Naomi held her close to her. She could feel the child's heart beating. Like a metronome out of control, Janie's warm chest felt as though it would burst.

"Sweetheart, go slow, go slow, tell what happened."

"I called the doctor." Becky, almost hysterical herself, was desperately trying to keep calm but the bottom had just fallen out of her world.

"Go on baby, let it out, cry it out baby. Go on, Janie." Naomi held her as tight as she could, pressing every ounce of warmth she had into her niece's body.

Janie sobbed hard. She almost lost her breath as she sobbed, the words swallowed up in her grief.

"Gina ran away. Gina didn't even stay to help me, she just ran away. But that wasn't the worst part, the worst part was that after I gave him the money, by the way I saved my Kennedy dollar that I always keep in my shoe. He didn't know I had anything in my shoe and I fooled him so I felt good about that, but Mommy—" she looked over Naomi's shoulder at Becky slumped in a chair in the foyer of her apartment—"Mommy, I did what you told me I didn't speak to him I never speak to strangers, it's a thing I never do, but that wasn't the worst part, the worst part was that his penis was out, his fly was all open."

"On Madison Avenue?" Becky screamed.

Naomi couldn't help laughing. "Makes no difference, babe, where you are. This was at three o'clock in the afternoon?"

"I had just gotten off the bus to go to Grandma's where Jasmine was going to stay with me for a while till Mommy got back, and I was walking along when this big man came over to me and said he wanted my lunch money. How did he know I have lunch money when it's after lunchtime and anyone could figure out I had my lunch? But he didn't know that I brought my lunch in a bag today and didn't spend my lunch money, so it was still in my pocket so he got it. And Naomi—" in order to give her more of the gory details face to face, Janie looked her straight in the eye, put her hands on her aunt's cheeks—"the fly was way open and he was just hanging out there with the sun shining on it . . ."

"Janie, that's enough about that now. Once is enough to describe the whole thing." Becky got herself up out of her chair.

Janie was obviously fascinated by the whole affair, and very traumatized by it. The child started to shake as she remembered it again, tantalizing herself as she conjured up the image. Then the tears started again. For real.

"What do you say we just take a nice hot bath and I'll make you some hot chocolate and whip up some real whipped cream? How would that be, sweetie?" Naomi smoothed Janie's hair.

"I want a bubble bath." Janie sniffled. "But it's getting to be spring and it's too hot for hot chocolate, but a fudgesicle might be all right. I've never eaten a fudgesicle in the bath. Maybe I could do that?"

"Great. Becky, why don't we run her bath? Do you have those bubble bath crystals I gave you?"

"I've got them in my room. I was saving them for Janie for special occasions."

"Well," said Naomi. "I guess this qualifies. Come on, honey, let's go take a nice long hot bath. That's what I do when I want to relax and let off some steam. A hot bath is the best."

"I'll take her in Naomi, thanks. Fix yourself a drink. I'll be right out." Becky wanted her daughter back. Yes. She's right. She is her child. What was she doing, Naomi thought as she relinquished Janie to her mother. Becky was Janie's mother. Naomi tended to forget that sometimes. So did Becky.

Naomi went into the kitchen and took a bottle of white wine out of the refrigerator and poured herself a glass. She shuddered when she thought what could have happened. Thank God she was in town, thank God she was home when Becky called her. Thank God she is cool in emergencies. Janie will be all right. But her heart had stopped for a moment when Becky had called, breathless, hysterical, out of control. If anything happened to Janie . . .

38

Naomi didn't leave her apartment for a week. She talked to Janie on the phone every day. It seemed she had come through her urban crisis rather well. Naomi unplugged her phone, put her notes all over the floor, pinned some to the wall. She transcribed her own tapes, and disappeared.

She would put Matthew out of her head, she would exorcize the man's energy from her. But she could not banish him from her dreams, she could not make him leave her heart. She understood now why she had gotten so angry, had reacted so violently to what he had said. He had touched something crucial in her.

But she had to do first things first. Helene was anxious for a first draft of her articles; she wanted to see something in ten days. She wrote Matthew a long letter, telling him what she was about. How she had to get her life in order before she could make any decisions about anything. She had to finish her work. She had to set some things straight with Sol and Esther. She told him the story about Janie. But she did not mention the four-letter word that began with *b* and ended with *y*. She had not heard from him.

Finally, in ten days, after warding off her parents and Becky, the *New York Times* piling up in the foyer, the mail overflowing in the kitchen, she got something respectable down on paper. She sent it out to the typist on Tuesday, made an appointment to have a messenger deliver it to Helene on Friday so she could read it over the weekend. They made an appointment to see each other Monday morning.

Naomi pulled the shades down and slept all day Saturday until ten in the evening. She got up, made herself something to eat, and began to feel human again. She waded through a week's worth of *New York Times* and *Saturday Reviews* and *Psychology Todays*. She glutted herself with periodicals, stuffed herself with being up-to-date, and fell into bed after three. But not before she plugged her phone back in. She was preparing herself for the reentry process.

Which didn't take long.

She couldn't figure out whether it was the church bells on the corner beckoning worshipers or the jangle of her phone that woke her so unceremoniously. In concert it was an abrupt return to the land of the living.

"Ten days."

"Ten days what."

"We haven't heard from you in ten days. If Becky hadn't told us that you had unplugged your phone I would definitely have called the police. The fire department at least."

"Hi, Mother."

"Can you come to dinner tonight?"

"Tomorrow maybe."

"What's the matter with tonight?"

"I want to be alone. Got a big meeting tomorrow, want to keep my head calm, my mouth serene. I finished my story."

"What story?"

"The one about . . . never mind."

"Don't be sulky. I forgot. Who can remember everyth . . ."

"It doesn't matter, Ma. I can't come tonight."

"The Kaspars are coming."

"Who's that."

"Shopping centers."

"Sorry."

"They have a son who just got divorced who . . ."

"Forget it. I thought you gave that stuff up when I was sixteen."

"Where did you get that lemon cake you had when you had your open house?"

"Lexington and something. Miss Grumble or mumble . . . Mom, I'm not up yet. I haven't gone to the bathroom. What time is it?"

"So when are we going to see you. I've got a list of things for you to do."

"For what?"

"For the anniversary. Your father and I have it all figured out. Now you . . ."

"Mother." She exploded. "I am in the middle of worrying about if my work on the story I just finished is any good. I am in the middle of worrying about a man in my life. I am in the middle . . ."

"What man, what middle? You never tell me anything. How do I know what's going on with you?"

"Because you never listen, that's why. Because you're just listening to yourself. That's why. Look, give me a break, will you, okay?" And with that, Naomi hung up.

She had just dozed off again when the phone rang.

"What did you do to your mother?"

"Hung up on her," she mumbled into the phone.

"You sure are a smart-ass. I think she deserves an apology."

"How about somebody apologizing to me for a change. Call me back, Dad, I'm sleeping."

"Don't you dare hang up. You have hurt your mother very much."

"I don't mean to, I really don't. Look, I'll come over tomorrow, I can't come tonight."

"Tonight is the night we are having the dinner party. We tried to get a hold of you all week but you made yourself totally inaccessible."

"Dad. Daddy. I'll see you tomorrow. I've got to get some sleep."

Naomi fumbled for the phone and hung it up. She opened her eyes and repeated her last words. "Dad, Daddy, I'll see you tomorrow. I've got to get some sleep." She was wondering if she sounded like a ten-year-old whining person, or a thirty-five-year-old career woman who has just finished a difficult magazine piece.

39

"Just be grateful you have them. My folks are long gone."

Helene was ravishing in maroon stockings, maroon shoes, maroon tweed suit, and pink silk shirt.

"How old were you?"

"I was in my twenties. The worst part was that they died before we made our peace. There was a time I couldn't stand the sound of my mother's voice. And then the years went by and I started unraveling the threads, pulling it all together, and finally started to understand where they were coming from. They'd had two babies before me who died. And I got all that pressure. Whoosh. It blew over me like a tornado. But your parents are so adorable I don't know what you're complaining about."

"They're great with nonrelatives."

"Anyway," Helene said, "I sort of envy you, having them around. I just wish I could have said some things to mine before they went. So they would know how I felt."

Naomi looked at Helene. "You almost sound wistful, and you're a person not ordinarily given to wist."

"Queen of the wists, that's me. Well look, let's get to this stuff, I've got a bitch of a day. And Dennis is coming at twelve sharp to take me to lunch, and I don't want to be late."

"Dennis?"

"He's new. Boy wonder. Head of the art department. Well, I mean he was the boy wonder of a few years ago. Now he's forty and fabulous."

"Married?"

"Of course. Who isn't? He and his wife have an arrangement."

"Are you part of the deal?"

"Naomi, do I question your questionable taste? This is all right. It suits me. And I like this man. He's funny, and he knows the business and he's not gay and his marriage hasn't been much of a problem yet. We'll see what we will see."

"I know." Naomi bent over to the couch where Helene was sitting and touched her knee. "Excuse me. It's none of my business. None. You know? I read an article in *TV Guide* this week about some reigning TV star who's been married twice, both times to older men. Gorgeous lady who, the article says, is making middle age an acceptably sexy time. At any rate she's thirty-eight, which I can't see being near middle age. But anyway she says at the end of the article, if a new man came along and swept her off her feet again she would fall heavy and give all this hard-won independence up. Maybe we should do a piece on that phenomenon."

"You know what I think?"

Naomi was sure she was going to disagree with her.

"Of course they . . . we still exist. We'd be liars if we didn't admit to it. Edna O'Brien, Jean Rhys wrote about us. We need men even though somehow or other they can make us crazy. We can be unbelievably strong, take a bleeding child to the hospital without blinking an eye, drive through a hurricane without being blown away, make decisions on the spot, hire, fire, handle hundreds of thousands of dollars. But along comes a man we want, whose touch and whose words move us, bam . . . we wait by the phone. And if we do call him, modern liberated girls that we are, and we get him to go somewhere Sadie-Hawkins-Day style, and we hold him and fondle him and arouse him. So what? What do we have? He can still move away, reject us. And you know what, Naomi, it's not even their fault. I don't blame the men. There's such a lot of fear between us. Like who's going to give up whose sovereignty first. You know? Like who's going to feel first."

Naomi leaned back in her chair and lit a cigarette.

"I've been doing a helluva lot of thinking lately, since I saw you last. I live in a world where I've got everything and still feel empty. Yes, I feel empty. It would be different if I didn't love children. Some of the girls in the office have decided they're not having them. Okay. Fine for them. As far as I'm concerned the women's movement, and even we in the media, misled them. I admit it. Mea culpa. But I'm finally identifying that emptiness for me and I'm just tired of being scared. I want a man I can love and I want to have a family. I decided."

"Helene, you really have been doing a lot ot thinking."

"I sure have. Approaching forty is on my mind all the time. Christ, even Betty Friedan's changing her tune."

Naomi was thoughtful. "It's confusing, that's for sure."

"Not at all. I decided, I'm going to work out a way to have my cake, the icing, the ice cream, and eat it too. If it kills me. Anyway, come on." She took a deep breath. "I want to talk about your work. Where are the photographs you took?"

Helene shifted gears like lightning. Naomi was made breathless by the onslaught.

"I gave them to the lab to be developed. Didn't you get them yet?" Naomi was impressed by Helene's passion. But found herself wondering whether or not a forty-year-old married man was the most appropriate facilitator for this newly identified dream.

"Well, they may be on my desk, I'm not sure, I haven't been to the bottom of it yet today. By the end of the day I will."

"Some of the interviews have to be anonymous. I explained that to you."

" Naomi, I think some of this is smashing. The psychiatrist is too long, and you may have to expand on the kiddie porn stuff, but the interviews are fascinating, exactly what I was interested in. Especially the one with Eleanor. She really opened up to you. I've made some notes for rewrites and gave Jeanie Deutsch a copy of the pages. She'll have her notes for you tomorrow. But feel good, kiddo. It's a job very well done."

Kiddo. A stab. That's who she was, just your common ordinary everyday neighborhood kiddo. Matthew, I miss you.

40

Naomi always got them. The cab drivers. This generous, erudite one had an enormous bag filled with candies attached to the back seat. The sign pinned to it said Take 3. He also had all sixteen Beethoven quartets attached to an elaborate hi-fi set up in the car, but at the moment, he took pains to explain, was listening to Paul Robeson performing Othello.

Her parents were in the living room, her mother seated at her desk surrounded by invitations and envelopes. Sol was banging a nail into the wall. He was moving his paintings around.

"Where have you been, Naomi? You know I like to eat at a certain time, Jasmine can't stay late." Esther was wearing a long dressing gown.

"Sorry." Naomi kissed her mother, then her father.

"Fix yourself a drink dear, and please freshen mine while you're at it."

Naomi fixed herself a stiff drink. She handed the drink to Esther.

"How did your meeting go, Naomi?"

Naomi sank into a red velvet couch. She put her feet up on the coffee table in front of it, and slipped off her shoes.

"Take your feet off dear, that looks terrible."

"My shoes are off."

"Your mother said take your feet off."

I have interviewed Rosalynn Carter, Naomi thought. I jumped out of an airplane, I will go to the moon. And you are telling me to take my feet off this travertine marble tabletop with the antique mahogany legs.

Naomi removed her feet from the table.

"How did you say your meeting was, Naomi?"

"Good, it was good. Helene really liked the first draft and . . ."

"Helene, Helene Stanley, that's the girl I want you to invite. She's very interesting and well read. We really do need some younger people."

"Especially some gorgeous numbers. What other beauties can you suggest, Naomi?"

"Can't think of any offhand. What's for dinner?"

"It's Monday, lamb chops."

"Right. When did you arrive at that system, fish on Tuesday, liver on Wednesday, chicken on Friday?"

"I hope you're not criticizing the menus around here." Sol looked around from his work.

Naomi gave up. She was determined to get through this evening, and the anniversary, make the famous peace with her parents and go on about her business. That was the plan.

Jasmine sounded the dinner buzzer from the kitchen. Dinner was served. Naomi fled into the dining room, taking a quick moment off to look at her face in the guest-bathroom mirror. Look on this as an assignment, she said to the lady in the mirror there. Look on this as something that will get you the Nobel Prize if you survive to the end of it. And you will have to go to Stockholm to pick up the award.

Everything was fine until the meat came.

"Too rare."

"Change with Naomi dear, she loves it rare."

"Hers isn't well done enough for me. Jasmine . . ." He bellowed into the kitchen.

Saint Jasmine arrived at the table.

"A few more minutes under the fire, please. Now you didn't put any garlic or crap like that on mine, did you?"

"I never do."

"Right. So, Naomi, what's new?"

"Well, I finished my story."

"Wonderful. So glad to hear it. Now there's a lot of detail work for this party, and your mother is really going to need your help."

"What is it exactly you had in mind for me, Mom? My time is really wild these days. I may have to go back to the coast, you know, before June. Or even to North Africa to do an update on the French Foreign Legion, you never can tell."

Esther was indignant. She never was famous for her sense of humor. "Well if that woman is going to send you to North Africa to see some poor French dropouts from society she ought to have her head examined."

"Mother, it was a joke."

"Well, I don't get it. If she's going to . . ."

Naomi put her hand on her mother's right one, heavy with rings.

"Forget it, Mother. It's not important. Your hair looks great, by the way."

Esther lit up like the sky. She patted it.

"You like it? I found a new place. He insisted I don't touch the color. Armando says I've gone white in the way women envy. Evenly. I'm really glad you like it. Like the cut?"

No mother person existed. This hungry little girl sat in her mother's chair.

"It's lovely, Mother. Very youthful."

"She's something else, isn't she? Your mother. She doesn't look a bit different from the day I married her. Cute as a button."

Esther poured herself a generous glass of wine and refilled Naomi's glass.

"Forty years. I can't believe it." Sol leaned back in his chair. "Jasmine, what's with the lamb chops."

"Coming." Jasmine's voice floated in from the kitchen. In a moment, two shriveled very well-done chops sat in front of Sol.

"Perfect." Sol began eating.

"I mean you should be very grateful we've all lived to see this day. That the two lovebirds are still alive and kicking to experience this day with their loved ones."

When she was sixteen that Saturday morning in June, Daddy was standing at the entrance to the bathroom and Esther was still in bed. The four-poster had posts that were thick and comforting, and Naomi was hugging one in her nervousness, in her consternation. The trunk of it was sturdy. A safe place at the moment.

Sol was very unhappy. His eyes were bulging and he kept pacing. "Dr. Jacobs told me, it had to come from a stranger, it had to come from someone outside the family." I told him not to tell. Naomi kept swinging with one arm on the post. "Naomi sit down, you're making me nervous, stop swinging on the post. Why couldn't you come to us, why couldn't you tell us?" If I hadn't gotten an infection no one would know. It was just one of those things. "Who is this boy?" Sol could barely get the words out. In some perverse way Naomi was enjoying hurting him, knowing how difficult this was for him. Why did she feel this way, he was her daddy. But he had been so odd lately coming up to see her at boarding school a couple of times a month, it wasn't necessary, none of the other kids' parents came to visit that much. She was glad to see him, but he talked loud and flirted with all the girls and she was embarrassed, and he kept sending his meat back three and four times in restaurants when he would take her and her girlfriends to dinner.

She knew they had a lot more questions to ask, but frankly she was so relieved not to be a virgin anymore, it had hung heavy, her virginity, and now finally she had given her love a cherry and it wasn't any big deal, and she didn't know where the love part came in anyway. Sol had looked stricken that day, Sol couldn't take it that his little girl wasn't a virgin anymore, and had gotten an infection on top of it. He knew because the hypocritical hippocratical Dr. Jacobs had spilled the beans. Esther had been better than Sol that day, stoical, not getting out of the four-poster with the heavy curtains on top, but Naomi had kept swinging on the post and Sol had kept looking stricken and somehow Naomi knew that that day should have been the beginning of the end of something, something that had started a long time ago and was now finished. It should have begun a new phase, a new time. But it hung on, like a spider on a decaying web. It hung on.

"Now." Sol put down his fork. "Naomi, did you apologize to your mother?"

"For what?"

"For what? For hanging up on her, that's for what."

"Dad, she woke me up. I'd been working around the clock for over a week. I was exhausted."

"Your mother was worried about you."

Naomi poured herself another glass of wine.

The best-laid plans.

"I've told you for weeks I had a deadline on this story."

"Your mother deserves the courtesy of an explanation."

"How about 'my mother' fighting her own battles? Are you aware of how many times you've called up berating me for some terrible indignity I have caused your wife, my mother. I mean, Mother, if you have a gripe how about just letting me have it?"

"All right. All right." There were tears in Esther's eyes. "If you really want to know what I'm feeling, I'll tell you. You hurt me all the time. Often by omission. You call, sure, but what do you talk about? I know nothing about your life, your feelings. You mentioned a new man. Who is he? We have nothing to say to each other once you and I have asked about each other's health."

"Mother, I came over here to see if I could be of any help . . ."

"If you think Sol has to talk for me, then why don't you just hear what I have to say for myself."

Jasmine came in with another bottle of wine, opened it, and refilled Esther's and Naomi's glasses. Sol still had his Scotch. Jasmine moved in and around family arguments. Not a blink, not an inkling of acknowledgment that all was not very sedate and Victorian at the table.

"I try and I try and, I don't know, I just don't think I have a place in your life anymore. We used to go shopping when you were little, and to the beauty parlor. We used to do things together. Now we never talk. I just never feel you are concerned about me and what I'm feeling. Maybe you don't think I'm as smart as your educated friends. But you're my daughter and I love you and I'll always love you, no matter what. I am going through one of the worst periods in my life now, since your father got sick, and there are other reasons that I can't talk about."

"Mother. Please. Please don't . . ."

"Let your mother finish."

"It's no use. You don't have to love your mother." Esther

stared straight ahead. "I will love you, no matter what. I feel like the poem, the old ballad. When the boy kills his mother, her heart which he's carrying murmurs, 'Careful, don't trip, my son. You are running so fast. You will hurt yourself.' "

"That's beautiful, Essie."

Naomi was determined not to cry.

"Mother, can I tell you something?"

"Go ahead, who's stopping you."

"I was talking to Mom."

"Go ahead."

"Every time, every single time we have one of these imbroglios . . ."

"Speak English, will you." Sol rang the bell shaped like a shepherdess. He yelled into the kitchen. "Tea and cake, Jasmine. Let's get rid of these dirty dishes, please."

Naomi tried again.

"Jasmine, bring in the lemon cake and the leftover prune danish for Mr. Lazurus. Go on, Naomi." Esther turned to her daughter and put the pained expression back on. It looked very real to Naomi.

"What I was trying to say is that we've been over all this before. And what I always end up saying after you say what you just said . . . "

"Just get to it, what's that got to do with it, if we've been all over it before." Esther was impatient.

"Because *nobody listens!*" Lost. Naomi lost the battle of the best-laid plans. Out the window, down the street they went, rolling assuredly by the Waldorf by now, skittering down Park Avenue like those rats who live underneath the streets, living some Jean Valjean existence deep beneath the avenues of doormen and delivery boys. Naomi's best-laid plans, along with her resolve, poise, grace, and charm, had left her for the rest of the evening.

"You exaggerate," Sol scoffed. He sipped his tea and savored his cake. "We listen to you, we listen to you all the time. You're long-winded and you know you are; in my business if I phumphed around as much as you do I would have lost the sale hours ago."

"Well, you know what, Dad, it may come as a surprise to you, but I'm not in your business. It may come as some sort of shock but I'm in my business. And I'm living, hard as it may be for you to accept it, I'm living my life. Not yours."

Sol exploded. "After all we've done for you, how dare you sit there and be the ungrateful person you are? Who sent you to college and graduate school? And who took you to Europe first-class when you were sixteen and let you go out with whoever asked you, and who let you marry Harry what's-his-name? All that schooling cost one pretty penny, and all we've ever gotten is your snottiness and ungratefulness. I think you ought to count your blessings, young lady. You're as wrong as anyone could be about your feelings. You're just dead wrong."

Naomi wanted to scream.

"If I feel a certain way, how can that be wrong? There is no wrong or right feelings. Feelings are fucking feelings."

"Watch your language. You are wrong. Just believe it. All I know is that ever since you got to be twelve or something you decided to be something other than what we wanted you to be. You always had to be different."

"Thank God."

"What does that mean? Just what does that mean? You don't want to be what your parents want you to be . . . ?"

Naomi turned it off. She probably should have hours ago. But she had fallen, hook, line, and sinker. They had pushed her buttons with a good hard nudge and she, like Pavlov's dog, had reacted accordingly. She was down there right along with Alice, and that rabbit hole was a lonely place, the place of her child-hood, the place where nobody heard, the place where there was no self.

She wanted to love them. She didn't know how. They god-damn wouldn't let her. If they would only hear her when she got angry, if she could somehow be heard when she explained how they hurt her, how she had had to build up an armor, like Eleanor, with pieces of glass sticking out of her back so they couldn't get to her. Because when a confidence was betrayed, a bond of faith ripped apart, there was nothing left but a little girl with pieces of glass sticking out of her back warding off all the marauders, all those who might want to get close.

She was right, her mother, there had been a time when it was fun to be with her; sundaes at Schraffts and a walk from Bonwits down to Lord and Taylor, sniffing all the perfumes and looking at the windows at Christmastime and watching the skaters at Rockefeller Center, and the silver-haired Christmas trees glistening in the icy sun. There had been a time when they were friends, but now the old resentments hung like a shroud.

" . . . And God knows Becky's got her problems, but she's a good dutiful daughter, I know I can depend on her."

Her mother's voice jogged her out of her reverie. The old compare-the-daughters routine. She remembered it well. Obviously it was Becky's turn for the gold star this week.

Now that Esther had released her feelings she felt much better. And now it was as though nothing had happened. This is the way it always was. An argument, a blowup, a summer storm, and it was all expected to be forgotten in a moment.

But the wine was fermenting Naomi's resolve. There were to be no more silences this night.

"You know what?" Naomi looked straight at Esther. "You know what I think? You're so hungry. The only person I know who's hungrier than you is me, and then Becky. She stuffs her face and I run all over the world chasing my own tail thinking that's going to fill up that cavern, that canyon inside me.

"You had Dad. He fed you and warmed you and took care of you for forty years and tried to be the mother that you never had. Well, sorry. I can't feel sorry for you. You had a good deal going there for a long time. Things have slowed down a bit lately but after all there's attrition. The years go by."

Somewhere Naomi knew that she had had too much to drink, that her defenses were down, that she was saying all the wrong things. But also somewhere she knew it was the only way she could get to the things that were on her mind.

"And you know what else . . ." She obviously did not wait for an answer, ". . . I've been thinking about babies myself now. I never did before. You know why I didn't? Too busy? True. Career-minded? Correct. You know what else? Scared shitless, that's why. . . . Good God, what kind of mother am I going to be? I'm as self-involved and self-obsessed as you are, as my own mother and hers before her."

Esther had had enough of this. She looked at Naomi as though all the skin had suddenly fallen off her daughter's face and only the bones remained.

"Let me speak," she said very quietly.

"Let your mother speak. How dare you have this monologue here. Just who do you think you are. You hog the whole floor."

"I don't know who I think I am, but I know what I'm not going to be. You listen to me for once, Sol Lazurus, and button your lip." God that felt good.

"I cannot believe my own daughter is talking this way."

"Believe it, Dad. Look, I'm sick of the games and the triggers and all the pain. You know. What happened to families who liked each other?"

Sol lashed out at her.

"If we don't have that kind of family it's your fault. You run, you started running away the minute things got a little uneasy for you. You were in high school and you started running."

"Right. And I'm still running. But I don't want to anymore. That's the difference. I've carried around resentments and bitterness till they have weighted me down like stones. I don't want them anymore. I have gone a week without going to the bathroom because I carry around the shit of my anger till even I know that I have to cough it out, and I don't care what end it comes out of."

"Now I think that this is about enough." It was throwing-down-the-napkin time. Naomi had hoped Sol had outgrown it. The napkin hit the little shepherdess bell with such force that she fell down. Jasmine thought the tinkling was for her and came to the door of the dining room. She heard the shouting and scurried back into the kitchen.

Sol did not like being defied.

"I will not be talked to that way in my own house. It's about time you realized that you are not the queen of everything. In my house I am king here, this is my house, and I think you should watch your mouth."

Naomi took a sip of her water, swallowing her tears.

"We have been wonderful parents. I don't know what you want from us."

"I don't want a thing from you."

"Oh yes you do, and obviously you don't get it. All I know is that my conscience is clear. I gave you and your sister everything a person could ever want. And I've got the bills to prove it.

All I want is a little respect in my own house. You don't know what love is. Just you wait till you have children. You'll see, you'll put out and you'll put out and then get nothing back."

"You've gotten nothing back, is that it?" Shut up Naomi, the grown-up person in her head said. Don't say a word, the big girl cajoled, silence is golden. But the little-girl voice, for some reason, was louder and somewhere Naomi heard that little girl screaming something about talking to them was like talking to walls made of glass covered with tar. Dark, impenetrable. She could feel the grown-up being drowned in thick pea soup. Soon she could not hear her at all, only some high little voice punctuated by tears and heavy breaths.

Sol pushed his chair to the ground. His eyes were not the loving cow eyes of the daddy she loved, he had gone away a long time ago. There was so much heat, so much intensity in that room that even Jasmine, standing at the edge of the kitchen door watching, looked fearful. It had gone beyond where it should have gone, and Naomi was sure that either Sol would hit her or push her or kill her or storm out of the room.

He was about to do the latter, when the little girl ran past him, collected her bag and her jacket from the hall closet, and rushed out into the night, a bit unsteady on her feet, a bit unsteady in her head. She didn't look back but ran down Park Avenue looking for a cab, vowing up and down, swearing inside and out she would never never return to that house again, anniversary or not.

41

"So I blew it."

Naomi had awoken Matthew out of a sound sleep. She had waited until he turned the light on, got a cigarette, puffed up his pillows, maybe got rid of a girl. Naomi couldn't be sure. Then she told him the whole story.

She had wanted to call him only after she had made peace with her demons. It hadn't worked out that way. She had blown it, that's what she had done.

"What happened, kiddo?"

It had been several weeks since they had spoken.

"I had too much to drink and I feel foolish and behaved abysmally. Some little girl just took over the whole show. And why didn't you answer my letter?"

"Naomi, I wanted us both to be alone for a while. I didn't want to hear your voice or even your written voice. And I wanted you to think some things out on your own."

Naomi sighed. Heavy weltschmerz of a sigh.

"They make me feel so helpless. I can't get a word in about my feelings. They want to run my life. Every time I spend some time with them I remember why I keep running off to a new country, a new continent. I have no sense of self when I'm around them."

She caught her breath.

"Matthew, are you missing me?"

"Yes."

Assured, she continued. "Sometimes I feel they're going to kill me. That I can't survive them. My sense of humor just disappears around them."

"What a lot of hogwash. What a lot of crap." Matthew had heard just about enough.

"Stop it already. Stop blaming them for your life. You're going to be thirty-six years old and it's time you take it on yourself, for who you are, what you do or say. I mean, Christ it's enough already. You can't keep on blaming. It's their ballgame for about the first five years and then there's a lot of decisions and actions we make on our own. Passé, blaming them, out of style. Get pissed, fine, tell them what it is you want them to know, then forgive. Forgive yourself, Naomi. You've got so much guilt it's pouring off you like sweat. Then forgive them."

There was silence.

"Are you there, kiddo? What are you thinking about."

"I'm here." Naomi was suddenly sober. "I'm listening. Helene wants me to do a story on women in Russia."

"Terrific. Don't change the subject. Listen, so your parents give you a hard time. So they don't know how to be different. It's too late for them to learn. Can you get that into your thick pretty head. *They are not going to change.* There's only one other person in that triangle, and that's you. So either you change, or keep holding on to all this shit. One or the other."

He kept listening for breathing.

"Are you there?"

"I'm here."

"Okay. The important thing is to let them know you're not them, that from here on out you do not need them for all the things they think you need them for, but that it is still possible for you all to live on this planet with some regard and possible respect for one another.

"What the fuck are you screaming about? What the hell do you want, that you do not have or cannot get? Cancer, war, choking to death on a piece of filet mignon, it's all the fucking same. You try to live with the knowledge you will die. By your age and mine we should have accomplished enough so that we can go gracefully into the great whirl of a beyond with a sense that we are indeed ahead of the game on almost every count."

Matthew was going for broke. Naomi bit her lip as she felt his trembling, his passion careening through the phone. It was an avalanche. But she listened. For once she did not try to interrupt.

"Naomi. I miss you too. There's a light that's gone out around here. But I'm not settling, kiddo. I'm sorry. I know that I want to make a complete commitment, it's the only way I can go now and hope to do so if I feel that's what I can get back. If that's the case, I know me, I'll go like a big tree.

"I don't know what's going to happen to us. I don't know. I am not happy without you. But you have to do what you have to do. Make your big party. Go and take a present, or don't go, and send a present. Let them sit there and piss and moan about the ungratefulness of their kids and see how they go into the long night full of shit like that. But also, Naomi, Naomi take the risk to do what the hell you want to for them, in their regard, lovingly, whatever it is that is truly in your heart. Do you honestly know?

"You make this all sound like World War III. It isn't. Naomi, you've got to let go. We don't have a chance if you don't. Let go of them, of your resentments, let them go, set them free like some pigeons on a Brooklyn rooftop. And forgive your folks. Listen to me. Are you awake?"

"Barely."

"Good. Listen hard. By not forgiving them, you stay irrevocably tied to them. You stay dependent on them. All your righteous indignation isn't worth a shit. All your retaliation fantasies, all your clever remarks designated to hurt, don't mean a damn. You think you get energy from all that anger? Well, it's sapping you dry, kiddo. Draining you. I know you think that if you forgive them it means they win. Kiddo, it's the other way around. If you forgive them, you're no longer attached. They got no more power over you. And you might even be able to love them, if you accept them the way they are. If you finally accept deep down that they're never going to be the fantasy parents you think you want. Accept, Naomi. Accept them the way they are. And go on about your business."

Naomi could not stop the trembling.

"That all sounds very Christian and turning the other cheek to me."

"Double bullshit. I'm not saying the Jews should forgive the Nazis. Fuck 'em. I don't even think they should ever forget, no less forgive. Don't get me wrong, some things can't be forgiven. But Naomi, a lot can. And it can give release. I'm telling you. I know."

"I hear you. Stop yelling."

"And you know what, to go back to the original theme we've been playing variations on, if he touched you, old Sol, deal with that, finally lay that to rest too, Naomi. Get rid of the ghosts. When I'm in bed with you I want you to know that that's me, Matthew Johnson, there holding you. Not your father and not your ox husband and not all the other schmucks who betrayed you or didn't betray you, who you know deep down are going to go off and leave you for some tootsie. No more threesomes, Naomi. Think about that.

"I can't talk anymore, my throat hurts. I'm even tired of the sound of my own voice. A kiss on the tip of your nose. Ciao."

Naomi was wide awake. His words were stinging in her ears. The man was such a know-it-all. So what if it all made incredible sense.

Actually, the simplest thing in the world would be to just go to Russia. Just hop on a plane. That's what Oriana Fallaci would probably do.

42

The June issue of *Woman Today* was on the stands. Helene had received phone calls from several congresswomen, half a dozen psychiatrists, and since the phone numbers of several incest survivor groups from all over the country were printed in the issue, several of the groups called to say that their calls had tripled. Helene was ecstatic. She wanted Naomi to get to work immediately on the story about women in Russia. But Naomi kept stalling. For the first time in her whole professional career, she didn't want to do anything. So she made a date with Janie, and Becky came along.

While Janie went up and down on the carousel at the zoo, the Lazurus sisters traveled in a more sedate manner, reclining on one of the chariots behind the dashing stallion Janie had chosen. They were on their fifth ride, but Janie was indefatigable. Saturday mornings, Sol used to take the girls to the very same carousel.

"God, I don't even think they've changed the music on this thing." Naomi put her feet up on the empty seat opposite them. "Sol used to love to take us here."

"Sol used to love to take *you* here. I never came much." Becky was tight lipped.

"What are you talking about? You were here every time I was here."

"Bullshit. I don't know what kind of memory you have, but it's off somewhere. I used to hate the carousel, and I'd get vertigo going up and down all the time, and Sol preferred being alone with you anyway."

Life was getting a little much for Naomi. What was all this about?

"Since when have you decided that?"

"I always knew that. Usually it's always the dumpling, the little roly-poly one that's the favored. Our family wasn't like that. I hear it's your turn on the black list this week."

"We're not speaking if that's what you mean."

"I have been to the Lower East Side with Mom where we chose the dried fruit, decided on flowers at the flower market. We chose the room in the hotel, the menu, we even auditioned four orchestras."

"We aren't talking, how can I help if we aren't talking?"

"I don't know why you always let them get to you. I just don't pay any attention. I'm not going to get an ulcer over them. I'm not like you, I can control my anger."

"Sure, it all goes into your food binges."

"So what. I don't care. I'll never forgive them anyway, so what's the difference."

"Forgive them for what?"

The man came around for the tickets. Janie turned around and waved as she gave the man hers. Becky gave him two.

"Oh, I've got a list a mile long. I'll never forgive them for letting me stay a fat kid, never forgive them for not giving me a trust fund." She looked hard at Naomi. "I'll never forgive Sol for loving you more than he does me."

"Becky. What are you talking about?"

"Look, I understand the whole thing. It's simple. You were the achiever, the smart one, the one he doted on. He always preferred you."

"But you were the baby, you were so cute. You were beautiful. Everybody loved you. God Becky, do you know I thought the bottom fell out of my world when you arrived on the scene."

"Yeah, well, I've still got the scar on my head to prove it, when you pushed me out of my high chair and I fell to the kitchen floor with a thud."

"You still remember that?"

"It's not the type of thing you forget. I mean, it took me years to forgive you."

215

Naomi was silent. She just sat there listening to "Dixie" being played over and over again on the merry-go-round. That's what happens when you stick around for a while. You start seeing things as they are.

"Becky, you can't keep blaming them, or anybody. After a while you have to . . ."

"Take responsibility for myself? If I hear that one more time I'll puke. I do blame them, and I love them and I feel sorry for them. But I was the victim. I was this innocent little kid . . ."

"Becky, but you're not now."

"Don't you blame them for all your neurotic tics?"

Naomi felt her heart beat faster.

"Not so much anymore. It's boring feeling the victim, Becky. I'm beginning to see that now."

"Bullshit, you were never a victim, you had it made."

"Becky, I could be in Afghanistan and they'd still have some power over me. But I'm beginning to see how crazy that is. Blaming goes nowhere."

"If the folks will spring for it I may go back to school," Becky said after a long silence.

"Becky, that's great."

"You think they will?"

"I don't see why not."

"He's so weird about money." The music was winding down. Janie turned around and mouthed "Just one more." Becky nodded all right. She got up and walked over to Janie's proud horse and gave Janie her ticket; she kissed the top of her head before she came back.

"Isn't this great, Naomi," Janie shouted over the music.

"Fabulous," Naomi shouted back.

Becky watched Naomi give Janie a loving glance. "You think you'll ever have any of your own kids?" Becky was never one to beat around the bush.

Too loaded. Naomi wasn't going to get into that.

But Becky moved right in.

"You know what I think? I think you're scared to have kids. I really think you look at Mom and you look at me and you are scared shitless about the kind of mother you'd make."

Naomi looked at her sister. She remembered the last time she babysat and had spent the weekend when Becky had gone to a fasting place upstate. She shouldn't have, but Naomi had peeked into the journal that Becky had neglected to put away. She read one paragraph and could never forget it. "I will not look at my body in the mirror," it began. "I am so grotesque that I repel even myself. I cannot stop eating. It is fascinating to me when this compulsion takes over, like some kind of demon who creeps into my brain. Eat, eat, my child, eat everything in sight. I cannot stop it. I have no power over it. Tonight I went into the freezer and ate four frozen apple tarts. They were freezing and the apple part hurt my teeth. I could barely taste anything except the cold and a little tartness from the apple. It wasn't enough. It is never enough, only when I cannot move, when my stomach feels as though there were a baby inside, when it is so taut and tight and pulled across my front, and the belly button distends, like when Janie was inside—only then can I move off the chair, only then when I know that I cannot put another bite into my mouth can I go to sleep. Only then am I full. Tonight I dragged myself upstairs and put my fingers down my throat and threw the whole thing up. And in the morning I will pray not to be hungry, pray that the demon in my head will have left me. But it never does . . ."

Naomi leaned over next to her sister. She did not want to shout over the music.

"Becky," she said softly into her ear. "I'm sorry I pushed you out of the high chair. It was really hard on me when you were born. I was Queen of the May, I'd been the only one there for four years. I had had them all to myself. And then this beautiful baby came and that's why I pushed you out of the high chair and that's why I used to get into the crib with you. I used to want to sleep in the crib so bad. God, I wanted to be a baby again."

Becky, her defense and her offense shattered, denied herself her resentment for the moment, and patted her sister's knee.

43

It had been quite a morning. First the man sitting next to Naomi on the subway had a fine time masturbating to her reflection in the window. Right there, under the lights, under the empty stares of weary riders, carrying paperbacks, cake boxes, newspapers. He thought he was fooling her because he wouldn't look at her, only at the glass. Who did he think he was kidding? She slunk down into her magazine, moved around, put on lipstick. But nothing deterred him from his morning constitutional.

Then on Fifth Avenue and Fifty-third Street, just as she was going to turn into the block, a young man twirling along with his radio to his ear looked her right in the eye, touched his penis with his free hand, taking time away from Blondie to muse, "Lookin' at you makes my dick get hard."

Naomi sought refuge in the cool and calm of the Museum of Modern Art, away from the masses and decadence of the street. She paused in the outdoor restaurant for a cup of coffee, when a well-dressed, bearded young man asked her if he could join her. She really wanted to be alone but reluctantly nodded her head yes. He was delighted and pulled up a chair and began to chat about this and that. He had an attaché case and a newspaper, certainly the accouterments of respectability. So Naomi felt at least buffered from the indignity of the streets.

Suddenly the drift of the conversation came around to didn't she think that a tank resembled a womb with a penis sticking out of it, and didn't the world remind her of one great ejaculation. Moments later, when he referred to his profession, writing books, as being like spreading your legs for whomever comes along, Naomi decided to excuse herself and move on out. New York, New York, it's a wonderful town. She took refuge in front of a cool Cézanne, whose blues and aquas proved to be the only sanity of the morning.

So she roamed. She walked out onto the street, content to meander. She wanted to hold Matthew's arm. She wanted to share the sweetness of the day with him, she wanted to go into a store and buy him an outrageous hat. She wanted to love him. She wanted to trust him.

But she kept her distance. And her silence. She caught a glimpse of herself in the Dunhill window. Tall, slim, lovely. She liked herself. Finally.

When she passed Rockefeller Center there was a crowd gathered. She was propelled toward the center of it, and there was one of the myriad of unexpected New York miracles. In the middle of everything, in the middle of a warm day with flags flying and out-of-towners gawking, awed by Saint Patrick's and excited by the pulse and preponderance of people, there in the middle of it all was Bobby Short. Sitting on a platform that had been erected for the day, there he was, suave and urbane, cool as a cucumber, singing and playing the piano.

As the crowd around him, not the usual Carlyle crowd to say the least, was applauding and mouthing "I'll Take Manhattan" with him, tears formed in Naomi's eyes for this lovely treat in the middle of the day in the middle of Rockefeller Center. She got so teary her mascara stung her eyes, and the back of her hand was black from wiping the wet off her cheeks.

Short was wearing black boots and well-cut jeans, a blue blazer with a jaunty red carnation in the lapel. "What I Did for Love," he sang to the rapt faces, his slim fingers snapping the beat when he would take one hand off the piano, and the old man next to Naomi carrying a newspaper knew every single word. She wanted Matthew to share this with her. She wanted to hold his arm and kiss his ear, she wanted to trust him, she wanted to love him.

Abruptly she went into the nearest coffee shop and called her service. Perhaps he had called, perhaps there would be a message from Matthew.

Two messages, the service said. Your mother called. And your father called. Naomi took a deep breath and started turning it over, the new leaf, that is. She closed the door to the telephone booth. Matthew's words were ringing in her ears.

"Hi, Mom."

"Oh sweetheart, I'm so glad you returned my call so promptly." Esther was speaking very fast, talking over the erased tape of the nightmare dinner. "I wanted you to know I just ordered twenty-five copies of your magazine with your articles in them. Naomi, I think they're wonderful. You do write well. You really do. I'm so proud of you."

"Well, thank you, thanks a lot, Mother."

"You know what I felt bad about? I just felt so bad Grandma wasn't alive to see your name plastered all over the issue and the wonderful picture of you. It is becoming. You know the way my mother loved that kind of thing. She would call up all her friends, you know? Naomi?"

"Yes, Mom."

"Do you think that's really true? Like you said in the story, that a lot of times the mother is collusive and knows what the father is doing to those poor little girls? That's so sad, Naomi."

"I know, Mom. I know."

"Well, I just want to congratulate you, dear."

There was a vague moment of silence. And Esther mumbled goodbye.

Naomi deliberated. She ran her fingers through her hair, played with her earring. She had to move on. She knew Matthew was right. She had to let it go. The ice maiden was beginning to crack. She had never loved before. Before Daddy. She had to forgive him, she had to be free. But Sol was Sol. Not the easiest person in the world to forgive, or to let go.

Naomi dialed her father's number.

"Hi, Dad."

"Who's this?"

"It's me, Dad. Naomi."

"Right. How are you, girl? Look, your mother showed me your articles in the magazine. I didn't get to finish them yet, but they seem really good."

"Thanks, Dad."

"How come the poor old dad is always the villain in those stories?"

"Well, it's just . . ."

"Anyway, I wanted to congratulate you." He sounded very guarded.

"Well, thanks Dad. Thanks a . . ."

"Well, that's about it, that's what I wanted."

Naomi shut her eyes, played with the hair on top of her head.

"Dad, what are you doing?"

"What do you mean, what am I doing? Today? Now?"

"Right."

"Have an appointment with Larry about some real estate, then have to go to the doctor. He checks me up every time I turn around."

"I'm planning to be at the zoo in about an hour, by the carousel."

"So?"

"So why don't you get to Sixty-fourth Street and buy me an ice cream cone?"

Never had Sol Lazurus been so taken aback.

"You what?"

"Ice cream. In a cone? Vanilla."

"Sure, Naomi. Sure. Just like the old days. Well, I can't possibly be there for another two hours. Can you be there in two?"

Naomi delighted at the thought of more roaming around.

"Two hours, at the carousel."

"See you." There was a note of excitement in Sol's voice.

Two hours later Naomi was riding a newly painted horse with a red and yellow mane. She was the only grown-up on the carousel but didn't feel odd at all. It was probably the first day in years she had no plans, no appointments, no assignments. She just moved, put one foot in front of the other, and wherever it took her that's where she went.

She had gone into Saint Patrick's Cathedral and had sat there, cooled, made quiet by the hum, and the height; she had gone into Tiffany's and priced a few things, with as much hauteur and Jackie O. imperiousness as she could muster; she had walked over to the Plaza and heard the tea-time musicians in their frock coats playing Fritz Kreisler. She was having the most romantic time, all by herself. She ordered a charlotte russe and made a request for the violinist to play "Core Ingrato." And then she had ridden the horse with the red and yellow mane till her father came.

There he was, standing there in the same spot. Every time she made the circle on the merry-go-round there he would be with his hat on this warm day, perched at a jaunty angle on his head. Sol's shoulders sloped, but his hair was very thick and white. He got smaller and smaller, standing in the very same place, every time she went round and round.

"So aren't you sorry you made such a fuss the other night? Meanwhile, by not talking to us, you got out of doing a lot of work. That was pretty shrewd."

"It would be lovely if we could keep the fights down to a minimum, Dad. Let's get an ice cream."

Naomi's father took her arm as they walked. He had to lean on her because it was hard for him to keep up.

"We make quite a pair, don't we? Speaking for myself, I'm proud to be with the best looking broad on Sixty-fourth Street." She flushed in spite of herself. He bought her vanilla ice cream on a stick with chocolate coating. He had an almond fudge.

"Years ago they had lucky sticks. If you got a stick that said lucky on it once you ate your way to the bottom, you'd get a free popsicle."

"You look tired, Dad. Want to sit down on the bench?"

Naomi shooed some pigeons away from an empty bench. They sat down and ate in silence. Neither quite knew what to do with this unexpected meeting. This enforced intimacy.

"When I was courting your mother all I could buy her was ice cream. That was the big treat. I was making thirty-five dollars a week when we got married."

"She must have been cute when you got married."

"As a button. Different. She was very feminine. Sexy."

He continued to eat his popsicle. Naomi took a Kleenex out of her bag and wiped his mouth.

"Thanks." He stopped eating for a moment.

"I brought you something." Sol took a manila envelope out of his pocket.

"What is it?"

"Something I found when I was cleaning my desk." Sol licked his almond fudge. "Don't open it now. Read it when you get home. And don't tell your mother I gave it to you."

Naomi couldn't imagine what it was. She put it in her purse. She forced herself to talk.

"I was really upset the other night, Dad."

"No kidding."

"It goes back a long time, a long way."

"Naomi. We're quiet This is really nice. Don't make waves."

Don't make waves.

"You really liked my pieces?"

"A lot. I can't believe that incest stuff happens. In Jewish families too it happens? That I doubt."

"All over. Rich, poor. All over. Crosses all economic and racial barriers."

"Unbelievable."

"Dad . . ."

"What? That was a delicious ice cream. I haven't had one of those in years . . ."

"How did you feel when I started to grow up, I mean like when I was twelve or thirteen and got my period and started to look like a woman?"

Sol was on the defensive. Like a cat he was.

"What do you mean, how was I? I was fine. You weren't any different. Only better looking."

"I mean, was it hard for you to have me grow up, and grow breasts and everything." Naomi didn't know where she was getting the courage for this conversation.

"What is this, am I being interviewed or something?"

"Of course not Dad, it's just that as I was writing this article and interviewing all those people, I started remembering stuff I had put away for a long time."

Sol put his hands in his lap.

"I don't know, Naomi. You're a queer bird. I mean, let's face it you are. Here you come from a happy home. How many people do you know whose parents are still married and still are crazy about each other like we are? Nobody. Kids who come out of families like that are supposed to be well adjusted and make great marriages and be loving, terrific people."

"Daddy. Sometimes I felt like the other woman."

"I have no idea what you're talking about. None. What other? What woman? You are my daughter, Essie's my wife. What other woman?" Sol was bewildered. He didn't, couldn't understand.

"And let's face it." Sol shook his finger at her. "Automatically when I say blue you say green. Let me tell you, that's kind of tiring to live with."

"We used to be very close when I was little."

"Listen, all the fathers used to play golf on Saturdays but I would take my little mommalee and we'd go everywhere. But everywhere. You were my first born, my little mommalee. We'd go to the horse races and I'd take you to the fights. Your mother hated the fights. And you were so cuddly and loving. Always gave me lots of kisses and hugs.

"And we were pals. You know? We were really pals. You'd confide all your secrets to me and hold my hand in the movies and how I loved my little girl. I loved you more than the world. I'd hold you and cuddle you and put you to bed at night and sing to you and read you to sleep. I did it more than your mother because she might have been busy doing something else, but it didn't matter because I loved doing it.

"So and then you started pulling away and started to talk to Jake Gold the optometrist, what a shtarke that guy was, and you trusted him with all your secrets and you hurt me. I felt left out. My little girl went and left me."

"Daddy, I was the one who . . ."

"And then you got sullen and kind of mean, and wouldn't let me come near you. I just wanted to hug and kiss you like I always had. You always make fun of me because I'm so sentimental and nostalgic. But Naomi, family, that's all we have in this world. I try so hard to hold on to what's left, so many gone, so many, and that's why when our little family fights it makes me so sick. I've only got two brothers left, a few cousins. That's it. And I never had sons. Now that was hard for me, Naomi. Nobody with my name. You were like a son to me at the beginning. You were so smart and picked up things so fast, and there was a time I thought I would leave the business to you, but you made it perfectly clear that the last thing in the world you wanted was to go in business with me. So I sold it."

He looked out into space.

Naomi put her hand on his arm. She forced herself to speak. The words came slowly and she could barely hear herself.

"Dad, can I ask you something. I have to know. I mean, it's a thing I have to ask you."

Sol looked at her.

"When I was, I mean before I grew up, did you ever touch me, hold me, I mean, as though I was a woman and not a girl?"

Naomi looked away. She could not look straight into his eyes.

"I get this feeling you did, that you didn't mean to. that you always loved me. I know you always loved me, but I get this feeling that you went too far, that you, you did something to me sexually, Dad? Daddy?"

There were tears in Naomi's eyes. The afternoon had broken in two for her. The sun burned a scarlet *N* onto her chest.

She turned and looked at Sol.

"Are you crazy or something? You mean like those men in your article?" Sol's cheeks were burning. "You're kidding, right? You always did have an imagination as big as an ice rink. I can't believe what I just heard. You were my baby girl, my love. I don't know what you're talking about, Naomi. Not at all. You really do have a crazy streak. You know that? Sometimes I worry about you."

"Dad."

"And besides, I always had my Essie, always. You were my daughter, Essie was my bride."

Daddy, you touched me. Somewhere, somehow where you shouldn't have. I know it. I just know it. You didn't know, you didn't realize. When you roughhoused with me, and held me too long maybe, it mixed me all up. You didn't know. You just didn't know. It doesn't matter now, I'll let it go. I swear I'll let it go. But I know that you moved on me in a way that made me so uncomfortable. I have no proof but it hurts me somewhere and I've had to undo it in a million ways ever since. Daddy, let's go to the races. Daddy, let's go to the fights and smell the sweat and the bodies in the Jamaica Arena and let's go to the movies and I will hide my head in your big strong arm. And we will hold hands in the movies and my daddy will always protect me and my daddy will always take care of me.

No he won't. No more. No more.

"See, you were this beautiful little girl, sensitive and kind. Dear, good-natured. The sweetest child I'd ever known. How I loved you, Naomi. And then how you hurt me. You retreated, you went away and you never came back."

Gone were the rages in the eyes, the cow eyes returned. Sol looked bewildered. He tried. He took Naomi's hand and kissed it. He was her daddy. She would forgive him.

Naomi kissed her father.

"Come on Dad, let's go home. I'll walk you home."

44

Naomi went to a movie by herself and reached her own apartment at about ten o'clock. She sat down at her dining room table, and remembering, took out of her bag the manila envelope, the one Sol had given her in the park. Without taking off her jacket she opened it. Inside was a small notebook with lined pages and some neat Palmer method writing in it. At first she thought it was one of her old school exam books, but when Naomi began to read she realized it was a yellowing journal Esther had kept when Naomi was a baby. She didn't remember ever having seen the book before. Once she began reading, she realized why Sol, on finding it, had wanted her to read it. It was Esther's baby book, the one she had kept when Naomi was an infant.

She began reading.

"June 5, 1947: Naomi crawls and turns around constantly in her playyard. She says da das and makes a funny horsey sound. Probably imitating Sol when he kisses her. She eats all kinds of vegetables, soup three times weekly, desserts, stewed fruits. She is a friendly baby. Seems to have a sense of humor. Smiles almost constantly. Not pretty but has loads of personality, so think her proud parents. She's brown as a nut and very firm, skin soft as rose petals, utterly delectable to kiss. Occupies herself continually. She is self-sufficient. Needs no restless amusement, a miracle to behold. I think myself very fortunate in having such a piece of joy. Only delicious babies make me believe in something immortal."

Naomi moved into the living room. She lay down on the couch, making the light a bit brighter. There was a tightening in her chest.

"June 21, 1947: Naomi is nine months old today. (Actually I am faking a little. It's really June 23 now, but to write on her birthday is kind of motherish and sentimental.) She stands. I'm thrilled to death. I love that kid. She shakes bye-bye at the mere word. She plays for hours and hours by herself. She tries to suck her thumb but I try to divert her attention, putting a toy in her hand or talking to her. We took her to the beach today and she was much admired. 'What a pretty boy' everyone said. She has the best nature. Good tempered and easy. Sol's undoubtedly. So happy she's ours. It hardly seems possible."

Naomi could read no more. She put her arm over her eyes. So many years ago. Thirty-four. Esther was about her age then. Why couldn't she remember that joy Esther had had in her? Why wasn't it a visceral recall? Why weren't they friends anymore? She felt overwhelmingly sad.

She washed up and changed into a pair of jeans. She threw her bag over her shoulder and went out again.

One half hour later Naomi walked into her mother's dressing room.

"Mom?"

"Here. I'm here."

Naomi walked into the room and sat down on the ottoman of the needlepoint chair opposite her mother. Esther almost disappeared into the vastness of the easy chair.

Esther reached over to a jar of cold cream resting on the table by the chair. She creamed her face absently, wiping the residue off with cotton balls.

"Feeling a little tired, Mom?"

"A little." She got up to go into the bathroom for her bottle of astringent. She was dwarfed by her silk nightgown. Esther faded into the voluminous folds of the gown. She was so small.

"How nice. Let's talk softly. Your father's asleep in the bedroom. Was there any special reason for this nice visit?"

"I don't know. I thought you might want to talk, the night before your big do and all."

Naomi got up to let her pass. She towered. As usual. It was

hard to tower over your mother. Esther returned with the bottle, put it on her desk and began wiping her face.

"Forty years," she said. "It can't be. I remember the night I was married. I remember I had so many dreams, Naomi. I felt we could do anything. You know?"

"I know, Mom."

"I believe in my dreams Naomi, and I'm a fighter. I'm fighting all the time. You know that about me. It's why your father needs me so. I help him believe in himself. I never let him give in."

"I know, Mother."

Naomi leaned back in the chair.

"Any chance of your staying over tonight, Naomi?"

A silence.

"Would you like me to?"

"Sol goes to bed so early. It's quiet in this big apartment. Lonely. I'm a little lonely."

Naomi had so much to do.

"Sure. Can I borrow a nightgown?"

"Take the blue one. Here." She opened her drawer and gave Naomi a simple cotton gown. "I'm going to have another brandy, want one?"

"No thanks . . . no, maybe I will. Might help me sleep."

Esther tried to bend forward to pour her daughter a glass, but, misjudging, almost dropped the crystal decanter filled with Courvoisier. Naomi caught it in time. She poured herself a drink.

Esther was tipsy. Nothing wild or outrageous. Naomi had seen her mother drink before; usually at dusk. Dusk was a hard time for Esther. For Naomi too. It was an impossible time and Naomi always made it her business to be somewhere on her way to, or coming from, no matter where she was in the world at that time of day. It seemed to be Esther's time to drink, delicately, carefully, the pinky always outstretched, nibbling a cracker with some Brie on it from a silver tray at the same time; it was all very acceptable behavior. But in these last years Naomi noticed that Esther, in her exquisite ladylike fashion, used Scotch as a way of dealing with a lot of feelings; feelings about a baby that grew up perhaps, feelings about a dusk that brought

229

with it not so much the promise of an evening but an organic sense of loss.

Naomi understood. That triggering automatic push-button pain of dusk. The clock striking six and down it ran . . . hickory dickory dock. And down it runs, the terror, from the inside of the brain to the pit of the stomach. Empty. Frightened. Of what. Dusk demons, those dragons of dusk.

In New York the trigger was worse. Alone. An astronaut alone, wandering floating in emptiness. In California the dusks had been gentler to Naomi, the pinks tender, making six o'clock a softer time. The clock struck six there too, but with a benign more cushioning sound. The purples were pale there, but not startling. There was no glare, no brilliance, the smog and exhaust muting the sky. California dusk came gradually; with grace.

But the trigger was there all the same, the stomach remembering something her mind could not. Coming home from school, cooking smells, Daddy not home yet smells, alone, suddenly dark smells.

And Esther, what was dusk to Esther?

"Mom, you ought to go to bed."

"I guess so. I'll have a little more brandy and then turn in. You want some? What is it that you came over for, Naomi?"

"Just wanted to say hello."

"Well that's nice. That's really nice, Naomi. Sorry I'm so tired." Esther smoothed the cream under her eyes.

"I'm tired too. I'll put the nightgown on. I'll be back in a minute to say goodnight. Okay?"

Naomi went into her old room. Wearily she took off her clothes and put on the girlish nightgown her mother had given her. It smelled of Esther. Naomi loved the smell. It smelled familiar, floral. She folded her slacks, looked around the room. So many days and so many nights planning and scheming in this room. Dreaming. Dreaming of fame and glory and faraway places, and now she had achieved much of it. She was back where she had started. And her mother was down the hall in a voluminous gown, needing to talk, unable to talk, needing her daughter who also seemed unable to reach out.

But perhaps it wasn't too late. Matthew said it was never too late. Matthew. Naomi stamped her foot. How she missed that goddamn man. Damn him. He should know how she is feeling. She wanted to be wise and whole for him. Matthew, I am thinking about you. I am thinking about my mother. So lonely in these big rooms, that bed. Shrinking. Everyone is shrinking. So little time to make up. So little time to be friends.

Naomi walked back into her mother's room.

"I'll see you in the morning, Mom. Have a good night's sleep." It was hard to say anything else, even though there was so much to say.

Naomi went to Esther. She had to bend to embrace her. Her mother's head came into the curve in Naomi's neck, between the chin and the chest.

Suddenly Esther shivered.

"Naomi, I'm cold. I'm so cold."

Esther seemed to need the brandies to reach out. To hold Naomi.

"Warm me. Make me warm, Naomi. You're so warm."

And so she held her mother that way, smelling the cold cream and the astringent, the perfume from the gown, the mommy smells, the nighttime smells.

Into Naomi's throat, Esther said, "Sometimes I don't know if he'll be alive when we wake up in the morning. I feel his body next to me to make sure it's warm. I need warmth from you to help keep him warm. There's life here. You have so much life, Naomi."

Naomi kissed her mother. She held her again. Felt her softness.

Esther was afraid of dying.

It wasn't until Naomi had brushed her teeth and cold creamed her own face and put out the light that she let it happen. The tears. So many tears. Esther had felt so small. There was so much shadow, so much dusk between Naomi and love, and her mother, and love.

45

Janie couldn't stop jumping.

She just kept making these little jumps in place. Naomi pinched her bottom, the bottom encased in white frilly panties under her light organza dress. Janie looked like Alice in Wonderland, hair evenly trimmed, shiny and clean, her dress simple, white Mary Janes freshly polished.

"Stand still," Naomi said in a hoarse whisper.

"I can't. I'm so excited I'm going to die. Bruce Springsteen's coming tonight, you know."

"Who said?"

"Grandpa."

"He's pulling your leg."

"He wasn't pulling anything. He said."

"Grandpa kids, you should know that by now."

Janie and Naomi were the first to arrive in the room. Esther and Sol were upstairs in the hotel somewhere, and Becky was home having trouble with her dress. It had ripped as she was dressing. Now she was sewing and ironing it at the last minute. Janie was all electricity, unable to sit still, so Naomi and she went early to the Pierre.

The room looked magical. Esther's taste had indeed been flawless. Yellows and greens, gossamer ribbons on each table, on the ceilings. Flowers, flowers everywhere, and again on each table an abundance of fruit and bread, bottles of wine. Janie caught her breath.

"It looks like fairyland."

"No thanks to me," Naomi said ruefully.

"What?"

"Just talking to myself."

"What did you answer back?"

"Don't be such a smart-ass."

They stood there, hand in hand, as waiters scurried about, laying the tables, sweeping the dance floor. Janie was unquestionably Princess Grace even though the party wasn't for her. She let go of Naomi's hand and walked slowly out to the dance floor which had been polished to a high gloss. The short jacketed waiters paused to see the blond little girl with the round belly hidden by her organza dress twirl herself on the shining floor, in the yellow and green room of princess dreams.

In a moment it would all change, in a moment the liquor would flow and the music would start, and mountains of food would emerge. In a moment Sol and Esther would have their day. But now, in this second, watching Janie dancing to the music in her head, holding her own elbows, Naomi felt calm. It was going to be all right. For the first time, she knew it.

And suddenly it began; there was music, and Sol and Esther were in the center of their magical room, kissing cheeks, greeting guests. From all over they came, from Denver and Paris, from Miami and Minneapolis. The few aunts who were left came. Naomi loved the aunts. The old ladies had worked hard all their lives, were tough, feisty and funny. Every year at weddings and funerals the aunts seemed to get smaller, their hair redder, their fingers bonier. But they squeezed Naomi and breathed cigarette breath onto her and told her how proud they were when they saw her name written in a magazine. Because she never felt comfortable with her new teeth, Aunt Tessie never bothered to wear them and this occasion was no exception. But it did not hinder her raucous laughter as she regaled whomever was in earshot with her ribald exploits as a young girl in the Yiddish Theater.

The champagne flowed and Naomi was pulled here by her mother ("my famous daughter, the journalist") pulled there by her father ("isn't she gorgeous"). Becky had arrived and was deep in conversation with a cousin from Arizona who said there were great investments to be made out there. Becky had wisely dressed very simply in black and had pinned her hair up, which made her face look slimmer. She looked very pretty. Janie dashed from one embrace to another, squeezed and pinched and bitten by the crush of attention squandered on her by doting relatives. There were a few young children her age, sons and daughters of distant relatives, so Janie hobnobbed, feeling very much the royalty of the day.

Matthew, you should be here. Matthew, it is not right that I should be here alone. Naomi was furious at him. She had called the day before and today several times and there was no answer. This was not a time to unplug the phone. The man was so perverse. What was he thinking about? To see what would happen, she had given Matthew's name and address to her mother and assumed the invitation had been sent along with the other zillion envelopes.

People drank and ate hors d'oeuvres for about an hour as Esther and Sol held court. Naomi watched them from afar; they glowed, their joy shone in the room. Forty years.

"They sure are having a ball, aren't they?" Becky appeared at her elbow.

"I can't imagine living with one person for forty years," Naomi said. "In the old days nobody expected to live that long, so marriages would last for a few years until people died off at thirty."

"Too long. I swear, it's unnatural staying with someone that long," Becky said. "Naomi . . ."

"Yes . . ."

"I decided to split custody. A few weeks at my place, a few weeks there. Some visits in between. We had a talk. The first good talk since the divorce."

"Becky, I'm so glad. How come?"

"Janie told me her friend Caroline had two beds and two toothbrushes. She thinks the idea's cool."

"Becky . . ."

"That's what she said. Look, we can't talk here. Go mingle. That's what she said, you know." And Becky wandered off.

"Here she is, the older one." Janette Graham, one of Esther's acquaintances from one of her charities, hovered over Naomi. "Your folks are really something else. You must be so proud."

"I am. I really am."

"Naomi, there she is." Esther rushed over, breathless. "Darling, the Granites. They came . . . All the way . . ."

Naomi kissed some familiar faces from eons ago, an elegant matched pair of diamonds and silks.

"I can't believe you came, all the way from . . ."

"Naomi, remember Stan. Stan Stan the ice cream man, we used to call him . . ." Sol was slapping Stan from Cannes, that Stan from many moons ago, as he dragged him over to see her. Sol put his hands on both their backs and pushed them together. "Stan's one of my oldest friends you know, you remember him, don't you? Last time we saw you was at Christmas, Stan."

In a moment Sol was gone, flushed from the wine, flushed from the loveliness of everything. Stan gave Naomi a small kiss on her cheek, admiring her dress.

"You look great, must be doing something right."

"I'm fine Stan, how are you?"

A lovely young thing sidled up to Stan's left elbow.

"Nicole, this is Naomi Lazurus, Sol's daughter."

"Enchantée."

She was beautiful, and very young.

"Hello, Nicole."

Stan was still very heavy, but he looked tan and prosperous, two things that made him happy. As Naomi looked at the space between him and Nicole the room became a blur of pastels and gossamer, the sounds of Russian folk music mingling with the hum of chatter, laughter and clinking glasses, and through the blur there was someone standing in the doorway who looked very familiar.

Casual, the person was casual, sort of leaning against the doorway as though he just happened to be passing through on his way to a roundup. In between Nicole and Stan, Naomi saw the person leaning up against the door shaking hands with Sol. He towered over Sol, but her father put his hand high on the person's shoulder and brought him over to Esther who presided in another corner. Naomi squinted and it seemed that the person was wearing a white jacket with a red tie but she couldn't be sure. She squinted again and it seemed that the person was Matthew.

"Still pounding the old typewriter, Naomi? Didn't see you at Cannes this year."

"I was in L.A., doing a series on child molestation."

"Wow, a far cry from the Croisette, right? Nicole was there, she's in the new Truffaut film."

The girl chattered on in French with Stan looking down on her as though she were the reincarnation of Jeanne d'Arc.

From the corner of her eye Naomi saw Sol and Esther coming across the floor, and between them was Matthew Johnson wearing cowboy boots and all his finery. What did Rodgers, or was it Hart, say? "My heart stood still." It did. Naomi's heart stood still. She defied medical history at that very moment.

"This young man says he's your guest, Naomi. You didn't tell me we were having so honored a celebrity, a gentleman who has been on the best-seller list."

"Paperback," Matthew offered modestly.

Naomi saw the blue eyes. Not too bloodshot, not too many bags under them today. She saw the blue eyes, and they were dancing. Merry Kris Kringle eyes today, full of mischief and conspiracy and love. She heard her heart start up its motor again as she put two and two together for once. The man loved her. He had come all this way to her parents' party.

"Say hello to your friend, dear." Esther was interested in protocol.

"Mrs. Lazurus, I want to thank you so much for inviting me to your beautiful party. Congratulations are certainly in order. May I?" And Matthew Johnson leaned over and kissed Naomi's mother on the cheek. The man was charming the pants off them. Regardless, they'd never accept a son-in-law who wasn't Jewish. Maybe he'd convert. Hell would freeze over before Matthew Johnson would do anything against his working class origins or anti-Judeo-Christian ethic. Naomi's mind was spinning. Meanwhile, Esther was blushing and sputtering like a teenager. The whole scene was out of Kafka as far as Naomi was concerned, watching her two worlds coalesce.

"Oh excuse me, Stan." Sol took over. "This is Naomi's friend the writer, Matthew Johnson. You've heard of Matthew Johnson, I'm sure? I'm surprised *Trager* was never made into a movie. Ever read that book, Stan? Damn good read. You should look into it as property for film."

"Nice to meet you, Matt. This is Nicole Lissette."

"How do you do, Miss Lissette." Matthew kissed her hand. Naomi couldn't believe this whole scene. "Is that with two *t*s?" he asked with great interest.

"Two *t*s and two *e*s," Nicole said, making the few words sound like a love poem by Lamartine.

"Have your books been translated into French, Matt?" Stan eyed Nicole with a proprietary air as Matthew went about pouring on the Celtic Viking charm.

"About twenty-two languages," he said with his customary modesty.

"Well, it certainly is a pleasure to have you here." Sol was in seventh heaven. "Drink up, food's being served, now, you all must be starved," he said, squinting at the door. "The lady from the Mayor's office just arrived and there's Dr. and Dr. Pomerance. Let's go greet."

They begged their excuses and then, hand in hand, walked over to the doorway.

"It was lovely meeting you both." Matthew shook hands with Stan. "Naomi, I wonder if I could have this dance?" Naomi looked at Stan as though he were the man in the moon, as though he were a man who never existed. One time she had walked into a room filled with people and realized that there were five men in her line of vision with whom she had slept. Held them, kissed them, fondled them. An intimacy of sorts. And she had hardly remembered their names, hardly recalled the color of their eyes. Stan, whose last name she had forgotten, was standing next to her and she couldn't see the color of his eyes because she didn't care what the color of his eyes were. How can we have that intimacy of sorts with strangers? Strangers. The man with the beard who is standing at her right, his name is Matthew Johnson and his eyes are blue. No more Stans. No more time killers and loneliness assuagers. She was backing into it. She gave in. Finally. No more lovelessness. Matthew, I love you.

"What do you say, kid. Want to do the Texas two-step to the hora?"

The orchestra was playing "Hava Na Gila" and there was a circle of smiles as young and old in all their finery danced around the dance floor. The room was flooded with sound, music, animated chatter at the tables where masses of food were being served, steaks and chicken and curried fruit, and the wine and the champagne flowed. Sol and Esther were throwing themselves one hell of a party.

On the dance floor Matthew bundled Naomi into his arms.

"See, you go one step forward and one step back and you just hug a lot. That's how we do it down home. Come here, kiddo." Matthew held her very tight, and there, in front of Aunt Tessie with no teeth, and Dr. and Dr. Pomerance, the sex therapists, and Helene who had just arrived late standing with Essie by the main table, and Stan and his starlet, and Janie in the middle of the hora line holding on to the waist of cousin Ira who was related to them by marriage because his wife was Esther's sister Ida's daughter—in front of all of them Matthew Johnson kissed his Jewish princess.

Helene came over and Naomi introduced her to Matthew and she kept talking about women veterans and Russia. She was whisked away by Uncle Ira, but not before she told Naomi to call her first thing in the morning.

The party was very gay and by the time they got to the dessert, an enormous extravagantly decorated cake with a skyscraper of a forty on top of it, everyone was loose, giggling and reminiscing and dancing.

Meanwhile, Naomi had had about two words with Matthew, one dance, one kiss, and that was all, since he had been whisked away from her on the dance floor by Esther who wanted him to meet Herschel Adler, literary critic on *PM* years ago, now retired, who still wrote occasional reviews for the Sunday *New York Times*. Herschel and Matthew hit it off immediately and disappeared into the bar, while Naomi sat at her table and sipped her wine and ate all her steak. She danced the fox trot with Janie who led with a firm hand, and chastised her for trying to lead, since Janie was being the boy tonight.

Tessie and Sadie were the belles of the ball, dancing together and twirling each other about like Fred Astaire and Ginger Rogers playing Irene and Vernon Castle. Tessie was light on her feet and cracking jokes between sets and Naomi was whirling with it all. Yes, she was having a good time. No, all the resentments about her parents had not disappeared in a puff of smoke. But she was lighter. She was so much lighter. And she was indeed happy they were happy. She didn't mind being dragged around to meet this one and that one. It was their night.

And Matthew had come.

And gone.

Where was that man?

He makes this outrageous romantic statement and then disappears, drinking beer at the bar with an eighty-year-old literary critic. She loved him. It didn't matter. She had decided. She loved him.

The drums rolled and the trumpets blared and the master of ceremonies or orchestra leader announced that Sol and Esther were going to dance alone on the floor. Everyone applauded as they got up from their seats at the main table. Naomi saw Herschel and Matthew walking into the room, summoned by the clarion call.

The orchestra began playing "The Anniversary Waltz," and Sol and Esther took to the floor. Little gasps could be heard as the couple began to hold one another. Sol tried to stand as straight as he could, it was hard since the stroke and he had become a bit bent. Esther was lovely. A tiny perfect figure, her skin shining, her eyes glowing.

Matthew arrived just in time to anticipate Naomi's tears. He handed her a handkerchief.

It was worth it all; with all the yelling and cajoling and all the fights and bitterness and all the anger and spleen splitting. Esther and Sol, after forty years, married, still together, still wanting to be together for better, for worse—a lot of times for worse. Naomi looked at them, and through her tears, she let them go.

She forgave; and if you forgive you take away the power of the forgivee, that great sage Johnson had said. And so be it. She let them go. And so she could cry as she watched them dance, holding each other. Husband and wife.

Esther danced with Naomi. Over a hundred people including old Johnson-and-Johnson watched as Naomi walked to the dance floor and, since she was the taller, gathered her mother around the waist and danced to "Oh Mein Papa." They just held each other and swayed. Esther wanted so hard for Naomi to know she loved her, in her own way, the way she was, not the

239

way Naomi wanted, but she couldn't be any different. It was too late, and if she operated on what Naomi called denial it was because it was the only way she could survive. Esther didn't have to say a word. Naomi knew that was what she was thinking. Exhausted, she held her mother in her arms and smelled her perfume, and let herself love her.

Esther knew.

Then Sol danced with Naomi. He was a bit wary of his crazy mercurial daughter, as though he thought this bean of a girl was some kind of sex maniac or something. Naomi still felt his urgency. The intensity of his feelings for her. She tripped over his feet as always. The orchestra played a hora, and they danced it slowly. The applause around them was deafening. Naomi kissed him when the dance was over. Whatever it had been between them, it was over. He was not the daddy she used to know. She was not afraid of him anymore. He was getting to be an old man. It was time. It was time to move on.

Everyone applauded when Naomi sat down. Sol then danced with Becky and that wasn't too bad, except that Becky was a sourpuss and sullen, but no one seemed to notice.

Sol then announced that he was going to "trip the light fantastic" with his granddaughter, and since he was not getting any younger, would his daughters please oblige and arrange for some more grandchildren, because he wanted some more kissing and smooching with pretty little girls like Janie.

Matthew started to rub Naomi's back when he heard that one and gave her a leering lascivious look. Dancing with her grandpa, Janie was free and loose, not fearful and wary as Naomi had been when she was that age.

Then everyone moved onto the dance floor and ate dessert after Sol and Esther had cut the cake and fed each other a piece and the flashbulbs popped, just as they had done forty years ago. And Matthew danced with Janie and Esther whispered to Naomi, "I like your young man," as they said goodnight at the door. Naomi kissed her father, and Matthew shook his hand, but Sol was very busy with Nicole Lissette with two ts and two es, explaining how he could help her break into the Hollywood scene with his connections.

46

Naomi, just out of the bath, was putting on her white satin dressing gown. Matthew was in the bedroom on the phone. He had had an uncontrollable urge to call his editor, figuring that since he had made this mad crazy trip here anyway it shouldn't be a total loss and they should have lunch tomorrow and he could give him the first sixty pages of his masterpiece. Naomi brushed her hair and noticed the time. It was three in the morning; obviously Matthew's editor was used to his habits.

It was a very warm night, but Naomi, hating the air conditioning, had opened all the windows in the apartment. She walked out onto her terrace and looked out over Central Park.

The trees were June full now, all the winter spaces had been filled in. At night she could see clear across to Fifth Avenue. It was a close night and very warm, and she lay down on a lounge chair with a glass of juice, hoping for a breeze.

Wearing only his trousers, Matthew came out carrying the quilt off her bed, her radio and a bottle of champagne.

"You cold or something?"

"I want to lie down and look at the stars."

He plugged in the radio, uncorked the champagne, took a sip from the bottle and lay the quilt down on the rug on the terrace floor. He lay down with a great sigh.

"Come."

Naomi lay down next to him. They were both very quiet, now that it was all over, now that the orchestra had taken its marbles and gone home, now that the aunts and the nieces and the nephews, and Janie and Becky and Sol and Esther were all full and dizzy and asleep in their beds.

"We haven't talked. We haven't said two words to each other," Naomi said without looking at him.

Matthew leaned over and kissed her behind the ear.

"Maybe it's better that way."

Naomi lay there staring up at a constellation. She didn't know which one it was, but she wasn't going to mention it because if she did she was sure to get a long lecture, and if that's what she wanted she could go down the street to the planetarium.

"I mean, Matthew, I'm so happy you came. I mean, it meant so much to me."

"I know. That's why I did it."

Frank Sinatra was singing "September Song" as Naomi got up to pour some champagne into her orange juice. As she sat up her robe opened to the waist.

"I feel like Carole Lombard out here, in my satin number and my bearded lover and my champagne. And my New York."

"Your nipple is protruding."

"I beg your pardon."

"There, through the satin, there are arrows that will pierce my heart poking out of your robe."

"Can't figure out why."

"Not good being apart. Doesn't work."

"I hate it."

"No more." He started smoothing the protrusion on her left breast out from the silkiness. He moved with slow even strokes. It was almost impossible to talk. But they had so much to talk about; they had settled nothing.

He softly opened the robe so her breasts could greet the stars, so the air could touch her skin, cool from the bath.

His mouth was on one nipple, his fingers on the other. She was adrift in a sea of marshmallow, she was sinking into the bubbles of her bath, she was so ready for his touch for the touch of the man she finally loves, for this man with whom she wants to be, for this man she wants always, whatever always is.

He gently removed the whole robe; she unbuttoned his pants, always the most indelicate interrupter, but he slid out of his trousers like an eel out of the water and slowly and smoothly he kissed her whole body. He liked to be high in the sky, Matthew Johnson did. Next they would be making love on the wing of an airplane on the top of Mount Everest.

"I think we will fight continually and yet I think both of us could get some damn good work done with the other around, and I think we will be all right."

Matthew continued his exploration of her body, kissing and smoothing, behind her neck, under her knees, he kissed each toe and put his tongue into the curve of her belly. She thought she would disappear, she was a fragile bubble in the bath all blue and gold, sly momentary blast of color blown away.

He entered her quietly, softly. He stared into her eyes from on top of her.

He made her cry. Her face was wet with tears. He dried her face with his.

It was all right. It was finally all right. Perhaps like Helene she would try for everything. Perhaps she would get to go to Russia. Perhaps she would have a baby. Perhaps . . . her mind went fast.

"Naomi, come with me high in the sky and we will go camping in the Sierras, and see the elephants in Africa and the Imperial Palace in Russia. Come live with me and be my love, and someday we will have a fine healthy child together. What do you say?"

But he covered her mouth with kisses before she had a chance to answer.